Shattered Emotions

to: Magie Connor 7/6/11

James Preston Hardison

Shattered Emotions

A Novel by

James Preston Hardison

authorHOUSE®

AuthorHouse™
1663 Liberty Drive
Bloomington, IN 47403
www.authorhouse.com
Phone: 1-800-839-8640

First published by AuthorHouse 10/9/2010

ISBN: 978-1-4520-8627-9 (sc)
ISBN: 978-1-4520-8628-6 (e)

Library of Congress Control Number: 2010914416

Printed in the United States of America

This book is printed on acid-free paper.

This novel is dedicated to my wife, Ann

My children

Grand-children

Great-grand-children

Sister Ruby

Also, this book is dedicated to the many readers

that have told me how much they have enjoyed

reading my novels.

Thank you,

James Preston Hardison

OTHER WORKS

BY

JAMES PRESTON HARDISON

Poem published in the National Library of Poetry-

"After the Storm:

Poem title- "My sister Ruby"

NOVELS:

ANDY BEECHUM

The Devils Daughter

Matilda- Novel

Relentless Pursuit

Golden Tooth

Miracles on The Poke-A-No

Breaking Andy Beechums Heart

Tears of Love

Contents

Chapter 1

It's May, 2009; Sgt. Joseph Edward Wilson was on his second tour of duty in Iraq. All his friends and military buddies referred to him as Joe. He and fifteen other soldiers were being fired on by at least forty Taliban fighters. Dust and debris steadily filled the air as bullets from automatic weapons pounded the five-foot brick wall where the American soldiers had taken refuge. The barrage of gun-fire from the enemy was constant as the soldiers returned fire, trying their best to stay alive. Sgt. Horace Sweeney fell against Joe Wilson's legs. Joe dropped to his knees beside Sgt. Sweeney. He pressed his hand against his friend's chest, trying desperately to stop the bleeding. "Sergeant Wilson, I'm not going to make it!"

"Please don't talk like that!" Joe answered, his hands trembling.

"Tell my wife and children that I love them very much," Sgt. Sweeney whispered. "Help them whenever you can." With tears in his eyes and barely able to speak, he looked up at

Joe. "Please tell Delores and my children that I love them!" Please!"

"I promise I will tell them." Three minutes later Sgt. Sweeney was dead.

With tears sliding down his face and without regard for his life, Joe stood up and started firing his gun. He killed five Taliban fighters before being shot himself.

*   *   *   *

"Sgt. Wilson! Sgt. Wilson, wake up!"

Joe moved his head back and forth several times, and then he slowly opened his eyes. He saw a female nurse looking down at him. Lieutenant Doris Henderson was Joe's assigned nurse during the present shift.

"Where am I?"

"You're in the recovery ward of a military hospital. Don't you remember getting shot?"

"All I remember is Sgt. Sweeney falling against my legs. How long have I been in here?"

"You have been here for five days. You were shot in your chest. To further complicate matters there were some bullet fragments in your body as well. You were operated on in three different places to remove the bullet and fragments. Fortunately for you, none of your vital organs were damaged. On a scale of one to ten, how bad are you hurting?"

"I guess about an eight or so."

"I'll ask the doctor if he will give you something for pain. Sgt. Wilson, do you want us to notify your family that you were wounded in battle?"

"Please don't do that!"

"Why is that?"

"I don't want to worry my wife."

"You must love her a lot."

"Lieutenant, I love Linda more than anything in the whole world. She is beautiful, sweet, affectionate, and I trust her like she was a Saint."

"I understand that your tour of duty is almost up. You will be going home in a few days. Have you thought about re-enlisting?"

"Not at all, I'm going to get my honorable discharge and then spend the rest of my days with my wife."

"When was the last time you talked to her or sent her a letter?"

"It's been almost two months since I sent her a letter. It's been over three months since I actually talked with her. All I've been doing during that time was trying to stay alive. I'm not going to let her know when I'm coming home. I intend to buy her a bundle of red roses and then ring my doorbell. Linda will be very surprised to see me standing there with those pretty flowers in my hand. I want to hold her in my arms, look her in the eyes, and tell her how much I love her. That's when I'm going to give her my most passionate kiss."

"It's hard to believe that you're lying here all shot up, yet you're still thinking about a kiss."

Twelve days later was an exciting day for Joe Wilson; he was on his way home. The thought of him seeing his beautiful wife after being away from her for thirteen months sent chills through his body as he looked out the window of the military aircraft. Not only would he get to see his wife, he would be discharged from the military in a few more days. He and Linda were married one month before his second tour in Iraq. Their plans were not to have any children until he finished his tour of duty in the United States Army.

"Sgt Wilson, what are you thinking about?" Sgt. John Bower asked, seated next to him.

"I was just thinking about my wife."

"How many children do you and she have?"

"We don't have any, yet. However, I'm going to change that situation soon as I get home." He reached into his pocket and pulled out his billfold. "Isn't she beautiful?"

"Yes, she's very pretty. I'm assuming this is your wife."

"Yes, it certainly is. Her name is Linda and I love her more than anything in the world."

"Where is your home?" Sgt Bower asked.

"Adamsville, North Carolina. It's about ten miles from Fayetteville. Most of my kin folks still live in or around Adamsville, including my parents, brother and sister. Linda's father retired from Fort Brag nine years ago. He and his wife were originally from the state of Maine, but their children, Linda and Doris were born in North Carolina. Linda's father, Melvin Jones was stationed at Fort Brag for several years. While stationed there he and his wife, Grace, bought a house in Adamsville. They decided to continue living there after his retirement."

"How did you happen to meet up with Linda?"

"That in itself is an interesting story. It happened on a cold wintry-night. I decided this particular night to go dancing at a place named 'The Wagon Wheel.' Every Saturday night a live band played music there. It was my fourth time going dancing at The Wagon Wheel. I had already danced several times from eight o'clock until nine o'clock when I saw this beautiful woman standing in line, waiting to pay for her ticket. Still sitting at my table I kept my eyes on her to see where she was going to sit. No sooner than she had sat down I hurried to her and asked her if she would like to dance."

"Did she dance with you?"

"I was dumbfounded with her answer."

"Don't keep me waiting—what was her answer?"

"She politely, smilingly, said, 'No thank you.' My mouth opened wide, and for several moments I just stood there baffled. What was left of my ego fell to the floor."

"What did you do then?"

"I turned quietly and walked back to my table."

"Maybe you gave up to soon."

"Well to tell you the truth—I didn't give up. I decided to observe her for a while to see if she was waiting for someone, maybe her boyfriend."

"Did anyone sit down with her?"

"As a matter of fact—they didn't. She sat there for over thirty minutes and didn't dance with anyone. I didn't dance with anyone else as I continued looking in her direction each chance I got. I didn't want to seem overbearing toward her."

"Well, how did you finally break the ice?"

"Well, finally I got up enough nerve to walk back to her table. I asked her again if she would dance with me."

"She said, 'I'm sorry, but I'm not a very good dancer.' That's when I told her she didn't have to be a good dancer because she was the most beautiful woman that I had ever seen. I told her that my name was Joe Wilson and that I would greatly appreciate her dancing with me. With a broad, beautiful smile she stood up and that's how I meet my Linda."

"Tell me this, how was her dancing?"

"She danced beautifully."

"What are you going to do after you get out of the Army in a few days?"

"After I get my honorable discharge I'm going to take Linda on a real honeymoon. After that I'm going to work for my father."

"What kind of business is he in?"

"He's a building contractor. He builds houses, apartments and some commercial buildings."

"When was the last time you talked with your wife?"

"It seems like forever, but it's been about three months or more since I've actually talked with her. I sent her a letter about two months ago."

"You mean she doesn't know you're coming home today?"

"Heck no, I want to surprise her real good! She'll be shocked to the core when she sees me standing in front of her with my uniform on. I'll be smiling while I hold the bundle of flowers in front of me. Sgt. Bower, are you married?"

"I am and I'm not."

"How can that be?"

"I received a Dear John letter five months ago from my wife, Denise. She told me that she didn't love me anymore, but she did love Terry Adams."

"Do you know Terry Adams?"

"I'm afraid I do. We went to school together and before the Dear John letter I considered him to be my very best friend. I was devastated when I received that letter. For several days I didn't care whether I lived or died. I cried and cried, and that's when I started taking careless chances on the battlefield. Now you know why I don't have my left arm anymore."

"I sure am sorry about you losing your arm. Tell me this, what happened to bring you out of that mode of thinking, not caring whether you lived or died?"

"I was lying in my hospital bed; tears were streaming down my face as I noticed where my left arm used to be. Sometime that particular day I received a letter from my sister. She and I have always been very, very close. In the letter she told me that my wife, Christine, had never been faithful to me. It seems that she had slept with at least three men since I've been dodging bullets in Iraq. I guess I was the very last one to know about her transgressions. My sister didn't have the heart to tell me prior to the Dear John letter."

"Sgt Bower, I'm very sorry that your wife was not faithful to you. Will you ever speak to her again?"

"I'll have to."

"Why is that?"

"I have a son and a daughter. It's a hell of a note; I've been in Iraq getting shot at while my wife has been pleasuring other men in my own bed. I don't know why I should feel ashamed, but I do."

"Why on earth do you feel ashamed?"

"I don't know, but I do. I can't understand why she did those things! She told me how much she loved me before I left for Iraq. For some reason I don't even feel like I'm a real man anymore. My heart becomes numb every time I envision her and that worthless friend of mine having sex in the room adjacent to where my children were sleeping. I should go home and shoot that bastard!"

"No! No, you shouldn't do that, Sgt. Bower! After all, it seems that your wife was a willing participant. Another thing, if you shoot that guy you will spend the rest of your life in the penitentiary. You will lose your children forever."

"I guess you're right, but I may still bust him in his mouth, and I'm going to let Christine know just how I feel about her cheating on me."

"Sgt. Bower, we'll be at Fort Brag in another hour, what are your plans?"

"I'm going to find out if Christine has moved out of my house or not. I want my children to live with me, if that's possible. For years I've been making the payments on the house where we live. I still plan to live in that house. How about you, Joe, do you live on or off the base?"

"Linda and I live several miles off base in a town named Adamsville. When I get to the base I'm going to call my in-laws to pick me up. We're going to surprise my wife about me being home. Linda thinks I'm coming home in a month or two. Boy, will she be surprised to see me standing there with a bouquet of flowers in my hand!"

An hour and fifteen minutes later the large aircraft landed at Fort Brag, North Carolina.

"Sgt Bower, when we get off the plane I'm going to call my in-laws and have them pick me up? What are your plans?"

"I'm going to call my sister, and then she's going to take me to my house. I can hardly wait to see my two kids. Sgt. Wilson, I'm glad you've got a beautiful, loving wife to come home to. If I were you I would do everything in my power to hold on to her. As with a lot of men, some women are not faithful at all."

After departing the aircraft, Joe Wilson phoned his father-in-law to come to the Non-commissioned officers club (NCO) in about two hours to take him home. That would give him enough time to check into his unit before going home.

An hour and fifty-five minutes later, Mr. and Mrs. Melvin Jones, Linda's parents, pulled in front of the NCO club. Joe Wilson was standing in front of the building. He was all smiles as his in-laws exited their car to greet him. "Goodness gracious, Joe, haven't you lost a few pounds?" Melvin Jones asked, hugging his son-in-law's neck. "Look, Gracie, Joe has a lot of medals. Oh my goodness, he's got a Purple Heart! Joe, we didn't know that you got wounded!"

"I stood up when I shouldn't have," said Joe smiling. "Answering your question, I have lost some weight, but I'm still not skinny. Mrs. Jones, are you going to give your favorite son-in-law a big hug?"

"I most certainly am! Anyway, you already know you're my only son-in-law. We're all glad that you're home, Joe. Linda will be thrilled to death when she finds out that you're home."

"Mrs. Jones, how is your other daughter doing?"

"Doris is doing just fine. She asked me to tell you hello. None of us told Linda that you were coming home early."

"Joe, let me have your duffle bag and I'll place it in the trunk of my car," said Mr. Jones.

"Everyone get into the car and we'll take my son-in-law to see his wife."

"Mrs. Jones, where can I get some beautiful flowers to take to Linda?"

"There's a nice flower shop on Maple Street. Melvin, do you know where I'm talking about?"

"Yes dear, in fact that's where I got you a dozen roses on your last birthday."

"Mrs. Jones, Linda hasn't been sick or anything has she?"

"No, she hasn't, Joe. Why do you ask?"

"It's been a long time since I received a letter from her."

"Well, Linda was working two jobs at one time. She worked on her regular job at Clemmons Pharmaceuticals. For three full months they went through some kind of restructuring process. For about five months she worked part time at Stapleford's Jewelry Store. Maybe that's why she hasn't been writing you very much."

"Melvin, don't forget to stop on the next block at Reed's Florist. Joe, what kind of flowers do you want to get for Linda?"

"I want to get her a dozen perfect roses. Mrs. Jones, will you go inside the florist with me since you know so much about flowers? I want to get some real fresh, very beautiful flowers for my wife."

"Of course I will Joe. I'm so glad you're home now. Maybe Melvin and I will finally get that grandchild that we've been waiting for."

"Grace, I can't believe you just said that!"

"Melvin, don't act so innocent," said Mrs. Jones. "You know as well as I do what's going to happen tonight at Joe's house. This poor man has been away from his wife for a very long time. He's got a lot of catching up to do," she smiled.

"Joe, don't pay any attention to my un-bashful wife."

"Mr. Jones, I love your wife as much as any son-in-law can. The same goes for you as my father-in-law."

It didn't take long for Joe and Mrs. Jones to purchase a dozen of beautiful roses. "I want you both to go into the house with me when I get home," said Joe. "Mrs. Jones, I see you've got your camera with you."

"Yes, I certainly do. I intend to take your picture when you hug my daughter and hand her those gorgeous flowers."

As Melvin Jones drove toward his son-in-law's home he noticed in his rear view mirror the broad smile on Joe's face. Melvin loves Joe as though he was his own son. Every once in a while Joe would smell the roses that he was carrying to Linda.

It was about five o'clock in the evening when Melvin Jones turned his car into Joe's driveway. "Well, Joe, we're at your house now," said Melvin. "Hopefully, Linda didn't see us drive up. Grace, let's be very quiet so we don't spoil Joe's surprise."

Melvin and Grace were standing directly behind Joe on the porch as he quietly inserted his house key into the door lock with his right hand, holding his flowers in his left one. He pushed quietly against the door, and then they tip-toed inside the living room. Linda's car was parked outside so they all assumed that she was inside the house. Joe and his in-laws were now standing in the hallway in front of the master bedroom. They all knew that Linda must be inside the bedroom because they detected some movement inside. Melvin and Grace held each other's hand as they watched Joe place his hand on the doorknob. Joe was very excited, his heart was pounding. He had a broad smile on his face, wondering what his wife's expression would be seeing him standing there with a bundle of red roses. Mrs. Jones nodded approvingly as Joe turned the doorknob quietly. He flung the door open; to his horror his wife and her supervisor, William Davis, were lying naked on his bed. William quickly grabbed the sheet to cover himself up. Linda was still in a deep sleep. Joe stood there motionless, in shock, still holding the roses. He held his head downward. Tears trickled down Joe's face.

"Linda Wilson, wake the Hell up!" Melvin Jones yelled. She awoke and then realized that she was lying naked in front of her parents. Linda hurriedly placed the sheet across her body; that's when she saw her husband standing there, tearfully, with roses in his hand.

"Why in the Hell are you lying naked in bed with that idiot?" Melvin asked. "You no-good son-of-a-bitch, William Davis, you've got thirty seconds to get your pants on before I go to my car and get my gun! Turn your head, Grace while I toss this piece of trash his clothes." Mr. Jones picked up William's clothes and then threw them into his face. "Half your time is already gone, you bastard. Now get out of my son-in-law's house before he comes out of his shock!" William slipped on his pants and then rushed by Joe as he stood there looking toward the floor.

"Linda, I have never been more disappointed in my entire life than I am right now!" Her mother said, placing her arm around Joe's neck. "Why? Why did you do this terrible thing? I don't understand! I don't understand at all!"

"Mother, I'm sorry! I don't know what to say! Joe, I don't understand any of this!"

"How long has this sort of thing been going on?" Her mother asked.

"I don't understand this! I swear to you, Joe—I don't understand what's going on! It's not my fault! Mother, it's not my fault!" Tears slid down her face as she looked toward her husband. Joe dropped the flowers onto the floor; he turned around and walked out of the bedroom. "Joe! Joe, I'm sorry!" Linda cried. "It's a mistake! You don't understand! I didn't know this was going to happen!"

Mr. Jones followed Joe to the living room. "Joe, I can't tell you how sorry I am about this! What do you want me to do? Joe, tell me—what do you want me to do?"

Sniffing back his tears, Joe looked at his father-in-law. "I'm going outside for a while and during that time I want you and Mrs. Jones to get whatever items your daughter needs together and then take her to your house. I love you and Mrs. Jones with all my heart, but your daughter is no longer welcome in my home. Whenever she is ready for the rest of her stuff please call me in advance so I can be someplace else."

"Joe, I hope we can still be friends."

"Mr. Jones, you will always be my friend, and so will your wife. I'm going to walk down the street for a little while now. Please get your daughter out of my house as quickly as possible because it will not be safe for her to be here." Joe started crying as he opened his front door.

Mrs. Jones and Linda hurried into the living room where Melvin was sitting on the couch, his hands pressed against his face. "Daddy, where did he go?" Linda asked, tears sliding down her face.

"He's gone walking for a few minutes. Grace, help Linda get some clothes together."

"Why?" Linda asked, tearfully.

"What do you mean why? You can't stay here now! You've got to go home with us before Joe gets back. He's grieving and in shock now, but when he comes out of it your life will be in grave danger."

"Daddy, I don't won't to go anywhere, I love Joe!"

"The Hell you do! If you loved him you wouldn't have done what you did! I'm so ashamed of you I don't know what to do!

Now—go get your things together before Joe gets back! Grace,
I feel like I'm about to have a heart attack!"

"Daddy, do you want me to get you something?"

"I don't want you to get me a damn thing! Just get your
things together so we can go home! Oh God, I feel so sorry
for Joe! I can't believe my own daughter would cheat on her
husband while he's over in Iraq getting shot. I don't think I'll
ever be the same again. I don't understand it! My daughter!
My own daughter lying naked in bed with her supervisor!
Get your clothes together!" Tears streamed down Melvin's
face.

"Your father is right, Linda, go get a few clothes and
whatever else you may need for a couple days. We'll have to
come back later for the rest of your stuff."

"It's not fair that I've got to move out of my own house!"

"Let me set you straight young lady," said her father.
"This house is in Joe's name and he's the one that's made all
the payments up to now! I've never seen a man more excited
than he was when he picked out those dozen roses for you!
He loved you with all his heart! Why on earth did you do
him this way? Why, for God's sake did you do it?"

"I don't know!" Linda cried. "I don't know why I was in bed
with William Davis!"

"It's not all that hard for me to understand why a man and
woman are naked in bed!" Melvin responded.

"It was not my doing, I tell you!"

"Linda, your father and me are getting old for sure, but
we're not senile or stupid! My God, I'll never forget the look on
Joe Wilson's face when he saw you and that man lying naked
on that bed!"

"Mother, it's not what you think!"

"Not only is my daughter unfaithful to her husband, she can't even own up to her infidelity!"

"Daddy, it's not what you think!"

"I don't want to hear anymore about it! Grace, help Linda get her clothes together so we can go home! I'll never have another happy moment in my entire life!" Tears slid down Melvin's face.

"Don't you both understand—I love Joe?" Linda said, crying.

"You might as well get over that right now young lady!" Her father snapped. "He'll never have you back now after seeing you lying naked in bed with your supervisor! Now, go get what you need so we can get out of here before he comes back! I've never seen a more pitiful man, him standing there with that bunch of flowers in his hands! He was totally devastated! Joe is like a son to me! I can't believe you betrayed his trust the way you did! You need a good ass-whipping for doing what you did! Not only have you broken your husband's heart, but you did the same thing to your mother and me! I'm your father, I'll have to overlook the situation to a certain degree, but I damn sure won't forget how you destroyed your marriage and broke our hearts!"

"Please, Melvin, don't get more upset than you already are," said Grace. "I don't want you to have a heart attack. Linda, let's get your stuff and then get out of here before he comes back."

"Mother, I need to tell him that I'm sorry!" Linda started crying uncontrollably.

"You should have thought about that before you had sex with your supervisor," answered her mother. "Now, quit wasting time and get your stuff together!"

Chapter 2

Thirteen blocks from his house, still in his uniform, Joe Wilson stopped at Bailey's Bar and Grill. He went inside and took a seat near the back of the building. He used a napkin to wipe his watery eyes. A few minutes later a waitress came to his table. "Soldier, how may I help you?"

"Could I get a beer please?"

"What kind would you prefer?"

"I don't care. I'll drink whatever you bring me."

"Are you alright? You look like you've been crying."

"I'll be okay—just bring me a beer. In fact, bring me two beers."

The waitress came back with two beers. "I hope you don't get mad with me for saying this, but you are the saddest looking man I've ever seen," said the waitress. "By the way, that blonde at the bar asked me if you might need some company."

"Please tell her that I don't care for any company right now."

"I'll tell her."

It was almost twelve o'clock that night when Joe Wilson walked out of the bar, and then on toward his house. He had only walked six blocks before he was confronted by four teenage gang-members. They demanded that he hand over his billfold. "If you sorry bastards want my wallet you're going to have to take it from me!"

"Well, Army man, that won't be a problem at all," sounded what appeared to be the ring-leader. He pulled out a switch-blade knife and started toward Joe. After having consumed four beers that night, Joe was in no condition to fight all four gang members, but he was not afraid of them.

"Either you give me your wallet or I'm going to cut you to pieces!"

"Well, sonny-boy, come on and start your cutting. I'll snatch that snake-shaped earring right out of your partly severed ear!" The eighteen year old boy rushed toward Joe with his knife, but Joe turned quickly to one side and then he grabbed the gang-leader around his neck with one arm while holding the knife away from him with his other hand. Joe easily over powered the teenager causing him to drop his knife. The other three gang members started closing in on Joe.

"You guys get him," said the boy that Joe was holding.

"So help me God, either one of you take one more step and I will break this punk's neck! I'm not joking—you yellow bellied cowards!"

"Don't come any closer," whispered the ring leader, as Joe squeezed harder against his neck.

"You had better do like this tough guy said because I'm in a bad mood and I will break his good-for-nothing neck in a heartbeat! Now, you morons start down the street in the opposite direction from where I was walking! I'll turn your buddy loose when you're out of my sight. Now get going!" The three gang members hurried off like Joe had told them. He still held onto the ring leader for about a minute and then pushed him aside. Joe picked up the switchblade knife from the street and threw it as far as he could into the darkness.

"You got the drop on me this time, Mister, but I know where you live! This thing is not over by a long shot!"

"It's going to be over for you if I ever see you anywhere near my house! Now, you get going or I'm going to bash your head in and then I'm going to break your neck!" The gang member realized he was no match for Joe Wilson so he hurried off in the same direction that his buddies went. Joe realized that the only thing that saved him were the street lights. Otherwise he wouldn't have seen the switchblade knife in the teenager's hand.

By the time Joe had walked another block he was thinking about Linda. He burst into tears as he continued walking toward his house.

It was eight o'clock the next morning when Joe Wilson was awakened when his doorbell rang. He slipped on his trousers and shirt as hurriedly as he could, and then he opened his front door. Standing on his porch was his father, mother and sister and brother. They were very excited to see him. His mother was the first to hug his neck as tears edged down her face. "Joe, we're so glad you're home! I've prayed each and every day that you would come home safely from that war-torn place." His mother commented.

"I'm glad to be home. Dad, how are you doing?"

"I've been doing just fine, son. Give your old daddy a big hug." They embraced each other for a few seconds. "Welcome home, Joe, I'm sorry about your marriage."

"Dad, how did you find out so soon about my marriage?"

"Melvin Jones called us last night and told us about Linda and her supervisor. I'm truly sorry that you walked in on such a despicable sight. Tears came into Joe's eyes as he reached for his sister and brother.

"We all love you very much," said Joan, Joe's sister. "I may never like Linda again for doing you the way she did."

"I sure am glad you're home," said Anthony, Joe's brother. "You promised me that we would go fishing some after you got out of the Army."

"I promise you that we will. For the next few days I've got to process out of the Army, but after that—we'll do a lot of fishing. Please everyone—come inside and I'll make a pot of coffee."

Everyone took seats in the living room, except for Joe and his mother. They were in the kitchen talking. Sarah stood next to her son as he nervously placed coffee grounds into his coffee maker. "What are you going to do about Linda?"

Tears slid down Joe's face as he filled the coffee maker with water. "Mother, I don't know what I'm going to do. I love her with all my heart. I don't know why she did me the way she did. It doesn't make any sense! Why would she do a thing like that?"

"I can't answer that, Son, but you deserve a lot better than a cheating wife! I don't know how she could ever show her face again after her own family saw her lying naked in a bed with another man! I love you, Joe. We all love you and we want you to be happy. I feel like slapping her across her face for doing you the way she did!"

"Mother, there's got to be a reason for what she did."

"The reason is quite plain to me—it was to have sex outside of her marriage!"

Joe wiped his eyes as he started pouring coffee into his mother's cup. "Mother, how do Joan and Anthony like their coffee? I know my father likes his coffee black."

"Joan likes two teaspoons of sugar in coffee. Anthony just likes cream in his. Joe, before we go into the living room, what are you going to do about Linda?"

"Mother, I don't know what I'm going to do. What would you have me do?"

"I can't answer that. I'm not sure anyone can advise you on that, but I know one thing—she did the unthinkable by sleeping with another man. I'll be surprised if both of them don't lose their jobs when their management hears about the situation."

"Mother, let's take the coffee cups into the living room. I really don't want to talk about my situation with Linda at the present time. I feel like my heart is broken into bits and pieces as it is."

Joe's father looked toward him. "We're thankful to God that you're home safe, Joe. More than once I had horrible nightmares that you were killed. We're all very glad that you're getting out of the military."

"How is your business doing?" Joe asked.

"It's doing fantastic! There's just one small problem."

"What's that?"

"My business needs you in it."

"You mean I'm already hired?"

"You were hired before you ever got off that plane at Fort Brag."

"Anthony, how have you been?"

"I've been fine, Joe, but I'll tell you one thing—we all missed you more than you'll ever know."

"You can't believe how much Anthony loves and admires you," said Mark.

"How about me, Father, I love Joe just as much as Anthony does?"

"Of course you do, Joan. I didn't mean to leave you out."

"Sis, you know darn well that I love you more than a hog loves slops."

Smilingly, Joan asked, "Are you comparing me to a hog?"

Joe smiled back answering, "You and I have always been very, very close. We're like two peanuts in the same shell."

"Mother, my eldest brother just reduced me from a big hog to a lowly peanut," Joan laughed.

"You two cut it out," said Sarah. "Joe, we want you to come eat supper with us tonight."

"Could we make it on another night?"

"We could, but we're having your favorite food tonight."

"What are you cooking?"

"We're having grilled pork chops, cabbage, boiled potatoes, string beans, whole-kernel corn, butter beans and home-made biscuits. Oh, did I mention that we're having your favorite dessert?"

"You're having banana pudding?"

"Not just any old kind of banana pudding. We're having a very large banana pudding. How does that sound to you?"

"I've just got one question."

"What is the question?"

"I'll need to know what time I should be at your house."

"You can come as early as you want, but the table will be set at six o'clock this evening."

"Joe, Melvin Jones said you were wearing a Purple Heart ribbon when he and his wife picked you up from the base. What happened? How come you got wounded?"

"I stood up when I shouldn't have. That reminds me that I've got to visit a fellow soldier's wife soon as I get discharged from the Army."

"Why is that?" His mother asked.

"He wanted me to tell his wife and children how much he loved them. It was Sgt. Horace Sweeney's last request as he lay dying by my feet."

"Where do Mrs. Sweeney and her children live?" Joan asked.

"Smithfield, North Carolina. That's one promise I will definitely keep."

"Okay folks, we need to go home now so Joe can get some rest before coming to dinner this evening."

"I want all of you to know that I love you very much."

"We know you do, Joe," said Mark. "We love you more than you will ever know. I can't tell you how sorry I am about your marriage. I don't know anything else to say."

"Thank you, Dad; I really appreciate all of you coming to see me."

After his family left, Joe took a seat on his couch. A little while later he noticed a picture frame on a small table at the end of his couch. Inside the picture frame was a photograph of him and Linda kissing each other. Hesitatingly, he picked up the picture frame and stared at the photograph for several minutes. Tears came into his eyes as he laid the picture face down on the couch. Like a young child—he began crying uncontrollably. A few minutes later, alone and heartbroken, Joe threw the picture frame against the fireplace. Broken glass was strewn about the carpet.

Joe got up from the couch, and then he went into his bedroom. With his eyes closed, head lowered, he remembered seeing his wife and her supervisor lying naked on his bed. Shocked and bewildered, he turned his attention toward his closet door. There was something in his closet that he needed to see. Without further hesitation he opened his closet door; he felt around on the closet shelf for a plastic box. The box was right where he had left it. He opened the box and removed a .45 caliber Smith & Weston pistol. Upon careful examination he determined that the pistol was still loaded. He took the pistol to the kitchen and laid it on the dinner table. Tears came into his eyes as he stared at the loaded gun. His hopes and dreams of having children with the only woman he ever loved had dissipated. He closed his eyes as he reached for the gun. He had barely touched it when the phone rang. He used the kitchen phone to answer the call.

"Joe, this is your Mother. I just wanted to let you know that your brother is on the way to your house. Tell Anthony to be sure and bring me about three pounds of ripened bananas on his way home."

"Anthony is coming here?"

"Yes, he's bringing you a welcome home present."

"What is the present?"

"He couldn't wait until you get here this evening to give you a new rod and reel that he bought you. Joe, Anthony absolutely worships the ground you walk on, and so does Joan. Guess what your father is doing at the moment."

"What's that?"

"He's looking at some of your old photographs. He's so unhappy about yours and Linda's situation. Joe, I don't think your father could take much more bad news."

"Mother, I'll have to go now; I believe that's Anthony ringing my doorbell."

"Joe, please don't forget that you're having dinner with us."

"I won't, Mother. I've got to go now." Joe hung up the phone, and then he rushed toward his bedroom with his gun in his hand. He placed it back into the plastic box, and then on his closet shelf.

A big grin was on Anthony's face when Joe opened his front door. "Joe, this is yours." He handed the rod and reel to his older brother.

"Anthony, this is a very nice rod and reel."

"There's nothing too good for my brother," said Anthony. "By the way, I've got a rod and reel just like yours. Joe, are you okay? You look like you've been crying."

"I'm just fine, brother. I really do appreciate your gift, but I'm supposed to tell you to hurry home with three pounds of ripened bananas. I'll see you later this evening."

"Joe, I'm so glad you're home now. I prayed almost every night that you would come back to us in one piece. If something were to happen to you I don't believe our father could handle it."

"I'll be just fine. Now you need to take some bananas home to Mother. I'm looking forward to eating banana pudding and some of that other stuff that she mentioned earlier." Anthony shook Joe's hand and then he hurried toward his car.

Joe Wilson arrived at his parent's house at 5:30 that evening. He was holding a neatly wrapped package in his arm when his father answered the doorbell. Mark and Joe went into the living room. "I see you brought something with you."

"Yes, Dad, I did bring something with me. I came to the conclusion that I no longer need what's in this box, but I do want you to have it as a Christmas present."

"Joe, it's a long ways off before Christmas."

"I know that, Dad, and that's why I don't want you to open it until Christmas."

"Won't you even give me a hint as to what's in it?"

"I'll just say this—inside this package is a plastic box. Your Christmas present is what's in the plastic box. I want you to place the package on your closet shelf until Christmas."

"That won't be a problem at all. I'll go do it right now." Joe walked toward the kitchen.

"Mother, I believe you are the very best cook in the whole country."

"It's unbelievable how you can be right about so many things," said his mother, smiling.

Joan, Anthony and Mark walked into the kitchen. "Joan, help me set the table now because everything is done. You men folks take a seat at the kitchen table."

"Mother, you weren't joking when you said you were going to fix a large banana pudding."

"No, Joe, I wasn't kidding. I know how well you and Anthony like my banana pudding."

Five minutes later everyone was situated at the table.

"I want each of us to join hands so I can offer a prayer to our Lord," said Mark. "Lord, my family thanks you from the bottom of our hearts for allowing Joe to come home alive and well from that horrible war in Iraq. Now, Lord, we ask you to help him during this stressful period of his life. Please inspire and guide him to make the right choices in the days, weeks and months ahead. Lord, you have always been very, very good to my family, and for that I want to thank you. I, also, want to thank you for this food that we are about to eat. I, especially, want to thank you for giving me the good sense to marry the very woman that cooked this meal. In Christ name I pray. Amen."

Chapter 3

At ten o'clock the next work day, Linda Jones and William Davis were called into Mr. Richard Jamison's office. Mr. Jamison is Vice President at Clemmons Pharmaceuticals.

"I've heard some very disturbing news about both of you," said Mr. Jamison.

"What have you been hearing?" William Davis asked.

"I think you already know what I'm talking about. Mrs. Wilson, what have you to say for yourself? I do believe you know what I'm talking about."

"Mr. Jamison, I know exactly what you are talking about. I don't know how or why, but I have committed a sin against my God, and I have lost my husband for sure." Tears started running down her cheeks.

"Mrs. Wilson, are you saying it's true that you and William Davis have engaged in sexual activity while being employed with this company?"

"Sir, it happened one time, but I don't know why it happened. I don't even remember it happening! I was found naked in bed with Mr. Davis and I don't even remember taking my clothes off! Mr. Jamison, I've lost my husband, home, everything I've ever dreamed of having! I know that Mr. Davis had intercourse with me, but I don't remember it. This thing should never have happened!"

"Mrs. Wilson, were you drunk at the time this happened?"

"Sir, I've never tasted a drop of liquor, beer or wine in my entire life."

"What you're saying doesn't make any sense at all! How does two people engage in a sexual activity and one not know what was going on?"

"Sir, I have told you the honest truth!" Tears slid down Linda's face.

"Something very fishy is going on here! I fully intend to get to the bottom of it! Mr. Davis, why wouldn't Mrs. Wilson know that you were having your way with her?"

"Mr. Jamison, that woman is lying! I don't know what she's talking about!"

"Mr. Davis, I want you to go outside and wait for me to call you back."

"I don't want that woman lying on me!"

"I want you to go now!" Mr. Davis left the room. "Mrs. Wilson, you are a married woman, your husband was fighting in a war to protect us from our enemies. You, also, knew about our company policy concerning adultery by our employees. For goodness sakes, what possessed you to lay with a man other than your husband?" Mr. Jamison handed her some tissues to dry her eyes.

"Mr. Jamison, I didn't want to sleep with Mr. Davis, but he tricked me!" Tears flowed freely from her eyes.

"What do you mean—he tricked you?"

"My husband thoroughly enjoys football and baseball. I knew he was coming home soon so I bought a wide screen television set for him, but I didn't know how to hook it up. Mr. Davis found out that I had bought the set from Lawson's Appliance Center. Someone in the office told him that I had the large flat-screen television, but I didn't know how to hook it up."

"Mrs. Wilson, continue your story, how did Mr. Davis trick you?"

"He came to my office and told me that he could hook up my television set in five minutes and it wouldn't cost me a dime. I was a little apprehensive, but I did want the set hooked up for Joe when he came home. I told Mr. Davis that it might not look right for him to come to my house, especially since I was married. He insisted that it would be okay, and that he would be in and out of my house within five or ten minutes. To my sorrow, I agreed for him to come to my house." Linda broke down and started crying.

Mr. Jamison handed her a box of tissues. "Mrs. Wilson, what happened when he got to your house?"

"When I answered my doorbell, Mr. Davis was holding a jar of juice. It looked like grape juice to me. I asked him where his car was and he told me he parked it down the street a ways to avoid neighbors gossiping. As soon as he got inside my living room he suggested that I get two glasses. He wanted me to drink some of the best tasting juice he had ever tasted. I really didn't want any, but he being my supervisor I tried to be nice.

I went into the kitchen to get two glasses. After I returned with the glasses, Mr. Davis asked me to go back to the kitchen and get some hand towels because he had spilled a little juice on my hardwood floors. By the time I got back with the hand towels he had already poured juice into the glasses. He handed me one and then told me to drink it. Mr. Davis said he would hook up the television set soon as we finished our juice."

"What happened then, Mrs. Wilson?"

"I only remember waking up and seeing Joe and my family standing in my bedroom. That's when I realized that I was naked on the bed with Mr. Davis." Tears flowed down Linda's face.

"Mrs. Wilson, why didn't you, immediately, tell your husband what had happened?"

"Mr. Jamison, I was in such a state of shock that I didn't know why or how come I was in bed with Mr. Davis."

"I'm assuming he never did hook up your television."

"I really don't know, but he probably didn't."

"Have you told your mother or father what happened to you?"

"No sir, you're the only person I've told."

"You worked a while this morning. Have you had any verbal contact with Mr. Davis today?"

"Yes sir."

"What was said between you two?"

"He came into my office this morning, closed the door, and then he threatened me."

"How did he threaten you?"

"He told me that if I ever told anyone that he had spiked my juice that I would be fired.

Mr. Jamison, I love my job, but I will resign today to protect this company from any embarrassment. What happened to me is partly my fault."

"Why do you say that?"

"I used poor judgment letting him come to my house. I should have realized that he was up to no good after seeing his car parked a block away from my house. Mr. Jamison, my heart is broken; I'm like an empty shell."

"Why do you feel like an empty shell?"

"My parents think I'm a tramp and my husband thinks I'm a slut. I love my husband with all my heart! Not once have I ever been unfaithful to him until I was drugged and then raped. I don't know what to do! My God, I hope I'm not pregnant! I've lost everything, including my self-respect!"

"Mrs. Wilson, excuse me a few seconds while I call my secretary."

"Do you want me to step outside?"

"No, I want you to sit right where you are." Mr. Jamison called his secretary and asked her to send Mr. Davis to his office. The secretary informed Mr. Jamison that Mr. Davis had left the building. Mr. Jamison asked his secretary if he said anything before he left. She informed him that Mr. Davis told her that he couldn't work here any longer. Mr. Jamison hung up the phone and then he stood up.

"Mr. Jamison, will it be okay if I go to my office and get my personal things?"

"Why would you want to do that?"

"You mean—you don't want me to quit my job!"

"No, Mrs. Wilson, I do not want you to quit your job. I believe you have told me the honest truth about your affair with Mr. Davis. From what you've told me that happened between you and Mr. Davis was not your fault. You should try to explain that to your husband before it's too late. Are you going to file charges against Mr. Davis? By the way, he is no longer employed with this company."

"How could I ever prove what I told you?"

"I see your point which would be very difficult to prove. Mrs. Wilson, your job is in good order. It is my sincere desire that you can get your marriage straightened out."

It was seven o'clock that evening when Joe Wilson's doorbell rang. He opened the door and saw Mrs. Grace Jones, Doris Jones and Linda standing on the porch. "Joe, I know we didn't call, but we do need to get some of Linda's clothes," said Mrs. Jones.

"That's okay I was just on my way to the drugstore so get whatever you need." Joe held his head down as he walked past his wife, and then on toward his car.

"Mother, Joe wouldn't even look at me when he walked by."

"Can you really blame him?"

"None of you understand what happened," said Linda, tearfully.

"I think we understand quite clearly what happened," her mother answered.

"Mother, it's not quite fair to say that!" Doris responded. "Not one person has asked Linda why she was in bed with William Davis!"

"What difference does it make why she was naked in bed with her supervisor? Now, you and Linda get whatever you need before Joe comes back. Your father will bring a truck Saturday morning to get the rest of her belongings."

Joe was standing a block away when the three women came out of his house. Grace Jones walked down the street to where he was standing. He held his head downward as his tears slid down his face. "Joe, Melvin will bring a truck here Saturday morning to get the rest of Linda's clothes and things."

"That will be okay, Mrs. Jones. I'll leave the house unlocked."

"Are you doing okay?"

"I'm alright, Mrs. Jones."

"I just want you to know that Melvin and I think you're a very fine man and we still want to be your friend."

"The same here, Mrs. Jones, I've always liked you both." Tears streamed down Linda's face as she sat in her mother's car observing Joe, his head held downward, him standing on the sidewalk a block away. Never before had she felt so heartbroken, alone and confused. She wanted to tell him why she was in bed with William Davis, but she feared he wouldn't believe her.

Grace backed her car out of Joe's driveway. "Did you see how pitiful Joe Wilson was?"

Grace asked.

"Mother, have you noticed how pitiful Linda looks? You seem to be more interested in Joe's feelings than your own daughter!"

"Doris, that's not fair! Joe didn't cause the situation that exists between him and Linda. She is the one responsible for their marriage problems. Joe will never want her back now."

"Linda, I'm your sister and I love you! I'll stick by you no matter what! Yes, it's true she was in bed with that man, but in my heart I know there was a good reason for it! I intend to find out what that reason was!"

*   *   *   *

Joe Wilson processed out of the Army over the next few days. He received an honorable discharge, and now he had to fulfill a promise before going to work with his father.

It was Saturday morning. Joe had on his new trousers, shirt and shoes that he had recently bought from Charlottes Clothing Store, located in downtown Adamsville. His plan for today was to drive to Smithfield, North Carolina and visit with Delores Sweeney and her children. He was anxious to tell Sgt. Horace Sweeney's widow what her husband said while he lay dying on the battlefield.

Two hours later, Joe was standing on Delores Sweeney's front porch. A note on the door indicated that she and her children had gone to Cedar Lake cemetery. Remembering seeing the cemetery on his way to Delores's house he decided to drive back to it and meet Sgt. Sweeney's family.

Joe arrived at the cemetery a few minutes later. It seemed obvious to him that the woman and two children standing in front of a fairly new grave site might be Delores Sweeney and her children. Joe exited his car; he walked quietly toward the grieving family. Joe's presence was first detected by a young boy.

"Mother, a man is looking toward us."

"Excuse me young man, I'm looking for Sgt. Horace Sweeney's family."

"My name is Delores Sweeney; these are my children, Michael and Gail. Who are you?"

"Mrs. Sweeney, my name is Joe Wilson. Until recently I was an Army soldier serving in Iraq along with your husband. In fact, Sgt Sweeney and I were very close friends. I have news from your husband."

"How can that be, my husband is lying here in this grave?" She wiped her eyes with a handkerchief.

"Mrs. Sweeney, I know that your husband is dead, but he told me some things before he was was killed. I'm not sure this is the appropriate place or time to tell you what he said. I saw the note on your door and that's why I'm here at the cemetery."

"The children and I are about to leave the cemetery. You're welcome to drive back to our house. We'll meet you there in a little while."

"Thank you, I'll do just that." He started walking out of the cemetery. While sitting in his car momentarily, he noticed Delores Sweeney as she wrapped her arms around her husband's tombstone. She and her children were crying. Tears came into Joe's eyes as he observed the heart-broken widow trying to console her children. He turned on his engine and drove off.

Joe Wilson was sitting on Delores Sweeney's front porch when she and her children turned into her driveway. He stood up as she and her children exited their car. "Mr. Wilson, this is my daughter, Gail. She just turned fifteen years old three days ago. My other child is Michael. He's eleven years old."

"I'm very pleased to meet you both," said Joe. "Mrs. Sweeney, you have two very beautiful children."

"Mr. Wilson, please join us inside the house. We're all very anxious to hear what you have to say about Horace." Joe followed the Sweeney family into the house.

"Would you care for something to drink? I'm going to make a pot of coffee."

"I'll have a cup of coffee since you're going to make some anyway."

"Please sit down at the kitchen table while I get our coffee perking. Children, I want you to sit down at the kitchen table, also. Your father's good friend has something to tell us concerning your father, isn't that right, Mr. Wilson?"

"Yes, Mrs. Sweeney, I certainly do have something to tell you and your children. First, I would like to tell you what Horace told me one time about his daughter, Gail. It was at an all boys' baseball game, except for one girl that had just joined the team. This girl was twelve year old Gail Sweeney. The young players couldn't understand why a girl had to be on their team. It was the bottom of the ninth inning; the bases were loaded with Gail's team at bat. The second batter had just struck out. Things didn't look good at all now for Gail's team with two outs, bottom of the ninth-inning and the other team with three runs ahead. Shouts from the bleachers demanded that Gail be given a chance to bat. Up until now she hadn't played a single inning. Hearing the boisterous sounds from the bleachers the coach reluctantly told Gail to don her helmet and pick up a bat. As Horace told it, the coach even walked away from the dugout as Gail positioned herself at the plate. The coach shook his head back and forth after Gail took the first two strikes without making a swing with the bat. That's when Horace hollered out to his daughter, 'Do it for your daddy, sweetheart!' Well, as luck would have it, Gail swung the bat as hard as she could. Contact was made; the ball seemed to go higher and higher as it sailed toward center field. Gail ran toward first as fast she could go, on to second base she went! The centerfielder misjudged the ball as it came fast toward the center field fence. He missed catching the ball, but Gail never stopped running. Stunned and surprised the coach tripped over his own feet as he raced toward his cheering team and their excited families. 'Run, Gail, run,' yelled the coach, jumping up and down in excitement. You can do it, sweetheart!" Gail's team mates were yelling and cheering as she rounded third base. At this exact moment, Horace Sweeney jumped from the fourth row of the bleachers, he ran to the fence cheering Gail on. The centerfielder threw the ball toward home plate, but Gail got there before the ball did. The entire team, one by one hugged Gail for winning the baseball game by one run. Horace dropped to his knees in excitement. Mrs. Sweeney, did I leave anything out?"

"You did a fine job of telling it like it was."

"Gail, your daddy told me that was one of the proudest moments in his life. The reason I was able to tell it so well is because Horace told me about that ball game at least six times."

Tearfully, Gail walked over to Mr. Wilson and hugged his neck. "Thank you, Mr. Wilson, for telling me what my daddy said about that game."

"You're welcome, Gail. Now I want to tell Michael what his daddy told me about him."

"I'll bet I know what it was, Mr. Wilson."

"What would that be, Michael?"

"You're going to tell about me wading in that old creek."

"As a matter of fact—that's exactly what I'm going to tell. According to your father, it was a hot summer day when you were about eight or nine years old. You and your father were fishing at Bower's Creek. The water wasn't very deep and the fish were not biting. You told your father that you wanted to wade into the creek to a shallow sandbar. At first he refused to let you do that, but after a couple false tears from you he decided to let you have your way. With no more than your underwear on, Horace watched attentively as you waded thigh-deep on the sandy bottom, shivering from the cold running water. After about ten minutes you told your father you were ready to get out of the water. He reached out his hand to you and that's when he saw an unsightly animal attached to your chest."

"Mr. Wilson, here's your cup of coffee," said Mrs. Sweeney. "What was it on my son's chest?"

"Horace said it was one of the longest, blackest, and ugliest blood-sucking leaches he had ever seen. Michael started screaming when he saw what was on his chest. Horace told him that he would burn the leach off him. Michael was not going to have any part of being roasted so he started running. Horace caught him. He told Michael that he was going to burn the leach, not him. After giving Michael a couple of reassuring hugs, he used his cigarette lighter to heat a small twig. Horace placed the hot end of the twig against the leach until it released his suction cup. Horace told me that's when he got down on his knees and said to Michael, 'See son, I would never ever hurt or burn you.' Horace told me how proud he was to see his brave young son wade off into that creek."

"What about my mother, Mr. Wilson? What did daddy say about her?" Gail asked.

"Mrs. Sweeney, as you well know—Horace didn't drink whiskey, beer, or even smoke cigarettes. On this particular night he and I were sitting at a bar. We knew that same night that we would be facing our enemy within three more days. I ordered myself a beer, but all Horace wanted was some fried chicken wings and a Pepsi Cola. That's when he told me about you, Mrs. Sweeney."

"What did he tell you?" She asked.

"He told me how he happened to meet up with you on a fishing pier."

Mrs. Sweeney smiled as she recollected their first meeting. "Did he tell you that he threw his hooks, line and sinkers across my fishing line? I didn't think we would ever get our lines untangled. At first I didn't know whose line had crossed over mine, but when I saw a man squatting down at the end of a bench I knew then whose line it was."

"You're absolutely right, Mrs. Sweeney, it was Horace Sweeney's line that was entangled with yours. He said when he got up close to you that chills went up and down his body."

"Why did he get chills?" Michael asked.

"Horace told me that Delores was the most beautiful woman that he had ever seen. Even though he had tangled up her line very badly she never seemed angry or upset. Mrs. Sweeney, do you remember what Horace asked you while you and he were separating your lines?"

"I believe he asked me if I was married."

"That's exactly what he asked you. Horace told me that he fell head over heels in love with you before you and he separated your fishing lines."

"I guess he did because he started asking me one question right after another. I never told Horace, but I've always been thankful that our lines got crossed that night."

"Mrs. Sweeney, there's something else that Horace told me. In fact, you probably don't know a thing about what I'm about to tell you."

"Why would Horace keep a secret from me?"

"He didn't want you or your children to ever go lacking for anything so he took out an insurance policy on himself just before entering the military."

"You mean his government insurance?"

"No, Mrs. Sweeney, I'm not talking about what Uncle Sam has or will pay you for Horace's death. I'm talking about a half-million dollar insurance policy. Horace told me several times that if anything were to happen to him that you would find that policy on top of his gun cabinet. Horace paid the premiums each quarter so the premiums should be paid up through next month. It's time for you to retrieve that policy and cash it in."

"Mr. Wilson, Horace's gun cabinet is tall; will you go with me to the bedroom and get the policy for me?"

"I certainly will." They walked toward Mrs. Sweeney's bedroom. Michael and Gail followed behind them. Joe placed his hand on top of the gun cabinet. After feeling around for a few seconds he found an envelope. He took the envelope down and then handed it to Mrs. Sweeney.

Sure enough, it was an insurance policy for a half-million dollars.

"Mr. Wilson, what should I do now?"

"Call the insurance company and tell them that you have your husband's death certificate and that you are ready to collect on the policy. In a matter of days you should receive a check for a half-million dollars."

"What about taxes on that money?"

"There won't be any taxes on that money, Mrs. Sweeney. That money is for you and these children." Mrs. Sweeney led everyone back to the kitchen table. She dumped the cold coffee out of Joe's cup and then she poured him another cup.

"Mr. Wilson, what happened to my husband?"

"About fifteen American soldiers, including Horace and myself, took refuge behind a five-foot brick wall as Taliban fighters fired automatic weapons in our direction. We were greatly outnumbered as the enemy came closer and closer toward that wall. Of course, we fired back and kept them at bay, but one of their bullets hit Horace in his chest. He fell at my feet, but before he died he asked me to do something for him."

Tears streaming down their faces, Michael and Gail ran out of the kitchen. "Mr. Wilson, what did Horace ask you to do?" She wiped her eyes with a kitchen napkin.

"Mrs. Sweeney, moments before he died he asked me to tell you and his children that he loved each of you with all his heart." Overcome with emotion, Joe burst into tears as he watched Mrs. Sweeney crying uncontrollably. Michael and Gail standing in the hallway had heard what Joe told their mother concerning their father. They ran toward their weeping mother, placing their arms around her neck.

A few minutes later, Mrs. Sweeney stood up. "Mr. Wilson, I'm so glad you came here today. I don't know how, but you have brought a certain degree of closure to our lives. I'm thankful to God that Horace had you as his friend. You will always be considered a dear friend to my children and me. Are you married?"

"Yes, my wife's name is Linda."

"Do you and Linda have any children?"

"No, Mrs. Sweeney, we don't have any children. I know it's selfish for me to ask this, but would it be okay for me to send the children a present or two over the coming years?"

"That would be very thoughtful of you, Mr. Wilson. You don't know this, but my children don't have an uncle. How would you like to be their adopted uncle?"

"I would consider that an honor. Does this mean that I could take Michael fishing sometime?"

"Yes, it certainly does."

"What about me, Mr. Wilson?" Gail asked.

"Do you like to fish?"

"Not really, but I don't want to be left out of anything."

"You'll never be left out of anything because it was your father's wish, and it's my sincere desire that his family he united and happy throughout their lives." Tears came into Joe's eyes as he looked toward the children.

"Mr. Wilson, why are you so sad?" Michael asked.

"I'm not sad, son. I'm just thankful that I had a good friend like your father." Gail and Michael gave him a big hug.

Chapter 4

It was Monday morning; Joe was at his parent's house. "Okay, everyone, breakfast is ready," said Sarah. "That means you too, Joe."

"Mother, I've already had a doughnut this morning."

"A doughnut, for Heaven sakes a working man can't survive on doughnuts! You might as well sit down to the table because I've already cooked for you."

"Your mother is always right, Joe. Anthony doesn't have to be asked, do you Anthony?"

"No, Father, I sure don't have to be asked," he smiled, reaching for another biscuit.

"Anthony, are you engaged to anyone?" Joe asked.

"No, I'm not engaged. In fact, I don't even have a steady girlfriend. I tell you who I would like to go out with."

"Who is that?" Joe asked.

"Doris Jones. That is one pretty woman to me."

"Have you asked her for a date yet?"

"Not yet, but I'm going to ask her very soon."

"I hate to break off this romantic discussion, but we've got to talk about today's work activities," said Mr. Wilson. "Anthony, I want you to take Joe to the Wellington project this morning and introduce him to the men. Let my superintendent know that Joe will, initially, be learning our procurement procedures for acquiring materials for our projects. I have big plans for you, Joe, especially after you have gained enough experience to manage entire projects."

"Father, what is the Wellington project?"

"It's a twelve story office building. When the superintendent needs materials, I want you to make sure that we are getting the very best deals on materials needed for the construction. The superintendent's name is Clayton Melbourne and he already knows you will be on the job today. He's a top-notch man and you'll like working with him."

"Joe, how did you like your breakfast?"

"Mother, it was delicious as always."

"Have you talked with Linda yet?"

"No, Mother, not yet. Well, Anthony, I'm ready to go to the Wellington project. By the way, why am I referring to you as Anthony? We've always called you Tony before."

"It's simple, Joe, my real name is Anthony, not Tony."

"Well, what's wrong with the name Tony?"

"He asked us to start calling him Anthony right after you went into the Army," said Mark. "He thinks Anthony is a much more sophisticated sounding name, and more-sexy sounding."

"You two leave him alone," said Sarah, smiling. "I'm the one that named him Anthony."

"My mother is always right," laughed Anthony.

"Father, where will you be today?" Joe asked.

"I'll be at the Park View Mall most of the day."

"I've never heard of that mall."

"That's because it will be a new mall."

"Are you the contractor for that mall?"

"Yes, I certainly am. Joe, we've expanded a great deal since you left for the Army."

"Are you still building homes as well as commercial buildings?"

"We're doing both. My company is building twelve nice homes right now. Anthony oversees all the private home projects. You will be more involved in commercial projects. Okay, let's hit the road. Anthony, tell Clayton Melbourne that I may not get a chance to see him today, but I will tomorrow."

"Mark Wilson, haven't you forgotten something?"

"What did I forget? Oh I'm sorry—I forgot to give you a hug before I leave for work." He hugged his wife and then kissed her on her cheek. It was all Joe could do to keep from crying, remembering how he and Linda would hug and kiss each other.

"Joe."

"Yes, Mother."

"I love you very much."

"I know you do."

"It breaks my heart to see you so sad. I wish I could make things better for you."

"I'll be okay, Mother."

Two days later, eight o'clock in the evening, Joe Wilson was sitting on his couch looking toward his television set, but it wasn't on. His discharge from the Army was becoming a faded memory, but night after night he sat in the same chair reliving the night he came home to find his wife in the bed with another man. Tears emerged from his eyes as he remembered his and Linda's wedding. Most of all, he remembered how much she seemed to love him. He kept asking himself why she would be unfaithful to him. His thoughts were interrupted, hearing his doorbell ring. He opened his door and saw three teenage gang members standing on his porch. "Remember me, tough guy? I'm the one you tried to choke!"

"What are you going to do with that gun?" Joe asked.

"Hell bells man—I'm going to kill you!" He shot Joe twice, and he fell in the doorway. The three hoodlums fled across the street and into the darkness. Mr. Macon Conway, Joe's neighbor was standing on his porch when the shots were fired. He hurried to Joe's house and found Joe lying unconscious on his porch. Without hesitation, he took out his cell phone and called 911. Two more neighbors hurried to Joe's house.

"Mr. Conway, is Joe dead?" Carlos Sanchez asked.

"I think he's alive, but he's in bad shape. My goodness, where is that ambulance?" Mrs. Blanche Conway came to the porch. "Blanche, Joe was shot twice by those no good scoundrels!"

"Did you see who shot him?"

"There were three of them, but I couldn't tell who they were. My God, I wish that ambulance would come on! I hear some sirens—that must be the ambulance and the police! Blanche, go to the house and call Joe's parents! Tell them that Joe has been shot and that he will be taken to Adamsville Memorial Hospital!" Blanche hurried toward her house.

Several onlookers backed off a short ways as the ambulance crew checked Joe's vital signs.

Within five minutes they had him on a stretcher, moving him toward the ambulance. The ambulance sped off with the siren blaring.

Three police cars were now parked in front of Joe's house. "Did anyone see what happened here?" Sgt. John Jenkins of the Adamsville police department asked.

"I heard the shots and then saw three people run off Joe's porch."

"What is your name?"

"Macon Conway, I live next door to Joe."

"Can you identify any of the perpetrators?"

"I'm afraid I can't, but I know one thing—all three of them were gang members."

"How do you know that?"

"They were wearing those black coats that have a glow-in-the-dark, coiled-snake printed on the back of them. I know who can identify them."

"Who would that be?"

"That would be Joe Wilson, himself. I heard just enough of the conversation to know that the shooter was getting even with Joe because of a prior confrontation between them. My God, Almighty, Joe has lost his wife and now he's mortally wounded! I hope his parents don't have a heart attack when they hear the news."

"Mark, what's wrong? You look like you've seen a ghost!"

"Sarah, we need to get to the hospital! Lord have mercy, I can't believe what has happened!"

"What are you talking about?"

"Joe has been shot!"

"What! How do you know that?"

"Mrs. Blanche Conway just called and told me! Let's get to the hospital as quick as we can!"

"I'm going just like I am!" Mrs. Wilson voiced. "Who in the world would have shot Joe?"

"I'll bet a hundred dollars it was those guys that tried to rob him a short time ago. Joe told me that one of them said he knew where he lived. Let's hurry, Sarah, we'll call Joan and Anthony on the way to the hospital!"

Joan and Anthony Wilson met their parents in the hospital parking lot. "Joan, when I called you a little while ago you already knew about Joe being shot. How did you find out so soon?" Mark asked.

"Mrs. Blanche Conway called my house and told me that he had been shot. Anthony happened to be at my house when the call came through. Let's hurry to the emergency room! My God, does anyone know why Joe was shot?"

"I'll bet anything it was those hoodlums that tried to rob him a while back," Mark answered.

Within a matter of minutes, Mark, Sarah, Joan and Anthony were in the emergency waiting room. "For goodness sakes, Mark, go somewhere and find out how our son is doing!" Mark stepped outside the waiting room and spotted a nurse in the hallway.

"Nurse, my name is Mark Wilson, my son is Joe Wilson and he's been shot! Can someone tell me how he's doing?"

"Mr. Wilson, there are two doctors with your son now. They're doing everything they can to save your son's life, but I'm afraid that is all I can tell you now. Soon as the doctors get through working on your son I'm sure that one of them will brief you on his condition."

"There's a policeman standing in front of that curtain down the hall. Is that the room that Joe's in?"

"Yes, it is. Mr. Wilson, I know the heartache and sorrow that your family must be going through now, but please go back to the waiting room and a doctor will brief you and your family as soon as possible." Mark returned to the waiting room.

"Father, what about Linda?" Anthony asked.

"What about Linda?"

"Well, she's still Joe's wife."

"So she is, but not a very good one!"

"Daddy, good or bad, Joe still loves Linda," said Joan. "Mother, what do you think?"

"What do I think about what?"

"Shouldn't we call Linda and let her know that her husband has been shot?"

"You all can do whatever you like, but I'm not calling her! In fact, I don't even want to speak to her!"

"Mother, I can't believe you even said that!" Joan remarked. "She did something terrible, but like Anthony said, Linda is still Joe's wife! I'm going to call her. She has a right to know that Joe has been shot." Joan opened the door and stepped into the hallway. She dialed Melvin Jones' house number.

A few seconds later, Mrs. Grace Jones answered the phone, "Yes, who is this?"

"Mrs. Jones, this is Joan Wilson, may I talk with Linda? It's very important!"

"Of course you can, Joan. Let me lay the phone down for a

few seconds and I'll get Linda for you." Mrs. Jones hurried up the stairs; she tapped lightly on Linda's door.

"Yes," Linda responded.

"Hurry downstairs, Joan Wilson is on the phone and she says it's very important!" Linda opened her door, she along with her mother hurried down the stairs.

"What's going on?" Melvin Jones asked as Linda reached for the phone.

"Joan, this is Linda. Mother said you had something important to tell me." Melvin and Grace Jones watched attentively as Linda listened on the phone. All at once, she dropped the phone; she started screaming as tears poured from her eyes. Her mother ran to Linda and tried calming her down.

"Linda, what's wrong? What did Joan tell you?"

"I've got to get dressed! I've got to go to the hospital! Oh, my God! I can't believe it!

I can't believe it happened!"

"My God, Almighty, Linda—what's wrong?" Her father asked.

"Joe! It's Joe!"

"What about Joe? Linda, what about Joe?"

"Daddy, he's been shot! Oh, my God, I've got to go to him! God—please don't let my husband die!" Linda pleaded.

"Who shot Joe?"

"Daddy, I don't know who shot him!" Linda hurried up the stairs to change her clothes.

"Grace, get ready real quick, we can't let Linda drive in her emotional state."

Linda and her parents arrived at the hospital twenty

minutes later. They hurried down the corridor toward the emergency waiting room. Tears were sliding down Linda's face when she opened the waiting room door. "Mr. Wilson, what is Joe's condition?"

"We're not sure, Linda. We haven't talked to a doctor yet. Mrs. Jones, you and Melvin have a seat. I guess we'll know something soon."

"Mark, do they know who shot Joe?" Melvin asked.

"Not really, but I'll bet anything it was the same individuals that tried to rob him the first night he came home."

"Sarah, I'm very sorry about your son," said Grace Jones.

"Thank you."

It was quite evident that Sarah Wilson was still mad with Linda, but under the circumstance she remained civil toward her.

Thirty minutes later, Doris Jones came into the waiting room. Her father had called her before they left home. Anthony got up and offered her his seat. "Thank you, Anthony, but where are you going to sit?"

"I'm tired of sitting anyway."

"Linda, have you found out anything yet about Joe's condition?" Doris asked.

"No." She answered, wiping her tears.

It was very obvious to Doris that Sarah Wilson was giving Linda a cold shoulder. It was as though Linda was despicable in her sight. "Anthony, would you mind walking with me to get something to drink?" Doris asked.

"I wouldn't mind at all. In fact, I would be happy to walk with you." They left the room, and then started walking down the hallway. Doris motioned for Anthony to follow her into a small waiting room.

"Have a seat, Anthony; I've got something to tell you that you should know. In fact, your entire family needs to know what I'm going to tell you. I really like your family, but I can't stand the way your mother looks at Linda. It's like she's a piece of trash or something! You or they don't know why Linda was found in bed with her supervisor!"

"Doris, I only know what my parents told me. They saw her naked in bed with someone other than her husband."

"That's true, but did anyone ever ask why she was in the bed with that low down scoundrel?"

"I don't know what you're getting at, but it seemed very obvious why they were naked in bed together."

"I want you to be quiet for a few minutes while I tell you something that you or your parents don't know! Linda knew that Joe was coming home soon, but she didn't know the exact date because he didn't tell her. I guess he wanted his arrival to be a surprise. Anyway, Linda bought a wide screen television set for Joe, but she didn't know how to hook it up. Her supervisor agreed to drop by and hook it up for her. Linda didn't like the idea of him coming to her house, but she did want the television hooked up before Joe came home. She agreed to let her boss come by her house to hook up the set. When he came he brought some kind of juice with him.

While Linda wasn't looking he poured her and himself a glass of the juice. At first she declined, but he insisted that she drink it. Anthony, he spiked her drink which made her pass out. When Joe and my parents entered your house my sister was on the bed still passed out. She only awoke after my parents and Joe entered the bedroom and Daddy started yelling at her. It was only then that Linda realized that she was naked on her bed with William Davis lying beside her. Confused and bewildered, she didn't know what to say or do, but cover herself up. It was never her intention to have sex with her supervisor. Whether you believe me or not—I have just told you the honest truth about my sister."

"Doris, why didn't Linda report this to the police?"

"Do you think the police would have believed what I just told you?"

"I guess they wouldn't have."

"How about you, Anthony, do you believe what I just told you?"

"Yes, Doris, I do believe that's what happened. When did you find out what really happened?"

"Linda told me and my parents three days ago. Linda loves Joe Wilson with all her heart. She's loved him from the first time she met him. I can't bear the thought of your parents' thinking she is a tramp."

"Doris, I will talk with them as soon as I can. I'll try to straighten this whole thing out."

"Thank you, Anthony, I appreciate that."

"Doris, before we go back to the waiting room, may I ask you something?"

"Yes, what is it?"

"Would you consider going to dinner with me one evening?"

"I was wondering when you might ask me out."

"Does that mean your answer is, yes?"

"That's what it means. Now, let's get back to the waiting room and see if there's any news concerning your brother."

Anthony and Doris saw Dr. William Jeffrey talking to Linda, Mark and Sarah in the hallway.

They stopped near the doctor to listen in on the conversation. Tears were running down Linda's cheeks as she listened to the doctor. "Mrs. Wilson, since you're Joe Wilson's wife it will be your decision whether we try to remove the bullet next to your husband's heart."

"Doctor, what are my options?" Linda asked.

"Joe's condition is critical. We've removed one bullet that was not too far from his spine, but the other one is lodged close to his heart. The operation is a very serious one. However, to leave that bullet where it is could prove to be just as serious and more probable fatal at some point in time."

"Dr. Jeffrey, don't his parents have any say in the matter?" Sarah Wilson asked.

"I understand your feelings, Mrs. Wilson, but I'm afraid this decision must come from Joe's wife."

"Dr. Jeffrey, may I have a few minutes to think about it?" Linda asked.

"Yes, but I need a decision within the next thirty minutes. I just want all of you to know that Joe is in a critical condition. It's a miracle that he's still alive."

"Well, it seems that my son's life is in Linda's hands!" Sarah Wilson said, sarcastically.

"That's not true, Mrs. Wilson," said Dr. Jeffrey. "I would say that your son's life is in God's hands." Dr. Jeffrey started walking down the hallway.

"Mother, that wasn't very nice what you just said."

"Well, that beats all! My only other son is siding with Joe's unfaithful wife!"

"Mrs. Wilson, you will learn later that I wasn't unfaithful to your son, but right now we've got to decide what's best for Joe. Mr. Wilson, we've only got two choices as far as Joe is concerned. Would you give me your advice as to what we should do about Joe?"

"I appreciate you asking me, but I'm afraid Joe won't have any chance of survival if the bullet is left lodged near his heart. It will be your decision, but I recommend removing the bullet."

"Mrs. Wilson, Joe is your son and I respect that. What would you have me to do?"

"I think my husband's recommendation is the right way to go."

"Anthony, Joe is your brother, what are your thoughts about the situation?" Linda asked.

"I think the bullet should be removed from near his heart."

"Okay, it's final—my decision is the same as Joe's family. I'll go find Dr. Jeffrey and have him remove the bullet. Mrs. Wilson, no matter what you think of me, I still love you and your family. I love my husband with all my heart and I always have." Linda burst into tears as she walked away.

"Doris, would you mind going to the waiting room," said Anthony. "I need to talk to my parents for a little while."

"Okay, I'll see you in the waiting room in a little while." Doris started walking down the hallway.

"Mother, Father, I want you both to follow me down the hall a little ways."

"Why?" Sarah asked.

"I need to tell you something."

"Anthony, I didn't appreciate you standing up for that tramp like you did!"

"Mother, Linda is not a tramp!"

"You don't know what you're talking about! Her own mother and father saw her lying naked on the bed with her supervisor. What do you think they had been doing? They weren't just counting sheep!"

"Mother, please keep your voice down! I want both of you to go to a waiting room around the next corner. I've got something that I need to tell you."

"You can say whatever you want to, but I'll never have any respect for that two-timing hussy that Joe married!"

Anthony and his parents went inside a vacant waiting room. Anthony closed the door. Mark looked at his son and asked, "We're here, Anthony, what is it that you need to tell us?" His father asked.

"I want to talk about perception."

"What in the Hell are you talking about?" Sarah asked.

"Mother, please let me finish what I have to say before interrupting me! Perception can be a very harmful thing. Sometimes individuals see situations or conditions and their brains lock in on what they believe to be a reality. In a lot of cases the actual situations or conditions are totally different from what the perceptions are. However, it's very difficult to see another side of the situation or condition once the perception is locked into our brain."

"Mark, do we have to sit here and listen at this nonsense?"

"Sarah, give Anthony a chance to tell us what's on his mind. I believe after he gets through with this perception thing he's going to tell us something."

"Father, Mother, I'm going to tell you something that's going to blow your mind. Linda is not a tramp and she's not an unfit or unfaithful wife. It's true that her parents and Joe saw her lying naked in bed with another man. Upon hearing that news, your perception was that she was in that bed because she chose to be there. Well, you're wrong! Dead wrong! Linda knew that Joe was coming home soon so she bought him a new wide-screen television set. She got the television home, but she didn't know how to hook it up. She wanted the television to be a surprise for Joe whenever he came home."

"What did a television set have to do with her being naked in bed with another man?" Sarah asked.

"She mentioned to her supervisor that she had bought a new television for her husband, but she didn't know how to hook it up. Linda's supervisor volunteered to drop by her house and get the television operational. Linda declined his offer at first, but he told her that he could be in and out of her house in a matter of minutes. When he came to Linda's house he brought a bottle of juice. Before hooking up the television he insisted that she taste his special juice. Somehow or other, the low down scoundrel spiked Linda's juice causing her to become unconscious. He carried her to the bed and stripped her naked. She only came to when Joe and her parents went into her bedroom and her father started shouting. At that very moment she was in total shock, in disbelief—realizing that not only was she naked, but she had been molested by her own supervisor. Only then did she realize that Joe was standing there with a bundle of flowers in his hand. Linda was speechless, she didn't know what to do or what to say since she hadn't figured out then that she had been drugged."

"That's the most ridiculous story I have ever heard!" Sarah said, standing up. "Who told you that lie?"

"Sarah, what if you're wrong?" Mark asked.

"I'll never believe that cock and bull story!" Sarah said.

"Anthony, what you've said does make sense. I saw a new television set in Joe's house and it wasn't hooked up."

"Thank you, Father. I'm going to prove to both of you that I'm telling you the truth."

"How are you going to do that?" Sarah asked.

"I won't get into that, but I know how I'm going to prove it."

"Anthony, I'm your father, I want to know how you're going to prove it."

"Well, if you must know I'm going to beat the living Hell out of William Davis! He's going to tell me exactly why he was naked in bed with my brother's wife!"

"You do that and you'll wind up in jail!"

"Your mother is right, Anthony. It will be much better if you let me handle it."

"Mark, what are you planning to do?"

"Sarah, I'm just going to talk with William Davis."

"Like Hell you are! You're planning to beat the crap out of William Davis! I can see it in your eyes right now! Don't you know you can't just beat that man like a pulp and then get away with it?"

"Sarah, whether you like it or not—I think the world of Linda Wilson! She's like a daughter to me! What happened to Linda is not her fault if it's true what Anthony told us! I'm not going to let that pig get away with ruining my son's marriage!"

"Mark, what if you're wrong about Linda?"

"I don't think I am wrong! Linda loved Joe way too much for her to have sex with William Davis or anyone else."

"Please, Mark, don't get into trouble with the law!" Tears came into Sarah's eyes.

"I'm not planning to get into trouble, but I am going to get to the bottom of this horrible situation. We deserve to know the truth! By golly, Joe needs to know whether his wife cheated on him or not! I won't rest until I have that answer!"

Chapter 5

Linda Wilson and Joe's parents were told that they could go into Joe's room for a few minutes, prior to him being moved to the operating unit. Linda was the first one into the room. Tears slid down her face as she observed her husband lying motionless on the small bed. She walked beside him, and then she placed her face against his. Sarah Wilson looked toward Linda in total disgust, nodding at her husband to notice Linda's behavior. Mark saw nothing wrong with Linda showing emotional feelings toward her husband.

"May I kiss my son?" Sarah asked, sarcastically, standing behind Linda. "Furthermore, I've never done anything to make him ashamed of me!" Linda moved to the other side of Joe's bed.

"Sarah, you have no right to be rude toward Linda?"

"Haven't I, Mark? You did hear about her being naked on the bed with her boss man. Well, Joe saw the same thing his parents did"

"Mrs. Wilson, you're wrong about me!" Linda cried.

"I'm well aware of that cock and bull story that you told your sister! I guess she told Anthony the story that you concocted about you being drugged or something! Well, I don't believe one word of it!"

"Sarah, this is not the time or place for you to be talking like that!"

"Mark Wilson, you're as crazy as Anthony if you believe that story she made up about sleeping with her boss." Tears flowed down Linda's face as she hurried out of the room.

"That was a cruel and unnecessary thing that you just did!"

"Listen here, Mark Wilson, only a fool would believe that story of hers!"

"Well, I guess I'm a fool because I believe what she said. It sounds perfectly logical to me."

"Why didn't she go to the law? Why didn't she say that she was drugged when they walked into her bedroom?"

"Sarah Wilson, would you have gone to the law if that had happened to you? Before you answer, do you think your family would have believed you if they had caught you in the exact circumstance?"

"I don't know if I would have gone to the law or not."

"Would you have explained to your family right then and there why you were in bed with your supervisor? Remember, according to her she only came to when Joe and her parents walked into her bedroom. That poor woman was still in a daze at that time!"

"You can paint any kind of scenario that you want, but I think she lied about the whole thing! I think our son found out exactly what she was—a cheating wife. It's her fault that he got shot like he did!"

"How in the Hell is it her fault that Joe got shot? I've never seen you this critical before about anything!"

"I'll never get the picture out of my mind of Linda lying naked on that bed next to William Davis while her poor husband, our own son mind you, standing there in his Army uniform holding a dozen roses in his hands! The very thought of it makes me sick! Do you hear me—sick?"

"Sarah, I don't know what has come over you!"

"Joe's been fighting in a war! He's been shot! She had no right to do him the way she did!"

"What on earth will you do if you find out that you've been wrong about the whole thing?"

"I hate to break up your conversation, but I need to take Mr. Wilson to the operating room," said Tammy Smith, a registered nurse. Mark and Sarah walked out of the room. Linda was in the hallway crying when Mark and Sarah walked past her.

"Nurse, please wait just a minute so I can say a prayer for my husband!" Linda asked. Mark and Sarah watched as Linda, tears sliding down her face, got down on her knees beside Joe and started praying. <u>"Lord God, please—I beg you to make my husband well! He's a good man and he deserves better than to come home from a war in belief that he's married to an unfaithful wife. He was wounded there and now he's been shot again by low down sneaking scoundrels! Joe, if you can hear me—I promise you with my life that I was not unfaithful to you! God, please grant me this one wish because I love my husband with all my heart! Joe, I'll be praying for you! Please don't die on me! Oh, God! Please! Please let him live! I love you</u>

<u>Joe. Amen."</u> Linda, still on her knees cried uncontrollably as the nurse moved Joe toward the elevator. It was obvious that the nurse was in tears, also.

Mark Wilson walked to Linda and helped her up. "Linda, for what it's worth—I believe you were telling the truth about what happened in your bedroom. Let's go back to the waiting room where your parents and sister are waiting."

"Mr. Wilson, I was telling the truth so help me, God!"

"I believe you. Now, let's get back to the waiting room so we can tell your folks that Joe has been moved to the operating room." Sarah Wilson turned and started walking ahead of Linda and Mark. It was still obvious that she didn't believe a single word that Linda had said.

After they got back to the emergency waiting room, Mark Wilson noticed that his son was no longer in the room. "Melvin, did Anthony say where he was going?"

"Yes, Mark, he said he was going to take care of some business."

"Did he say what kind of business it was?"

"Not exactly, but I do believe he's gone somewhere to find William Davis."

"What makes you think that?"

"Out of the clear blue while sitting in that chair you're in, he got up and said, 'William Davis is a low-down, conniving, sneaking-bastard and I'm going to prove it!' I asked him where he was going, but he didn't say anything. Mark, I hope Anthony doesn't get himself in any trouble with William Davis."

"Melvin, do you know where William Davis lives?"

"Yes, Mark, I sure do. Are you going looking for Anthony?"

"I plan to. Would you mind coming with me and show me where he lives?"

"I wouldn't mind at all. Grace, you, Doris and Linda wait here until we get back."

"Mrs. Jones, all of you need to go to the waiting room near the intensive care unit," said Mark. "They're going to take Joe near there sometime after his operation. "Sarah, you and Joan go with them upstairs. Mr. Jones and I are going to find Anthony before he gets himself into some serious trouble."

"Mark, do you have to go now?" Sarah asked.

"Yes, Sarah, we need to find Anthony."

After accompanying the others to the intensive care waiting room, Mark and Melvin left the hospital to go find Anthony. "Mother, may I get you something to drink?" Joan asked.

"I'm not thirsty."

"Doris, would you, Linda, or Mrs. Jones care for something to drink?" Joan asked.

"I believe I would," said Doris. "In fact, I'll walk with you."

"Linda, would you like to walk with us?" Joan asked.

"I appreciate you asking me, but I'll wait here."

Joan and Doris hadn't walked very far before Doris asked Joan why Mrs. Wilson disliked Linda so much.

"Doris, my mother's nerves are all to pieces now. She's terribly worried about Joe and she still thinks that Linda was cheating on her son. Father told me what Linda said that happened. I see no reason to disbelieve her story, but my mother seems to have her mind made up. Before this situation my mother always said very nice things about Linda."

"Here are the vending machines," said Joan. "What kind of drink are you going to get?"

"I think I'll just get a bottle of orange juice."

*   *   *   *

"Mark, that two-story brick house up ahead is William Davis's house. Isn't that your son's car parked in the driveway?"

"Yes, it certainly is. Pull up behind Anthony's car. I hope my son hasn't done anything foolish." They parked their car, and then hurried up the front steps. Melvin rang the doorbell several times.

"Yes, may I help you," said a lady, standing in the doorway.

"Are you Mrs. Davis?" Mark asked.

"Yes, my name is Melissa Davis. How may I help you?"

"Mrs. Davis, my name is Mark Wilson and this gentleman is Mr. Melvin Jones. By chance, is my son Anthony inside your house?"

"Yes, please come inside." Melvin and Mark followed Mrs. Davis inside her home. Anthony was sitting on her couch observing her two small children."

"Father, Mr. Jones, how did you know I was here?"

"That's a good question, Anthony, why are you here?"

"Mr. Jones, I believe I can answer that question. Your son came here looking for answers, and he found out what he wanted to know."

"I don't understand, Mrs. Davis," said Mark. "Just exactly what did Mark find out?"

Tears came into Mrs. Davis's eyes. "Mr. Wilson, my husband

lost his job, or more specifically he quit his job because he did a very bad thing. Children, go to your bedroom for now. I will come see you in a little while." Nelson was ten years old and Heather was eight. They each kissed their mother, and then they went to their rooms.

"Father, I want you and Mr. Jones to hear what Mrs. Davis has to say," said Anthony.

"Okay, Mrs. Davis, we're listening," said Mark.

"My husband turned himself into the law two hours ago. He told me that he couldn't take the embarrassment and guilt any longer for what he did to Mr. Jones' daughter. He told me everything. Four days after he spiked Linda Wilson's juice and molested her he purchased a handgun and a box of bullets. His intention, according to him, was to kill himself for his despicable deed. Mr. Jones, all three of you have a right to hate William, but I have two children, and I am partially paralyzed. Not only do I need my husband, but I still love him. He got down on his hands and knees on this very floor, crying like a small child. He told me how sorry he was for deceiving Linda Wilson. William told me that he had ruined his life by destroying my trust for him. I had no idea what had happened until he told me himself. He went to Linda Wilson's house with the sole intention to spike her drink and then have sex with her.

Before turning himself into the law he withdrew most of our savings to give to Linda for the wrong he had done. The money is in that manila folder that's next to where Anthony is sitting."

"Mrs. Davis, why did William turn himself into the law?" Mark asked.

"He told me that he needed to be punished for doing such a cruel thing to Joe's wife. I believe he wants Linda to press charges against him."

"Mrs. Davis, I can't speak for Linda, but I do not think she will be pressing charges against your husband, especially now," said Mr. Jones. "Also, I don't think my daughter would want to take your money that you need to take care of you and your children. Mark, is that the way you feel about it?"

"I couldn't agree more, Melvin. Mrs. Davis, the reason all three of us are here is to find out the truth. I believe we have found out the truth and the truth will be all that Linda and my son will need to know."

"Sheriff Nathan Corbett was here earlier and he said that my husband wouldn't likely go to prison unless Linda pressed charges against him. However, he won't get off scot-free either. He most likely will be required to attend some sexual behavior classes for a few weeks."

Anthony handed the manila envelope containing the money to Mrs. Davis. "Mrs. Davis, you've got two wonderful looking children."

"Thank you, Anthony. Please tell your sister how sorry I am about what happened to her. I feel like I'm partly responsible for what my husband did."

"Why do you say that, Mrs. Davis?" Mark asked.

"I've got some serious health problems and I didn't want to do anything but go to sleep when I went to bed. Night after night, William would lie next to me, tossing and turning, but all I did was ache and sleep. I should have been a better wife to my husband. He has never thrown this up in my face, but I should shoulder some blame for his conduct."

"Mrs. Davis, make no mistake about it, you had absolutely nothing to do with his behavior at my daughter's house that day. However, I am pleased to hear that William is very remorseful for what he did. Mark, Anthony, let's get back to the hospital and see how Joe is doing."

"Mr. Wilson, Anthony told me about Joe getting shot. I was very sorry to hear that news. I promise to pray for him tonight and more nights to follow."

"Thank you, Mrs. Davis. Please take good care of your lovely children," said Mark. "I'm anxious to get back to the hospital and tell my daughter-in-law that we all know that she was telling the truth about her ordeal."

Chapter 6

By the time Mark, Anthony and Melvin got back to the hospital, Sarah and Joan had left to go home for a little while. "Why did they leave?" Mark asked Mrs. Jones.

"Your wife accidentally spilled some tomato juice on her clothes. They'll be back shortly."

"Mrs. Jones, Doris, may I go get you something to eat or drink?" Anthony asked.

"I've got a better idea," answered Doris. "Let's all go out for a few minutes and get something to eat."

"I'm not very hungry," Mark answered. "Why don't the rest of you get something to eat and I'll wait here for Joan and Sarah to return. By the time they get here and by the time all of you return I might be hungry. By the way, where is Linda?"

"She said she was going to walk around the hospital one or two times. " Grace answered. "She said she's too nervous to sit down. Anyway, we'll bring her something to eat." Anthony,

Melvin, Doris and Grace left the hospital, and then they drove toward Marston's Family Restaurant.

"Grace, I want you and Doris to know that Linda was telling the absolute truth about why she was in bed with William Davis. William has already told his wife about the whole thing. In fact, he's already turned himself into the law for doing what he did."

"Melvin, I already knew she was telling us the truth," said Grace. "Have you ever known Linda to tell a lie about anything?"

"No, I surely haven't. When we get back to the hospital I'll tell Linda what Mrs. Davis told us about her husband. I just wish Joe was conscious so we could tell him that Linda was not unfaithful to him. I'll pray that he will be okay."

"We all appreciate that, Mr. Jones," said Anthony. "Joe has always liked your family, and I know for a fact that he loves his wife. Linda is a very beautiful woman, and so is your other daughter." Anthony looked toward Doris and smiled.

"Guess who's asked me out on a date, Mother?"

"I already know that, Doris. Anthony has had an interest in you for a very long time."

"Anthony, is my mother correct in saying that?"

"She's telling you the truth, Doris. You look like an Angel to me."

"Mother, Father, did you just hear what Anthony said?"

"We heard, dear," answered Melvin. "Anthony Wilson, do you know how precious my daughters are to me?"

"Yes sir, I do. Mr. Jones, I'm no William Davis, and I will always treat Doris with respect and dignity."

"Well, that's all any parent can ask for."

Mark Wilson was sitting alone in the intensive care waiting room when a deputy sheriff opened the room door. "Sir, by chance are you Mr. Mark Wilson?"

"Yes." Mark stood up.

"Sir, your wife and daughter have been in a wreck."

"What! Where did it happen? Are they alright?"

"Sir, they were brought into the emergency room fifteen minutes ago." Mark hurried out of the waiting room. He hurried as fast as he could toward the emergency room desk. By the time he got there his wife and daughter were being attended to by two doctors.

"Nurse, my name is Mark Wilson, my wife and daughter just came into the emergency room! I need to see them!" Tears were in Mark's eyes. "My God, how could this have happened?"

"Mr. Wilson, your wife and daughter are being treated right now. If you will wait in the adjacent waiting room for a little while you will be allowed to see both of them." The same deputy that told him the news concerning the wreck a few minutes ago was now standing behind Mark. "Sir, it wasn't your wife's fault. Another vehicle ran a stop light and plowed into your wife's car."

"How bad did my wife and daughter get hurt?"

"Sir, I'm not privileged to tell you about their condition, except that they were both alive when they left the wreck scene."

"Oh my God, my son is lying unconscious on an operating table, and now my wife and daughter are lying in the emergency room!"

"Mr. Wilson! Mr. Wilson, are you alright?" The deputy asked.

"I don't feel so good. Officer, call a nurse!" Mr. Wilson dropped to his knees while clutching his hands against his chest.

"Nurse! Nurse!" The officer yelled. Mr. Wilson fell over on his side. A doctor and two nurses rushed to him.

"Doctor, I really belief Mr. Wilson has had a heart attack," said the officer. "He just found out that his wife and daughter were in a wreck." Within minutes, Mr. Wilson was moved to an emergency room stall same as was his wife and daughter. Tests were started to determine what had happened to him.

Forty-five minutes later, Anthony, Melvin, Grace and Doris returned to the intensive care waiting room, but Mark wasn't there. "Sir, do you know where my father went?" Anthony asked a gentleman that was in the waiting room when they left.

"I'm not sure, but I think he might be at the emergency room."

"I wonder why he went to the emergency room."

"Are you his son?"

"Yes sir, my name is Anthony Wilson."

"Son, I hate to tell you this, but I believe your mother and sister were in a wreck. A sheriff's deputy told your father that his wife and daughter had been in a wreck. Your father hurried out of the waiting room. I'm just assuming that he went straight to the emergency room."

Melvin, Grace, and Doris tried to stay up with Anthony, but couldn't—he was running down the hall toward the elevator. When Anthony got to the emergency room he quickly inquired about his mother and sister. "Sir, your mother, father and sister are being treated by doctors as we speak," said a nurse.

"You say my father is being treated, also?"

"When he found out that your mother and sister had been in a wreck, he had some kind of spell."

"Spell, what do you mean—spell?"

"I'm not supposed to say this, but it's possible that your father had a heart attack when he heard the news about his wife and daughter."

"For goodness sakes, nurse, what about my mother and sister?"

"Mr. Wilson, I can only say that your mother is unconscious and your sister has a broken arm and a broken leg."

Doris held Anthony's left hand as he wiped his tears with his right hand. "Anthony, let's go to the waiting room," said Doris. She held onto him as they walked down the hallway.

Anthony no longer could conceal his emotions, he commenced crying. Doris placed her arm across his shoulder.

"Grace, I'm going to find Linda. She needs to know what's going. While she's here, maybe you can get her to eat something."

"Okay, Melvin, I'll go to the emergency waiting room and see if there's anything I can do for Anthony," said Grace. "Try to find out how Joe is doing. We should have heard something by now."

By the time Melvin and Linda got to the emergency waiting room, highway patrolman Derek Meadows had just begun talking with Anthony Wilson concerning the wreck that his mother and sister were in. "Mr. Wilson, one reason I'm here is to see how your mother and sister are doing, and the other reason is to let their family know that the accident was not their fault."

"Did the driver in the other car get hurt very badly?" Anthony asked, tears flowing down his face.

"There were two people in the other car; both of them were killed in the accident. The driver didn't have any identification on him, but we were able to recognize him right away because he had a snake-shaped earring in his previously disfigured ear. His name is Wally Benson, a gang leader and he was wanted by the sheriff's office and the police department. His passenger was Monty Gaylord, he, too, was a gang member and wanted by the law. Mr. Wilson, I'm sorry that your mother and sister were in a wreck, but I will pray for both of them."

"Thank you, officer; I really do appreciate you talking with me and for your prayers."

The patrolman left the room. "Linda, how is my brother doing?" Anthony asked.

"He's still in the operating room. They're going to move him to an intensive care unit after he comes out of surgery. Daddy told me about the wreck and that Mr. Wilson may have had a heart attack. Anthony, I'm truly sorry that your mother and sister were in a wreck. I'll pray for them and your father. Is there anything that I can do for you or them?"

"Will you go find out if I can see my family?"

"I certainly will. There is no reason that you can't see them all! I'll be right back." Linda asked an emergency room doctor if it would be okay if Anthony could briefly visit with his father, mother and sister. He told Linda that he and two more individuals could see each of them for a very brief period.

Linda returned to the waiting room. "Is it alright for me to see my family now?" Anthony asked.

"Yes, you can visit each of them for a little while. You can let two more people go with you if you want to."

"Mr. Jones, Mrs. Jones, is it okay if Doris and Linda go with me first? After their visit, both of you can visit with my folks."

"That will be just fine, Anthony," said Melvin. "We'll wait until Doris and Linda gets back to the waiting room."

Anthony, Doris, and Linda walked quietly into Mr. Wilson's room. Mark, with tears in his eyes was looking toward the ceiling as Anthony touched him on his hand. "Father, are you hurting anywhere?" Mark shook his head, indicating no. "What did the doctor say about your condition?"

"Don't cry, Anthony. I'll be okay."

"I'm very worried about you."

"I know you are, but I'm going to be fine. How are your mother and your sister doing?"

"I really don't know yet, but I'm going to check on them in a very short while. Look who came into the room with me."

"Linda, Doris, it was good of you to come see me. Linda, how is Joe?"

"Mr. Wilson, Joe is still in the operating room. His operation should be over with very soon. I have prayed and prayed that he will be okay."

"Doris, you're a very beautiful woman. You may not know this, but Anthony likes you a lot."

"Well, Mr. Wilson, I like Anthony a lot, too."

"Father, didn't the doctor tell you anything about your condition?"

"Yes, son, he told me that I did have a minor heart attack, but with medication, rest and avoiding over excitement that I should be just fine. Now, I want you to go check on your mother and sister. Linda, will you remain here for a couple minutes, I want to tell you something?"

"Sure I will, Mr. Wilson." Anthony and Doris walked out of the room, and then they headed toward his mother's room.

"Linda, you're a good woman, and a fine wife. I can hardly wait until Joe and my wife finds out the real truth about you and William Davis. He's already admitted to his wife and the authorities that he spiked your drink and then he took advantage of you. For what it's worth, he's now a very troubled man for treating you the way he did. Linda, Joe still loves you very much, but he was devastated when he thought you were cheating on him. I want you and him to get back together. The last thing is this—please don't hate Grace for her harsh actions and cruel words toward you. After she finds out the truth about what happened between you and William Davis she will apologize to you for her behavior."

"Mr. Wilson, I don't hate your wife. In fact, had I been in her shoes I would have reacted the very same way." Linda leaned over and kissed him on his cheek. "Mr. Wilson, not only do I love Joe more than you can imagine, but I, also, love his parents and sister. I want you to quit worrying so much so you can see your son, wife and daughter walk out of this hospital."

"Tell Anthony to come back to my room after he's seen Sarah and Joan. Someone has got to look after my business."

"I'll tell him."

A nurse was checking Sarah Wilson's vital signs when Anthony and Doris walked into her room. "Nurse, how is my mother?" Anthony asked.

"Are you her son?"

"Yes, my name is Anthony."

"Her vital signs are nearly normal. Dr. Ben Starling will be meeting with you in about an hour. He will discuss your mother and your sister's condition."

Tears slid down Anthony's face as he observed his mother lying motionless in the bed. She had twelve stitches on her forehead and her left arm was in a cast. Doris placed her hand on Anthony's shoulder as he looked down at his mother. "She's going to be just fine, Anthony."

"Doris, I sure hope you're right. I can't believe what has happened to my family. It's like we've done something wrong, but what?" He looked toward the ceiling and said, "God, we need some help! Four members of my family are lying here in this hospital! Please! Please help us!" Doris handed Anthony a box of tissues as she wiped tears from her own eyes.

A few minutes later Anthony was down on his knees beside his mother's bed. "Mother, Mother, can you hear me, this is Anthony? Nod your head or say something if you can hear me. Mother, I love you very, very much! Please get well—your family needs you!"

About three minutes later Anthony and Doris met up with Linda in the hallway. They were on their way to Joan's emergency room stall. "Well, I'm finally getting some company," said Joan. "I'm glad to see all three of you. Linda, how is Joe doing?" Tears were in Joan's eyes.

"He's still in the operating room. He should be out very soon now. Joan, I have prayed so much that I feel confident that he will be just fine."

"Anthony, what about Mother?"

"We just left from her room. She's still unconscious, but

we're hoping to hear some good news soon. They're performing some kind of test on her. I don't want my sister worrying herself silly." He placed his face against hers. "I love you, Sis!"

"I know that already. I guess you know that I love you, too."

"I do—indeed!"

"What about Father? Is he going to be okay?" Joan asked.

"Father has had a mild heart attack, but he's going to be just fine."

"Linda, I just want you to know that I believe what you said happened to you with William Davis."

"Heck fire, Joan, everyone can believe it now," said Anthony.

"Why do you say that?"

"William Davis has already admitted to his wife and to the law that he spiked Linda's juice and then took advantage of her while she was unconscious and without her consent."

Linda leaned over and kissed Joan on her forehead. "Thank you for believing in me. It meant so much to me to have someone believing I was telling the truth." Tears slid down Linda's face. Anthony handed her some tissue.

"That will be wonderful news for Joe," said Doris. "Besides, I don't believe God is going to allow anything else bad to happen to the Wilson family, and that includes Joe."

A nurse walked into Joan's room. "Nurse, you were in my mother's room earlier," said Anthony. "Is Dr. Starling going to talk with us pretty soon concerning my mother, father, brother or my sister?"

"Sir, I believe the doctor is still waiting for the final results of a test being performed on your mother. He should be getting with you in a short while." The nurse left the room.

"Joan, we're going back to the emergency waiting room so Mr. and Mrs. Jones can visit you, Mother and Father, but we will be back to see you after a while." Anthony leaned over and kissed his sister on her cheeks.

"Anthony, I just remembered something. Your father wanted you to go to his room after you visited with your mother and sister," said Linda.

"I'll go there now. Doris, Linda, I'll see you both back at the waiting room in a little while."

Anthony walked hurriedly back to his father's room.

"How are your mother and sister doing?" Mark asked.

"Father, Joan seems to be doing just fine."

"What about your mother?"

"She has some stitches in her forehead, but other than a cast on her arm she looks okay."

"My question is this—is she still unconscious?"

"Father, I'm afraid she is."

"What did the doctor say about her?"

"He hasn't told me anything yet. He's waiting on some kind of test. Maybe we'll find out something real soon."

"Yes, you definitely will," said Dr. Ben Starling, walking into the room. "First, we'll discuss health issues concerning your father. Mr. Wilson, how are you feeling?"

"Well, I'm not having chest pains anymore. Dr. Starling, how bad was my heart attack?"

"Mr. Wilson, any kind of heart attack can't be taken likely, but as heart attacks goes—yours was diagnosed as a mild one. I've already written orders for you to remain at the hospital for

83

about three more days. We'll be administering a rather new heart medicine to you during that time and we need you close at hand for observation."

"You mean I'll be a Guinea Pig?"

"No, Mr. Wilson, that's not the case. In fact, the heart medicine that I'm talking about is the same kind I would want if I were in your condition."

"Speaking of condition, Dr. Starling, what condition is my father in?"

"My professional opinion concerning your father is this— with proper medication, avoiding very stressful situations, the right nourishment and proper exercise he will be just fine."

"That sounds great!" Anthony said, smiling.

"What about my wife, Dr. Starling? Anthony tells me that she is still unconscious."

"Mr. Wilson, your wife sustained a very bad head injury. We never know how these kinds of cases will turn out, but the internal swelling inside her head has gone down quite a bit. That in itself is a very good sign. Mrs. Wilson has a very strong heart beat and that's a real plus for someone in her condition. She will be intensive care until her condition changes for the better."

"What about my daughter?"

"Miss Joan Wilson is doing just fine. However she does have a broken arm and a broken leg. I haven't told her yet, but she will be able to leave the hospital in two or three more days. She will need a lot of help when she gets home, especially until those casts come off her arm and leg. Mr. Wilson, there's something else that may make your day."

"What is that?"

"Your son, Joe came through his surgery just fine. The bullet we had great concerns about was successfully removed from his chest. He has been moved to the intensive care unit of the hospital. He's still unconscious, but he should be just fine from the gunshot wounds."

"Dr. Starling, why is Joe still unconscious? Is it because the anesthesia hasn't worn off yet?'

"That's not the case at all. His head hit something hard after being shot by his assailants."

"Well, Joe does have a cement porch. Could that have been what his head hit?"

"It may have been, but I'm not sure. As I said before, I may have some news that may brighten your day."

"I really do need some good news."

"Dr. Benjamin Sawyer is Joe Wilson's doctor. He specializes in head injuries. Not more than twenty minutes ago he told me that Joe had moved his right fingers on at least two occasions."

"Good Lord, that does sound good news, Dr. Starling, but what does that mean?" Mark asked, anxiously.

"All I can say is this—it's a very favorable sign. Mr. Wilson, do you have any other questions concerning you, your wife or your daughter?"

"No, Dr. Starling, but I do want to thank you for that tidbit of information concerning Joe."

The doctor walked out of the room. "Father, Linda said you wanted to talk with me."

"Yes, Anthony, I do want to talk with you. I need for you to go see Clayton Melbourne and let him know what has happened to me and my family. Tell Clayton I want him to handle all my business dealings until I get out of the hospital. Anthony, I know you want to be at the hospital, but I really need you to work with Clayton and keep my business going. He will desperately need your help with everything we've got going on. Will you do that for me?"

"Yes, I will call Mr. Melbourne within the hour, and I'll start working with him tomorrow morning. Now, if you don't mind I'm going to bring Mr. and Mrs. Jones into the room to see you. After that I'm going to take them to see my mother and sister."

"How is Linda doing?"

"Father, she's doing just fine."

"I really love that girl. I can hardly wait to see the expression on Joe's face when he finally learns that she was not unfaithful to him." Tears came into Mark's eyes.

"Please Father, stop worrying so much!"

"Son, I'm not worrying. I'm just happy that Linda was telling the truth the whole time. Now, go bring me some company, and then make your phone call to Clayton Melbourne."

As soon as Anthony left the room, Mark Wilson commenced praying, "Lord, my daughter and I seem to be doing okay now, but I desperately need your blessings for my wife and son. My wife is such an important part of my life. I pray that it be your will that she fully recovers from her injuries. Lord, I don't know how much more my son, Joe, can withstand. He's a very good man, Lord, and at this very moment he's lying unconscious in the intensive care unit. It seems that bad luck has followed him for a good while now. Lord, I'm asking—no, I'm begging you to lay your healing hand on him. He deserves the right to know his wife was not unfaithful to him. Thank you, Lord. Amen."

Chapter 7

John Maynard, his wife and two children were on their way to Adamsville to do some shopping. They rounded a curve about hundred and fifty yards from the Turkey-Quarter Bridge.

"Good heavens, John, what is that man doing on the bridge railing?"

"It looks like he's going to jump!" John stopped his car as quickly as he could do it safely. He exited his car and then called to the man on the railing. "Mister, what are you planning to do?"

"I'm no good!" Tears streamed down the man's face as he looked downward at the fast moving current.

"Please! Please don't jump off that bridge! That's a very long ways down! You will surely be killed!"

"I can't live anymore!"

"Sure you can, Mister! You don't have to kill yourself!" John said, walking closer and closer to the tearful man. "Don't you have any family?"

"I've got a wife and two children!"

"For Heaven's sake then—think of your wife and children! Can you even imagine the sorrow and pain that you would inflict on them if you killed yourself?"

"They wouldn't care!"

"Sure they would care! Mister, what is your name?"

"I'm nobody, but my name is William Davis. I had a great job, a wonderful wife and two precious children and now I have nothing. In fact, I destroyed a man and woman's marriage.

I need to be punished!"

"Please come down off that railing, Mr. Davis! Please don't let my wife and two small children see you commit suicide! Come down, nothing is worth killing yourself! I want to help you!"

"No one can help me!"

"Sure they can. Now, please—I'm begging you not to jump from that bridge."

"Don't you understand I have nothing to live for?"

"You're wrong, Mr. Davis! You have everything to live for! My wife and children are looking this way; please don't kill yourself in front of them."

After about two minutes William stepped down from the railing. He wiped his eyes with his shirt sleeve. "What is your name?" William asked, sniffing back his tears.

"My name is John Maynard. My family and I are on our way to Adamsville. How did you get here at the bridge?"

"My car is parked across the bridge inside a woods path. Mr. Maynard, I'm very sorry that you and your family had to see me like this. I'm an educated man and I should know better than to attempt what I just did. I want to thank you for talking me out of it."

"Mr. Davis, may I ask what you did that would warrant you killing yourself?"

"For the first and only time in my life I committed adultery. However, it's much worse than that."

"How is that?"

"I spiked a woman's juice which caused her to pass out, and then I had sex with her. The woman's husband happened to be a soldier that had been fighting a war in Iraq. That poor soldier came home with a bundle of roses in his hand. I was in his house totally naked, lying next to his unclothed wife when he and her parents walked into the bedroom. He should have killed me right then and there!"

"Mr. Davis, what you did was very, very wrong, but you have owned up to your bad judgment. That means that you are truly sorry for what you did. People make mistakes all the time, but very few are willing to own up to their misguided actions. You have done just that! I believe you deserve a second chance. Anyway, I need to get back to my family." He pulled out his wallet and then handed William his card. "Mr. Davis, my number is on my card in case you ever need to talk to someone."

"Mr. Maynard, what do you do for a living?"

"I'm in the sporting goods business. I own several stores. In fact one of my stores is located near Adamsville. The name of it is Maynard's Sporting Goods. Have you ever been there?"

"Yes, I certainly have! Mr. Maynard, that's the biggest sporting goods store that I have ever been in. You've got everything there, boats, guns, knives, bows, arrows, reels and rods, clothes, hunting equipment and a million other things. That's where I always buy my fishing tackle and bait. Again, thank you for stopping here at the bridge." Mr. Maynard shook hands with William Davis and then he walked toward his car. All of a sudden he stopped, he turned toward William and asked, "I do have your word that you're not going to jump, don't I Mr. Davis?"

"Yes sir, you have my word on it."

As John Maynard drove past William Davis, his wife Gloria asked, "What was the matter with that man, John? Do you think he would have jumped from that railing?"

"To answer your first question, he did something that he shouldn't have. Realizing his mistake now he seems tormented by it. Yes, definitely he was going to jump from that bridge."

"Daddy, you saved that man's life," said Timmy, ten years old.

"Well, son, I sure hope I did. That was one pitiful man. He was truly sorry for what he had done. According to him—he had lost his job, wife and children."

"Were they in a wreck or something?"

"No, Gloria, his wife and children were not killed in an accident."

"For goodness sakes, why did he say he lost his family?"

"Apparently William and his family are no longer living together."

"John, why is that, and what did that poor man do that made him suicidal?"

"I'll tell you later."

"Daddy, it looked like that man was crying," said Tricia, thirteen years old.

"Yes, sweetheart, he was crying."

"Well, I didn't know that grownups cry."

"Tricia, grownups cry more often than you might realize. They shed tears for different reasons. One kind of tears is when someone hears very happy, exciting, news or maybe they win money or discover something they didn't know. Adults often cry when there is a death in their family or when someone loses their job or savings."

"Daddy, did that man lose his job?"

"Yes, Timmy, Mr. Davis did lose his job."

"Well, can't you help that poor man?"

"That is something to consider."

*   *   *   *

Marie Davis asked her son, Nelson, to see who it was at the door. Nelson opened the front door.

"Mother, its Daddy!"

"Marie, is it okay if I come inside?"

"What do you mean is it okay if you come inside?"

"I don't consider this house mine anymore. I don't deserve the house, you, or my children. I have sinned against God, you and my children. I don't have a job and I don't know what I'm supposed to do!" Tears came into William's eyes as he looked down toward his children.

"William Davis, if you have come here looking for pity— you're not going to get it from me! However, for the children's sakes I am prepared to forgive you for what you did! Just make sure you remember that I said I would forgive you, but I didn't say a thing about forgetting it happened! You're very lucky that Linda Wilson hasn't brought charges against you! You wouldn't be so lucky if I had been her instead of who I am!"

"Marie, I'm truly sorry for what I did! I'll never do another thing that would bring shame on me, you or our children—so help me God!" William dropped on his knees and then asked his children to come give him a hug. "I love you children. I love you more than anything."

"Daddy, why are you crying?" Heather, his eight year old daughter asked.

"I'm crying because I love my wife and my children so much." Heather handed her father a table napkin for him to wipe his watery eyes.

"Daddy, what did you do that was so bad?" .

"Nelson, I promise to tell both of you one of these days what I did, but right now you're too young to understand."

"I've already heard what you did," said Nelson.

"What did you hear, Nelson?" Marie asked.

"Tommy Herring said you kissed another man's wife. Why would you want to do that?"

"Nelson, I love your mother with all my heart and soul, but I did something that brought shame and disgrace on me, and it broke up someone else's marriage. You have no idea how sorry I am for what I did, but I can't undo what has already been done."

"Just tell the woman you're sorry for kissing her?"

"I would love to do that, Nelson, but I'm afraid an apology wouldn't make any difference. In fact, it might make things even worse."

"I still love you, Daddy."

"I know you do, Heather. I love you and Nelson more than anything in the whole world."

"In that case, why don't you get cleaned up and then go look for a job?" Marie asked.

"I'll do just that. Marie, I want to thank you for not kicking me out. Before I came here I drove down to the river." Tears came into William's eyes.

"Why did you go to the river?"

"I never thought you would live with me after what I did. I thought I had lost my children as well as you."

"Why did you go to the river?"

"Oh God, I hate to even say it, but I was going to end my life in the river!"

"That is the most selfish thing I've ever heard! What about your children? What about me?"

"I'm sorry, Marie! I shouldn't have mentioned that! I promise to never end my life by my own will! I have you and my children now! Please don't be mad with me, Marie! I will spend the rest of my life trying to make up for the hurt that I've caused you and my children."

Chapter 8

Linda Wilson was sitting inside her husband's intensive care room. Tears were visible in her eyes as she lightly rubbed the back of her hand against Joe's face. Three days in a row she had been in and out of his room. Even the monitoring-nurse outside Joe's window was saddened as she observed Linda crying some times, and praying at other times for her husband to open his eyes. "Joe, this is Linda—Linda, your wife. I love you very, very much. Joe, what you saw when you came home is not what you thought! I was drugged!" Linda started crying. Noticing the agony expressed on Linda's face, the nurse wiped her own eyes with a tissue. "Joe, I have prayed and prayed that you will wake up so I can tell you the truth about me! Oh God, I love you so much!" She was down on her knees, her head lying against Joe's chest.

"That is one pitiful woman," said Mark Wilson, standing behind the nurse.

"Mr. Wilson, I didn't know you had been released from the hospital."

"Dr. Starling gave me my walking papers about an hour ago. I've seen my wife and daughter this morning. In fact, as soon as they get Joan ready to leave the hospital I'm going to drive her home."

"How will she be able to walk with that cast on her leg?"

"She's got two brand new crutches."

"How is your wife doing?"

"She's about the same. As with my son, Joe—everything is now up to the Lord. Nurse, have you noticed any change in my son's condition?"

"I'm really not supposed to tell you this, but I've seen him move his right hand twice. On another occasion I saw him twitch his left fingers. Mr. Wilson, I'm not a doctor, but I sincerely belief he's getting better all the time."

"You don't know how much that means to me for you saying that. Is it okay for me to go inside his room for a couple minutes?"

"Yes, it will be just fine." Mark went into the room. He reached for Linda's arm and then helped her stand up.

"Have you eaten anything today?"

Sniffing back her tears, Linda answered, "Mr. Wilson, I'm not very hungry."

"I'm going to tell you something very important. I want you to listen very carefully! If you don't start eating something you're going to be sick. When Joe comes out of his unconsciousness you wouldn't want to look weak and frail would you? Of course you wouldn't. I've got to take Joan home and then I'm coming back. I want you to promise me right here and now that you'll go with me to a restaurant somewhere. Linda, I want your promise!"

"Mr. Wilson, I promise that I will go with you when you get back."

Clayton Melbourne was talking with Anthony Wilson at a construction site. "Anthony, its three o'clock in the afternoon, have you been by the hospital today?"

"No, I haven't. We've got so many jobs going on now that I felt like I needed to be at work."

"We do have a lot of work going on, but you need to go see your family at the hospital. Anthony, you're a great asset to your family's business, but for now my men and I have got everything under control. The most important thing in your life is your family. I can't tell you what to do, but I am suggesting that you take off now and come back next Monday. Tell your father that it was my suggestion for you to do that."

"Mr. Melbourne , are you sure it will be alright for me to leave now?"

"I'm quite sure. Your family needs you now more than this job does, and besides—I'm not about to let anything go wrong on these construction sites."

Anthony handed Mr. Melbourne a set of blueprints that he was holding. "Now I know why my father promoted you to be the number one man underneath him. Thanks, Mr. Melbourne, I'll head toward the hospital now."

Mark and Linda Wilson were in the intensive care waiting room when Anthony came into the room. "Daddy, before you even say anything, Mr. Melbourne suggested that I be here with my family."

"Anthony, I seldom question Mr. Melbourne's judgment. Are all the projects moving along as scheduled?"

"To tell you the truth—they're not."

"What?"

"They're moving ahead of schedule." Anthony smiled.

"You had me going there for a moment." Mark said with a sigh of relief.

"Linda, how is my brother doing?"

"He's about the same, but he did move his right hand a little. Also, he twitched his left fingers several times."

"Goodness gracious, that's great news! Well, I'm going to check on my mother. Daddy, do you want to walk with me to see Mother?"

"Sure, Anthony, I'll go with you. Linda, are you going back to Joe's room now?"

"Yes, I am. Mr. Wilson, thank you for taking me to Benny's restaurant."

"You're more than welcome. Anthony, don't I have myself a pretty daughter-in-law?"

"Yes, you certainly do. In fact, she's prettier than a speckled puppy."

"That's not true, Anthony. She's prettier than two speckled puppies. Look at that pretty little smile on her face? Linda, that's how you used to smile all the time."

"You two are making me blush. Anyway, thank each of you for your compliments. Now, I'm going to go visit with my husband."

Mark and Anthony walked to the intensive care unit to see Sarah Wilson. They were both shocked when they stared through the glass window and didn't see her. Even the nurse that had been monitoring Sarah's vital signs was gone. "It can't be!" Mark mumbled.

"Daddy, don't you have a heart attack! I'm sure there's a reason for her not being here!"

On weak knees, Mark propped himself up against the glass widow. Anthony grabbed hold of his father to keep him from sliding down to the floor.

"Mr. Wilson! Mr. Wilson, it's not what you think!" A nurse yelled out as she hurried down the hallway toward Mark and Anthony. "Your wife is alive! Mr. Wilson, did you hear what I just said? Your wife is alive! Not only is she alive, but she is no longer unconscious! Help me get Mr. Wilson to the intensive care waiting room so he can sit down." Anthony and the nurse assisted Mark to the waiting room.

"My wife is awake?"

"Yes, Mr. Wilson, she certainly is. Dr. Starling is having some tests performed on her now. Mr. Wilson, I've never been more excited in my whole life than when your wife opened her eyes. The first thing out of her mouth was, 'Where am I?' I was so happy that I tripped over my own feet when I ran for the doctor."

"Why in the world are you crying now, Daddy?"

"It's because I'm so happy. I do believe that God has answered one of my prayers."

"Nurse, will my mother go back into the intensive care room when she gets back?" Anthony asked.

"I really don't think so, but Dr. Starling will come here to the waiting room when your mother's tests are completed. He will explain everything to you and your father. Mr. Wilson, I know I'm a nurse, but I, also, prayed that your wife would get better. I am very happy for you and your son."

"What's going on?" Joan asked, coming into the room on crutches.

"Miss Wilson, I was just telling your father and brother some good news."

"What good news?"

"Your mother is no longer unconscious."

"You're not kidding me, are you?"

"No, Miss Wilson, I heard her say something when she came to."

Tears came into Joan's eyes. "What did she say?"

"She said, 'Where am I?' I told your father and brother that I became so excited that I tripped over my own feet when I ran for the doctor."

"Where's my mother now?"

"Dr. Starling is having some tests performed on her now. You will be able to see her real soon. Well, I've got to go now, but I will still pray that Joe Wilson comes out of his condition."

"All three of us thank you for your prayers and for being a wonderful nurse," said Mark.

"Thank you, sir. I really appreciate those kind words. Now, I really must get back to my duty station." A couple minutes after the nurse left the room, in walked Melvin, Grace and Doris Jones.

"Mark, I particularly noticed that each of you had smiles on your faces when we came in," said Melvin.

"I just received some very good news! Sarah is no longer unconscious! God has answered another one of our prayers!"

"That is wonderful news, Mr. Wilson."

"Thank you, Grace."

"Doris, you look very pretty today."

"Thank you, Anthony. You look quite handsome yourself."

"Melvin, have you noticed that gleam in my son's eyes every time he's around your daughter?"

"In fact, I certainly have. Mark, what does that gleam mean?"

"Well, I don't know for sure, but I had the same kind of gleam in my eyes just before I married Sarah."

"I declare, Daddy, are you trying to embarrass me in front of Doris's family?"

"Don't be embarrassed, Anthony," said Melvin. "I had that same look just before I popped the big question to Grace."

"Melvin, go ahead and tell them what you found out about Sarah and Joan's wreck," said Grace.

"Mark, the gang leader that shot Joe is the same one that wrecked her car. The police arrested three gang members for armed robbery. In a plea bargaining arrangement one of the gang members swore under oath that Wally Benson, gang leader, was the one that shot Joe twice. Wally and the other gang-member were both killed when they ran a stoplight and plowed into Sarah's car."

"Do you suppose they ran into Sarah's car intentionally?"

"Mark, I'm afraid we will never know the answer to that question."

"Mr. Wilson, where is Linda?" Grace asked.

"She went back to Joe's room."

"Mr. Wilson, I hate to be too inquisitive, but something doesn't add up to me concerning Joe's condition," said Grace. "Since he was shot in the chest area, not his head, why is he still unconscious after all this time?"

"Upon being shot he fell backwards onto his concrete porch. Joe sustained severe head injuries when he fell."

A nurse opened the waiting room door. "Mr. Wilson would you and your family please walk down the hallway to the family room? Dr. Ben Starling will talk with you down there in a few minutes."

"Nurse, I want the Jones family, our good friends to be with us when the doctor talks to us."

"That will be just fine, Mr. Wilson, but please hurry to the family room. Dr. Starling will be there very shortly."

There was total silence when Dr. Starling opened the door to the family room. "I'm sure all of you are very anxious to hear what I have to say about Mrs. Sarah Wilson. First of all, as some of you already know, she's no longer unconscious. We've run another head scan on her and she no longer has the amount of swelling that she did have. Mr. Wilson, I believe your wife is going to be just fine now in a few more days. Now, now, what are those tears for?"

"Dr. Starling, these are happy tears. I'm very thankful that she's going to be alright."

"When can we see my mother?" Joan asked.

"You can do that now. Mrs. Wilson is on the fifth floor, room 526."

"Daddy, you all proceed ahead, I'll be there soon as I can," said Joan, leaning on her crutches.

"No, sweetheart, we're all going to be at her room at the same time."

A nurse was checking Sarah Wilson's vital signs when the group, led by Mark Wilson, entered Sarah Wilson's room. "Sarah, I can't tell you how happy I am to see you wide awake with that beautiful smile of yours."

"Mark, the doctor told me that I was in a wreck. I don't remember being in a wreck. What happened?"

"Sarah, the wreck was not your fault. The driver of the other car ran a stoplight."

"Are they okay?"

"I'm afraid not, they were killed instantly."

"That is awful! Do you know who they were?"

"Yes, Sarah—I do know who one of them was."

"He was the same gang-member that shot Joe," said Mark.

"Oh, my goodness, why would he want to hurt me?"

"Sarah, the law feels like it was a coincidental situation. Look over there by the door; do you know who that is?"

"Joan! Joan, you're all hurt up!"

"I'm just fine, Mother." Joan made her way to her mother. "Mother, why have you started crying?"

"Just look what I've done to you? You're on crutches, all scratched up and you've got a cast on your leg and one on your arm!"

"Mother, the wreck wasn't your fault. Besides, I'm doing just fine."

"How are you feeling, Sarah," asked Grace Jones.

"I'm not hurting anywhere. Grace, it's so nice of you and Melvin to come visit with me.

Oh, there's Doris, too. Hello, Doris, you're as pretty as ever. Anthony, I hope you don't let that pretty woman slip away from you."

"I'm doing my best to hold on to her, Mother."

"Mark, how is Joe doing?"

"He's about the same as he was before your wreck. However, he did move his hand and fingers two or three times."

"Who's with him now?"

"Linda sits in his room nearly all the time."

Tears came into Sarah's eyes. "Mother, are you okay?" Joan asked.

"Yes, I'm okay."

"Sarah, why are you crying?" Mark asked.

"It's nothing, I'll be just fine in a little bit. Mark, what did the doctor say about Joe's condition?"

"His vital signs are normal. The doctor said Joe had a strong heart beat and that the swelling in his head had gone down some. His head hit the cement porch when he got shot."

"Mother, you will be out of the hospital in two or three days," said Anthony.

"I'll be very glad of that. Mark, why aren't you at work?"

"Sarah, you're a lot more important to me than my work is."

"Well, goodness sakes—you can't just let your business go downhill!"

"Don't worry, dear, Clayton Melbourne is taking care of everything for me."

"You're very fortunate to have a man like Mr. Melbourne working for you."

"Yes, I certainly am. By the way, Clayton told me to tell you hello when I was able to talk with you."

Linda Wilson entered Sarah's room door, shouting, "Oh, my God! Oh, my God, I can't believe it!" Tears streamed down her face.

"What's wrong? What's wrong, Linda?" Melvin Jones asked.

"It's Joe! It's Joe!"

"What about Joe?" Mark asked. "Linda, what's wrong with Joe?"

"He's awake! Did you hear what I said, my husband is awake!"

"Are you sure, Linda? Are you really sure?" Mark asked.

"Yes! Yes, I'm sure!"

"Where is Joe now?" Anthony asked.

"They've taken him to MRI. Doctor Starling will talk with us soon as Joe's tests are over with."

"Linda, have you talked with Joe?" Anthony asked.

"No, I haven't. When he awoke I was downstairs drinking a cup of coffee. Can you believe that—I was drinking coffee? In fact—I don't even like coffee! When I got back to the intensive care floor a nurse hurried to me! She was very, very excited! That's when she told me that Joe was no longer unconscious! I'm so happy I don't know what to do! Mrs. Wilson, I'm also very, very glad that you're much better now. Doris, please do me a favor!"

"What is that, Linda?"

"Take me to a florist. I want to buy Joe a bundle of flowers. Will you take me?"

"Of course I will. Anthony, would you like to ride with us?"

"Yes, I would love to ride with you and Linda." The three of them exited the room.

"Sarah, Mark, Joan, we've got to leave now and take care of some business, but we'll be back tonight to see how well you and Joe are doing," said Melvin. "That was very welcomed news concerning Joe."

"Yes, it certainly was. Mr. Jones, I really do appreciate you and Grace coming to see me."

"Sarah, we're just thankful that things are looking better now for you and your entire family."

"Mother, as much as I hate to leave now I've got to go by my office for a little while."

"Joan, is there something wrong where you work?"

"No, Mother, I need to go by there and pick up some papers."

"How in thunder are you going to drive a car with your arm and leg in casts?"

"Mother, you do have a good point. I'll just wait until Anthony gets back."

"When are they going to take those casts off your leg and arm?"

"I hope it's sooner rather than later," said Joan, smiling.

After Melvin and Grace had left the room, Mark asked Joan to take a seat in a lounge chair. He closed the room door very quietly, and then he pulled a chair close to Sarah's bed. With a very solemn face he looked toward his wife and said, "Sarah, I want you to listen to what I've got to say. First of all, I want you to know how much I love you. Life without you and my children would have almost no meaning to me."

"I know you love me, Mark. Dr. Starling told me that you had a heart attack when you found out that Joan and I were in a wreck. Are you doing okay now?"

"Yes, I'm doing very well now, especially since hearing the good news concerning you and Joe."

"You look like there's something on your mind, Mark. What is it?"

"It's concerning Linda. I want you to listen very carefully at what I'm going to tell you. William Davis has already told his wife and the law that he slipped something in Linda's juice causing her to pass out. He went to her house on the pretense that he would hook up her new television that she bought for Joe. He took advantage of her when she was unconscious. Sarah, what I'm trying to tell you is this—you were wrong about Linda. It was not her intention to have sex with William Davis. Now, what's wrong, you're crying again?"

"I was so mean to her! Mark, she will never like me again!"

"That's not true, Sarah! That's not true at all! Linda is a fine woman. She loves Joe with all her heart."

"Mark, will you ask her to forgive me?"

"I will, but it would mean a lot more to her if you were to tell her that you're sorry for not believing her."

"I'll tell her that I'm sorry! Mark, why didn't I believe her story? Why?"

"It's very simple, Sarah, it's because you observed your son, heart-broken, devastated by what he saw the day he came home. Linda is a good woman; she loves her husband as much as any woman can."

"That awful William Davis should be in the penitentiary for what he did to Linda!" Sarah said.

"From what I hear he's punishing himself for what he did."

"What do you mean?"

"The law didn't come after him. After telling his wife, he went to the law and told them what a low-down, awful thing he had done to Linda. There's no doubt about it, Sarah, he's genuinely sorry for what he did."

"He might be sorry, but it did happen and he's to blame. I'll bet his wife kicks him out of the house!"

"Not from what I heard. Marie Davis is a very fine lady. She's got two young children and Mrs. Davis has some physical problems. It seems that she has forgiven him for what he did, but I'm sure she will never forget that it happened."

"It's a good thing he was not my husband!"

"Why is that?"

"I would never have forgiven him! In fact, I would have put a broom handle across his conniving head!"

"In this particular case, that's what I call short-sighted thinking, Sarah. I just told you that the poor woman has some physical handicaps, and there are two small children to consider. It was shameful of him to spike her drink and then have his way with her, but I do believe the man is truly sorry for doing what he did."

"Sorry! What are you talking about—sorry? That man should be tarred and feathered!"

"Who should be tarred and feathered, Mother?" Anthony asked, as he entered the room.

"That no-good William Davis!"

"Daddy, I see you've told Mother what really happened that day at Linda's house."

"Yes, he told me. I don't know how in the world I will be able to face Linda Wilson now."

"Please don't get yourself upset now, Sarah. Linda understands why you felt the way you did."

"Daddy is right, Mother. Linda loves you a lot. I've heard her say that several times."

"Anthony, where is Linda and Doris? The three of you went after some flowers for Joe."

"They stopped by the ladies room. Linda wanted to freshen

up a bit to look her very best when she sees Joe. In fact, here's Doris and Linda now."

"Mrs. Wilson, I'm very glad that you're doing better now," said Linda, tears in her eyes, holding a dozen roses in her hand.

"Mark, would you please hold Linda's flowers for a little while?"

"Sure I will, Sarah." Mark took the roses from Linda.

With tears emerging from her eyes, Sarah motioned for Linda to come near her. "Linda, Mark told me what happened to you the day Joe came home. I've acted like a fool toward you every since that day. I just want you to know that I'm ashamed of myself and I'm sorry for the way I've treated you! How will you ever forgive me for the way I behaved?"

"Mrs. Wilson, I understand why you acted that way. There's nothing to forgive. Had I been in your shoes I would have reacted in the same way." Linda bent over and gave Mrs. Wilson a big hug. "I just want you to know that I love Joe with all my heart."

"I already know that, Linda. Mark and I love you too." Mark placed his arms around Linda's neck as she continued hugging Mrs. Wilson.

"Doris, everybody is doing some hugging, but us."

"We'll eliminate that problem right now," said Doris, placing her arms around Anthony's neck. "Is this better?"

With a broad smile across his face, Anthony answered, "Yes, indeed, it certainly is."

"Well, don't this beat all, I'm sitting in this recliner with a broken leg, broken arm and no one is giving me a hug," Joan smiled.

Chapter 9

"Seeing all of you smiling and hugging each other today is a wonderful sight, indeed," said Dr. Ben Starling, entering the room."

"We do hope you've got some good news concerning my son."

"Yes, Mrs. Wilson, I believe I do."

"Is Joe going to be okay, Dr. Starling?" Linda asked, tears in her eyes.

"Mrs. Wilson, your husband is a very lucky man. Including his war wound he's been shot three times now. Either one of those wounds could have been fatal, but Joe overcame each of them. His head injury was equally serious, but it looks like he's going to overcome that problem according to our tests. Joe is awake; his vital signs are normal, but something mentally or emotionally is wrong with him. I asked Joe what was worrying him, but he wouldn't answer my question."

"Dr. Starling, do you suppose it has something to do with his head injury?" Mark asked.

"It could, but I don't think so."

"Good Lord, Joe is remembering the day he came home!" Sarah remarked, sitting up in bed. "Linda, you need to go talk with him!"

"I don't think that is a very good idea at this time," Anthony remarked. "Linda, will it be okay if Daddy and I go see Joe first so we can tell him what really happened the day he came home?"

"Sure, Anthony, that will be just fine. Doris, Joan and I will visit with your mother until you and your father get back here. Just one thing, when I do see Joe I want to see him alone."

"Of course she does," said Sarah. "Linda, you be sure to take those beautiful flowers with you when you go into his room."

"Mr. Wilson, your son has been moved to the fourth floor, room 428."

"Thank you, Dr. Starling for the good news. Thank you for taking good care of my family."

"Most of the credit should go to the Almighty, but I do appreciate the compliment. Mrs. Wilson, I'm going to finish my round now, but I will see you tomorrow morning. You should be out of the hospital in a couple of days or so."

"That's wonderful; I'm quite ready to go home."

Mark and Anthony hurried toward the elevator. "Anthony, which one of us is going to tell Joe about Linda and William Davis?"

"I think you should."

Mark tapped quietly on Joe's door, and then he and Anthony

entered the room. Joe had his eyes closed as they neared his bed. "Joe, Joe, this is your father," Mark spoke softly. "Anthony is with me."

Joe awoke, he looked toward his father, and then toward his brother. Tears came into his eyes. "The doctor said you were getting along very well," said Mark. "What is this, you've got tears in your eyes, what's wrong?"

Joe shook his head back and forth, indicating nothing was wrong with him. Anthony reached over and held his brother's hand. "I love you, Joe. We all love you."

Joe shook his head from side to side, indicating not so. "That's not entirely correct," Joe whispered. "Not everyone loves me." Tears ran down his cheeks.

"Son, that's why Anthony and I are with you now before anyone else comes in here." Mark pulled a chair close to Joe's bed and then sat down. "Joe, I have never lied one time to either one of my children. In fact, I've always been up front with each of you whether it was good news or bad news. Anthony is my witness that everything I'm about to tell you is the truth and nothing but the truth. Linda Wilson is a good and honorable woman. Not once did she ever betray your trust or do anything willingly that would affect your marriage."

Joe shook his head back and forth. "No! No, that's not true!"

"Listen to our father, Joe! He didn't have a chance to tell you why he said those things were true! I'm your brother, I know what he just said is true! Now, hear Daddy out!"

"Son, William Davis has already turned himself into the law for spiking your wife's drink. He's already admitted that to his wife. Mr. Wilson, Anthony and I were sitting in William

Davis's house when his wife, Marie told us about her husband. Joe, Linda was still passed out when you and her parents walked into the house and saw her and William lying naked on the bed."

"Daddy, if that were true—why was William Davis in my house to begin with?"

"Linda had bought you a large flat screen television so you could watch your favorite ball games when you came home. She didn't know how to hook it up and that's when William Davis formulated his plan to have his way with Linda. He agreed to go to her house and hook it up in a matter of minutes at no charge. Somewhat reluctant for him to do that, Linda finally agreed that he could go there and connect the television and its accessories. William brought a jar of juice, maybe grape juice, to her house and insisted that she drink some of it. She declined at first, but he sort of insisted. Him being Linda's supervisor she drank a glass of juice and then passed completely out. William proceeded to do what he had planned to do all along."

"That dirty son-of-a-bitch! I'll kill that bastard when I get out of this hospital!"

"No, no, son! That's the last thing you should do! I'm your father and I'm telling you that it would be wrong to do that!"

"Look what he did to my wife?"

"Joe, I know what he did was bad, but William Davis is punishing his own self for doing what he did. He has a guilt feeling that he can't erase. He's been to the law. He's attempted suicide at least twice. He lost his job, his dignity, and he almost lost his wife and two small children. Joe, he took out nearly all his savings to give to Linda, but I told his wife that Linda wouldn't accept any of his money. What that man did to Linda was absolutely unforgiveable. His wife is not healthy at all and then there are those two children to consider. Mrs. Marie Davis is one of the finest ladies that I have ever met. I, truly, feel sorry for her and those children."

Tears streamed down Joe's face as he turned toward the wall. "Joe, what's wrong now?" Mark asked.

"I can't get that image out of my mind!"

"What image is that?"

"The thought of seeing Linda lying naked in bed with William Davis makes me feel sick."

"I'm going to tell you one more time, it was not her fault! The sooner you accept that the sooner you and she can get on with your lives! When someone is unconscious they have no control over what someone does to them. Take you for example, when you were unconscious anyone could have done anything to you, anything at all, but you wouldn't be held responsible for what they did. It's the same way with Linda. I love that woman just like she was my own daughter! If you've got any sense at all you'll forget about what you saw! You'll never—I said never find a woman that loves you more than she does! On top of all that, she's intelligent and a very beautiful woman! She's waiting in your mother's hospital room right now with a handful of roses. Don't make her cry anymore, Joe. She was so excited when she found out that you were no longer unconscious."

"You said something about Mother being in a hospital room."

"Joan and Sarah were in a car wreck, but they're both doing fine now. By the way, the gang member that shot you is no longer living."

"Why is that?"

"He and another punk were killed in the collision."

"Are you telling me that those hoodlums wrecked my mother's car?"

"The law thinks it was totally coincidental. They ran through a red light and plowed into your mother's car."

"Joe, what about Linda?" Anthony asked.

"I've never known our father to be wrong about anything. Anthony, before she comes in here will you help me clean up a little?"

"Of course I will, Joe. What do you want me to do?"

"I want you to comb or brush my hair, and then I want you to help rise up my bed."

"Why do you want me to raise your bed?"

"Are you kidding me? I need to brush my teeth with something. Daddy, will you get me a toothbrush and some toothpaste from the Wellness Center?"

"I'll go right now, but you'll have to hurry with your grooming. Linda is very anxious to see you."

Anthony held a small mirror in front of Joe's face after he had combed it. "Well, how do you feel and look now?"

"I'm not sure. Anthony, I feel like an idiot now."

"Why is that?"

"I really thought Linda was cheating on me. Now I find out that she was an innocent victim. I've acted like a fool toward her."

"Joe, it's understandable why you acted the way you did, but the whole thing is over now. Don't dwell on it any longer. Guess what, Joe?"

"What?"

"Doris Jones and I are going together."

"You're dating Doris now?"

"Not yet, but I'm going to. Joe, every time I look at that woman I get a tingle in my stomach."

"That's fine, but remember this—be sure and keep that tingle in your stomach until you decide to get married or something. Make sure that your tingle doesn't get down to your Wong-dong."

"Wong-dong, I've heard it called everything in the book except for that."

"Except for what," Mark asked, coming into the room.

"My brother thinks I have a Wong-dong."

"Of course you do. All men have Wong-dongs." Mark handed the toothbrush and toothpaste to Joe. "Anthony, get Joe some water and that container so he can gargle some."

"Joe, I believe you're going to put a lip-lock on your wife when she gets in here," said Anthony, smiling.

"I'm going to do my very best to do just that. Another thing, I don't want anyone in my room when she gets in here."

"Joe, your brother and me didn't just fall off a dead tree or something. We know that you and Linda need to be alone when she comes into this room."

"Daddy, where is Joan?"

"She's in the room with your mother. In fact, after you and Linda have your visit together, Joan, Anthony and I will come back to visit with you."

"Daddy, I just want you to know that I love you a lot."

"I know you do, Joe. Now, I want you to hurry up and get well. Clayton Melbourne is working himself into an early grave with all three of us away from work."

"I'll do my best. I need to go to work soon as possible so I can get a paycheck."

"Joe, you're a salaried man. In sickness, rain or shine your paycheck is not affected."

"I'm glad to hear that. By the way, when I get out of this hospital I'll need about a week off to take Linda on a real honeymoon."

"I would be extremely angry if you didn't do just that. Anthony, let's go tell Linda that she can see her husband now."

"I appreciate you and Anthony telling me the truth about Linda's situation."

"Why are you tearing up again?" Mark asked.

"I'm just happy, Daddy. Now I've got something to look forward to."

Wiping her eyes with a tissue, Linda Wilson stood in front of Joe's room door for a few seconds. She held a dozen roses in her left hand as her right one slowly turned the doorknob.

Tears were visible in Joe's and Linda's eyes as she walked slowly toward him. Joe held his right hand toward his wife. Linda laid the flowers on the sink and then she hurried to his side. Joe reached both his arms toward her. Linda leaned forward into his arms. Like two small children, they cried as they hugged each other. Joe was the first one to speak. "Linda, I'm sorry for not trusting you. Daddy told me the whole story. I love you more than life itself! Will you ever forgive me?"

"Joe, there's nothing to forgive. You saw me in a very bad situation. At the time you saw me I was totally confused, not initially knowing why I was in the bed with William Davis.

I wish it hadn't happened, Joe! I had rather be dead than lose you!"

"Please don't talk like that Linda! I will never leave you again! You're the only woman that I have ever loved."

"Joe, I brought you something."

"I know you did. I see those pretty flowers that you brought me. Where did you get them?"

"The very same place that you got mine the day you came home."

"Do you know who gave me the very last kiss I've had in months?"

"Could that have been me?" Linda asked, smiling.

"It certainly was. May I kiss you now?"

"You can't imagine how long I've waited for this kiss." Linda lowered her head, placing her lips against his.

"Uh-oh."

"Joe, what's the matter?"

"I got a hot flash."

"You're silly, men don't get hot flashes."

"Oh yes they do! When I get out of the hospital you and I are going on a real honeymoon."

Linda beamed with joy. "Are we really?"

"Yes, we certainly are. That's when I'm going to prove to you that men get hot flashes."

"How will you do that?"

"It's kind of like self-rising flour, the more you heat it the more it rises."

"You silly thing, I knew what you were talking about the whole time."

"Linda, would you give me a long drawn-out kiss this time?"

"How long drawn-out would you like it?"

"I want you to kiss me until my hot flashes start coming in close intervals."

"You're a naughty, naughty boy."

"Yes, Linda, I believe I am."

Chapter 10

William Davis has been turned down for employment on five job interviews in the last seven workdays. He hoped the situation would be different today as he sat, nervously, waiting to be called into the Mr. Fielding's office.

A few minutes later the receptionist told William that he could go into Mr. Fielding's office which was down the hall, first office on the right. Nervous, his hands trembling, William tapped lightly on the door and then he opened it. "Mr. Davis, I'm sorry that I kept you waiting beyond your appointment time. I had an important phone call and I had to take care of it. Please have a seat." Mr. Fielding opened his desk drawer and retrieved William's resume. "Mr. Davis, according to your resume you worked at Clemmons Pharmaceuticals for seven years. That is a very fine company. In fact your former supervisor there, Richard Jamison, is a close friend of mine.

May I ask why you no longer work at your former place of employment?"

"Mr. Fielding, I loved my job at Clemmons Pharmaceuticals, but I did something very, very wrong."

"Goodness, Mr. Davis, did you steal something, give away trade-secrets or what?"

"It was none of that. I would never have done anything like that!"

"Let me ask you this, how did you go about terminating your employment with the company?"

"What do you mean?"

"Well, did you give a week's notice or maybe even two weeks?"

"No, Mr. Fielding, I didn't."

"Why not, don't you think it would have been appropriate to give the company some kind of notice?"

"Yes sir, it would have been appropriate, but I was too ashamed of what I had done to face Mr. Jamison. Mr. Fielding, have you talked with Mr. Jamison about my employment with the company?"

"As a matter of fact—I have, Mr. Davis. It seems that you were a model employee until you spiked your co-worker's drink and then you sexually assaulted her."

"Mr. Fielding, I'm guilty for doing exactly what you just said, but I'm truly sorry for what I did. I can't imagine why I did such a low-down, conniving thing like that, but I did. I can't undo what I've already done, but I am very, very sorry for what I did."

"Mr. Davis, I understand that you're sorry now for what you did, but I don't understand why you couldn't have faced Mr.

Jamison and your accuser the day he wanted you to come into his office. That didn't show any remorse, courage or leadership on your part."

With the most solemn look a man could possibly display, William Davis stood up and said, "You're absolutely right Mr. Fielding, everything you just said is true! I was a coward that day! I was so ashamed of what I had done that I couldn't face Mr. Jamison or Mrs. Wilson! Another thing, as long as I live I will never forget the horror I saw in Mr. Wilson's eyes as he stood there with those roses in his hand. His wife and I were naked when he walked into the room. In fact, she was still passed out from being drugged. Yes, Mr. Fielding, I did a very bad thing! You want to know something else; that poor man was an Army soldier who had just returned from Iraq where he had been shot by the enemy."

"Mr. Davis, you don't have to tell me all this."

"The Hell I don't! I know I'm not going to be hired with your company and I don't blame you one bit! I wish I could undo what I did, but I can't!" Tears came into William's eyes as he walked quietly toward the door.

It was two hours later when William Davis arrived at his house. His wife, Marie Davis was in the backyard looking at her rose bushes when he walked out to where she was standing. "How did your interview go?" She asked.

"I didn't get the job. It seems that everyone knows that I'm no good."

"William, I will not listen to that nonsense! Yes, you made a big mistake, but you can't spend the rest of your life dwelling on it! You've got to get over it somehow or other!"

"Marie, why do you still put up with me?"

"What are you talking about?"

"I took advantage of that woman, I lost my job, and now I can't find employment anywhere! You're the only one that seems to care whether I live or die!"

"That is crazy! You've got two children that love you more than anything in the world! You have got to get over losing your job and what you did to Mrs. Wilson! If you don't, sooner or later it's going to drive you mad! If that happens you'll wind up in an asylum somewhere or even worse by killing yourself! William, starting today I want you to think toward the future. You and I have two children to rear and I need your help. Our savings will only last so long and I'm physically unable to hold down a full time job. Whether you feel like you can or not you have got to find employment somewhere."

"Marie, I have tried and tried."

"I know you have, but I don't want you to give up. William, I still love you with all my heart."

"I can't imagine why."

"There you go again! I can't stand anymore of your whining and you feeling sorry for yourself! Now, for the last time— get on with your life! Remember, I didn't say a thing about forgetting what you did, but now it's time to move on!"

"Marie—."

"Yes, William."

"I love you very, very much!"

"I know you do. Now, where are you going next to look for a job?"

"I'm going to Mr. John Maynard's office tomorrow."

"Who is that?"

"He's the gentleman that talked me off that bridge railing."

"I remember you telling me now. The best of my recollection, he was married and he had two young children."

"That's right, he does have two children."

"Do you know where his office is?"

"No, but I know how to find out."

"How can you do that?"

"He owns Maynard's Sporting Goods store, near Adamsville. I'll go there first to find out where his office is."

"His office is probably in that same building."

"Maybe not, Mr. Maynard owns several Sporting Goods Stores."

It was quite obvious that afternoon that ten year old Nelson Davis had been in a fight at school when he came into his house, followed by his younger eight year old sister. "Good Heavens, Nelson, what happened at school today? Your face is scratched and your new shirt is torn."

"Please don't be mad with me, Mother. Old Billy Ham was poking fun at my daddy."

"For goodness sakes, what did Billy say?"

"He said my daddy was a wife cheater, that's when I punched him in his mouth. I didn't know that Chuck Rouse and Perry Hawkins were going to take sides with Billy Ham."

"Go to the bathroom so I can get you cleaned up before your father comes home. Nelson, you shouldn't have been fighting."

"Mother, I'm not going to let someone talk about my daddy!"

"Son, you can't fight someone just because they say something you don't like."

"I tried not to fight him, but something happened."

"What happened?"

"After saying what he did about my father he stuck his tongue out at me. Mother, I couldn't help myself then, I just had to sock him in his mouth."

"What did the teacher say?"

"Just five little words, 'You two—come with me!' Right then and there I knew we were in for it."

"What happened then?"

"She took both of us to the Principal's office. You will never believe what he did to us!"

"Did he spank both of you?"

"A lot worse than that, a lot worse!"

"What did he do, Nelson?"

"He and my teacher took both of us back to our class. He made us shake hands, and then smile while we were made to hug each other in front of the class."

"Is that all?" His mother asked, laughingly.

"No, that wasn't all. We had to stand in front of the class and tell each other that we were sorry for fighting."

"Nelson, I don't want you fighting anymore. All you need to know is three things."

"What three things?"

"Your father loves you and your sister as much as any father can. No matter what you hear, your father is a very good man."

"What's the third thing?"

"I love your father and he loves me."

*   *   *   *

It was six o'clock that evening when Joan and her father entered Joe's hospital room. Linda was already in the room.

"Joe, I prayed and prayed that you would be okay," said Joan, tears in her eyes. After handing her crutches to her father, she hobbled over to Joe's bed and gave him a hug. "I love you very much."

"I know you do, Joan. I love you, too. When are you going to get rid of your casts?"

"I've got several more days to wear these blasted things. Hello, Linda, have you been taking good care of my brother?"

"I'm doing my best. Mr. Wilson, I sure am glad that your wife is no longer mad with me. By the way, when will she be released from the hospital?"

"She's going home tomorrow. I can hardly wait to get her out of the hospital. Joe, Anthony will be going back to work tomorrow. Clayton Melbourne called me about an hour ago and told me he had to take his wife to the doctor tomorrow. I don't think it's too serious. It sounds to me like she might be coming down with a virus or something similar."

"Daddy, I'll go to work soon as I get out of the hospital."

"Joe, you will do no such thing! You've promised to take Linda on a well-deserved honeymoon and that's what you're going to do! I'm your boss and boss men can get away with putting pressure on their employees." Joan and Linda laughed out loud.

Dr. Ben Starling entered the room. "I'm delighted to see everyone smiling this evening. Joe, how are you doing?"

"I'm not hurting anywhere, and I feel just fine."

"That's wonderful, but I don't want you forgetting that you've had some surgery. Don't even think about going to work or doing any strenuous exercises for another couple weeks."

"Two weeks!"

"Yes, does that seem to be a very long time for you?"

"It's a lifetime for a young man that's been away from their wife for months and months." It was obvious that Linda blushed when Joe said that. Mark gave his son the thumbs up. Joan shook her head back and forth.

"I can see your point, Joe," said Dr. Starling said. "I see no reason that you can't go home tomorrow, same as your mother, but on several conditions."

"Dr. Starling, what are the conditions?" Joe asked.

"You will not go back to work for two weeks. You will come to my office near the end of the two weeks for a checkup. You will need someone to assist you in your house for at least a week."

"You mean there are no other conditions?" Joe asked, smiling.

"If there are I'm sure you will find out soon enough."

"Dr. Starling, not only are you a fine doctor, but you give the best conditions of anyone I've ever heard of," said Mark, giving his son the thumbs up sign again.

"Men, I swear!" Joan shook her head back and forth.

"What did you say, sweetheart?" Mark asked.

"Oh, it was nothing."

"Joe, please don't get shot again."

"I'll try not to, Dr. Starling. I really appreciate you taking care of me and my family."

"You're quite welcome. Mrs. Wilson, after tomorrow I'll release this big guy over to you. I hope you and Joe have many, many happy days, weeks, and months ahead of you."

"Thanks, Dr. Starling, I believe we will."

*   *   *   *

It was ten o'clock the next morning when William Davis parked his car in front of Maynard's Sporting Goods Store. It was located about a mile from the town of Adamsville. William's confidence in getting employed at the Sporting Goods Store was extremely low. Why Mr. Maynard would want to hire a loser like him, William was thinking. He walked around one side of the building, and that's when he determined that the property contained several specialty stores which were not connected to the Sporting Goods Store. He kept walking, enjoying the beauty of the flowers, shrubs, trees and wildlife. William stopped when he noticed three women and two young children standing near a large pond. One lady was taking pictures of two mallard ducks swimming in the pond. Something caught William's attention in the top of a dogwood tree. It was a grey squirrel eating little red berries from the tree. At that very moment the silence was broken by a woman yelling for help.

"Help me! Help me!" A hysterical woman cried out. William ran as hard as he could toward the women. He already knew what they were hollering about. Without a second thought he jumped into the deep pond and felt around for the child that had fallen into it. The mother and another woman were screaming as loud as they could, but the other woman was snapping pictures as William kept going under the water searching for the child. Finally, he located the child; he brought him to the surface, holding his head above water. William got the child to the bank, that's when the mother reached for the lifeless acting child. "Let me have him! Let me have him!" William yelled, pulling himself out of the mossy pond. "Call 911! Do it now! Do it now!" William demanded. The mother was hysterical, screaming as she observed

William performing Cardiopulmonary Resuscitation, CPR) on her small child. As luck would have it, William had previously taken several CPR classes. He gently performed mouth to mouth resuscitation. He swept the child's mouth with his finger to ensure nothing was in it to prevent the water to come out. Again and again he checked the child's pulse, but always continued to employ life-saving techniques, trying desperately to save the young boy's life. His mother was frantic, she was screaming out loud, 'Don't let him die! Please don't let my son die!' Finally, with the child's face turned to one side, water flowed from his mouth. Then the little fellow's eyes opened up. William helped him up into his mother's arms. At least forty people had gathered around by the time William had performed his CPR skills successfully and flawlessly.

"Mother, I'm sorry for falling into the water," cried the little boy.

"Oh, my God, Timmy you frightened me half to death," cried the lady. "Mister, what is your name?"

"My name is William Davis." He stood there completely soaked. Green moss and algae covered a good part of his clothes and exposed skin. The lady with the camera kept on snapping pictures of William.

"Lady, here comes the ambulance, you should definitely let your son go to the hospital and get checked out."

"I'll do that. Mr. Davis, you saved my son's life. How will I ever be able to thank you?"

"You don't have to thank me, lady I'm just thankful to God that it turned out like it did."

"Timmy, you go to Mr. Davis and hug his neck for saving your life."

"Mr. Davis, I sure am glad you happened to be here when I fell into the pond. May I hug your neck?"

"Timmy, I would like that very, very much." All the spectators, including the little boys' mother clapped their hands.

"Mr. Davis, may I buy you a new suit of clothes or something?"

"That won't be necessary, but I do appreciate the offer. Good luck with your child. He sure is a nice boy."

"Mr. Davis, I'll never forget what you did for my child." The lady took her son toward the ambulance.

"Mister, that was the bravest thing I've ever seen," said the lady with the camera.

"Thank you. Well, I guess I need to drive home and change my clothes. By the way, what kind of fish are those in that pond? Some of them are very big."

"Yes, they certainly are, Mr. Davis. They're called koi fish. Mr. Davis, you may not think so, but you are a very generous, courageous and caring individual. Are you married, and if so, do you have children?"

"Yes, my wife's name is Marie; I have two small children, a boy and a girl. Nelson is ten years old and Heather is eight."

"Is Heather's name spelled like feather, but with an H.?"

"Yes, it certainly is."

"You may not know this, but the little boy you saved was ten years old just like your boy. Mr. Davis, do you always read the morning newspaper?"

"Yes, I generally do."

It was 11:45 that morning when William Davis arrived home. Marie was startled when he walked into the kitchen.

"My goodness, William, you're wet from head to toe! What happened? Why are you wet?"

"A little boy fell into a pond and I helped get him out."

"Is the boy alright?"

"Yes, I believe he will be just fine. Well, I'm going into the bathroom and take off these wet clothes. Will you get me a pair of underwear and a tee shirt?"

"You're dripping water all over my carpet. Hurry to the bathroom and I'll get your underwear and shirt. Did you get a chance to talk with Mr. Maynard?"

"No, I got wet before I even got inside the store. I'll try again in a day or so."

"Guess what your son said about you last night?"

"What did Nelson say?"

"He said you were the best father in the whole world."

"There are a lot of people that wouldn't agree with that."

"William, that boy absolutely idolizes you. Why don't you take him to Mr. Danny Sutton's pond this Sunday afternoon?"

"That's a great idea! Well, into the shower I'm going."

"William, whose child was it that fell into a pond?"

"I don't know, but he was a cute little boy. Marie, I'm very sorry that I ruined my suit that you bought me last Christmas."

"Well, William, suits can be replaced, but children can't be. I'm glad you messed the suit up in order to help that young child."

Chapter 11

Joe Wilson and his mother were released from the hospital by one o'clock that same day. It would be another week before Joan could go back to work at Hudson's Clothing Store. Mark Wilson and his son Anthony were back to work, trying their best to fill the temporary void left by Mr. Clayton Melbourne's absence. He was taking a couple days off to take care of his sick wife. Linda Wilson had driven her car under the shelter at the hospital. Joe and his mother were each being pushed out of the hospital in a wheelchair. Linda opened the front door and then the back door on the passenger side of her car. Mrs. Wilson was helped into the front seat. Joe got into the backseat by himself.

"Mrs. Wilson, is there anywhere special that you would like to go?"

"Yes, there certainly is!"

"Where is that?"

"I can hardly wait to get to my house."

"Mother, will you be okay at your house with no one to help you?"

"Of course I will. I don't even need those crutches anymore."

"Mother, you're still in a cast."

"So what, I can still cook, wash dishes, and do my laundry."

"Linda, I'm surprised that you haven't been called back to work by now."

"Mrs. Wilson, my supervisor gave me another week off to take care of my husband."

"I wouldn't pamper him too much. If you do he'll be expecting it all the time."

"Mother, I'm due a little pampering," said Joe, smiling.

"I know what kind of pampering you have on your mind." Linda was a little embarrassed. She looked straight ahead as she pressed her foot against the accelerator.

"I've always told you how perceptive my mother was."

"Mrs. Wilson, would you care to stay at our house for a few days? I could look after you and Joe at the same time."

"I appreciate your offer, but I rather go to my own house. Everything I need is already there."

It was three o'clock that afternoon when Joe and Linda arrived at their house. A fifteen-foot banner was displayed in the front yard. It read, 'WELCOME HOME, JOE'. A letter was stuck inside the screen door. Linda handed it to Joe. She released his hand so he could open the letter. Tears came into his eyes as he started reading. It was written as follows: 'Joe, day in and day out, week after week, month after month I have prayed that you would return to me. With all my heart

I love you more than words can say. I've lain in bed many, many nights, tossing and turning, often crying—yearning for you to be here next to me. No matter, day or night, this is a lonely old house without you being here. Your mother, father, sister and brother are all doing fine. Please be careful, Joe, you're all that I've got. You mean everything to me. I'll close for now because I know you don't have a lot of time to read, dodging bullets and trying to stay alive. You're loving wife, Linda.'

"Sweetheart, this letter was mailed, but I didn't get it!"

"I know you didn't. I had the wrong address on the box that this letter was in."

"You sent this letter in a box?"

"Yes, along with five more letters and a variety of cookies. Joe, I was devastated when the box was returned by the mailman."

"That explains why I didn't get some letters from you." Joe placed his arms around his wife and then whispered in her ear, "I love you very, very much." He kissed her, passionately.

"That was just about the best kiss I've ever had," said Linda, smiling.

"Should we do it again?"

"Let's do it inside the house since one of our neighbors is looking straight at us."

"Mr. Larry Peabody can't tell who we are."

"Why is that?'

"He's ninety years old and he can't see more than thirty feet in front of him."

"He sure did lean forward when you planted that wonderful kiss against my lips."

"I'll bet another kiss like that would sure get his rudder going," Joe laughed.

"You men—you have the most names for certain parts of your body. Now, let's you and I go inside our home before Mr. Peabody falls off his porch."

Once inside their house, Linda pointed toward the wide screen television set that she had bought him. "Joe, whenever you can I want you to adjust the color on your television set, but this time there will not be any offering of juice of any kind."

* * * *

The next morning local and state wide newspapers were headlined with the heroic effort of an Adamsville man that pulled a ten year old boy out of a pond. The paper read, 'Unhesitatingly, an without a moments concern with his own safety, William A. Davis ran to a pond, jumped into ten-foot of water and retrieved a ten year old boy. Mr. Davis managed to get the young child on the embankment. He then pulled himself out of the pond, immediately asked someone to call 911. Trained already in cardiopulmonary resuscitation (CPR), Mr. Davis wasted no time in taking charge and administering CPR to the unconscious little boy. Even when it seemed hopeless to revive ten year old Timmy Maynard, the man would not give up. All Mrs. Gloria Maynard could do was watch as a man that she had never spoken to use his life-saving skills, trying relentlessly to revive her son. Finally, with ultimate relief for everyone watching, the little boy discharged water through his mouth. That's when Timmy Maynard opened his eyes. Mr. Davis, a real genuine hero in everyone's eyes that were watching, helped little Timmy Maynard stand up. Seeing him hand Timmy's hand to his mother brought tears to many of the bystanders.'

'Soaked from head to toe, grass and moss on his clothes, Mr. Davis seemed as humble as any man could be. The boys' mother offered to buy him a new suit, but the kind-hearted man politely refused. Mrs. Gloria Maynard is the wife of John C. Maynard, multi-millionaire and owner of property in three states. Mr. Maynard, also, owns the ten acre properties where the three-quarter acre Koi pond is located. There are twelve specialty stores located on this tract of land, not including the mammoth sized Maynard Sporting Goods Store that he owns.'

'Before Mr. Davis left the Maynard property yesterday someone asked him how he happened to be at that very spot, at the exact time that Timmy fell into the water. The inquisitive bystander was stunned when Mr. Davis told him the answer to his question. Strangely enough, he was there to see Mr. Maynard about employment. As far as this newspaper reporter is concerned, you can't have a better resume than saving a potential employer's ten year old son's life!'

'Mr. William A. Davis is married and has two young children, a boy and a girl. It just so happens that his son, Nelson, is the same age as Timmy, the very one that he revived from drowning. The town of Adamsville should be mighty proud of this very heroic man.'

"I can't believe it! I just can't believe it!" Mark Wilson said, as he sat at the kitchen table.

"What can't you believe?" Sarah asked.

"William Davis is the town hero."

"Why? What did he do?"

"Here, read it for yourself." He handed the newspaper to her.

Sarah read the entire article. "No matter what we or anyone else says about William Davis that was a very remarkable thing he did."

"Sarah, I'm very glad that you said that. William Davis did a very bad thing to Linda, but I truly believe he's deeply saddened by what he did. I know his family must be very, very proud of him for saving that little boy's life. I wonder what Joe and Linda will say when they read the article."

"I have no idea about that, but I do know one thing for sure!"

"What is that?"

"When John Maynard finds out that William Davis saved his son's life I can guarantee you that he will have a job."

Marie Davis had driven into Adamsville that morning to go grocery shopping. Her children, Nelson and Heather were at school. Marie had hardly entered the store when Mrs. Glenda King walked up to her. "Marie Davis, do you know what the town should do about your husband?"

Embarrassed and shocked that Mrs. King would ask her a question like that in a public place was very annoying to Marie. "Mrs. King, what do you mean by that remark?"

"Didn't you read the morning paper?"

"No, the paper is still in my mailbox."

"Mrs. Davis, your husband is the town hero!"

"He's what?"

"The town hero, the news is all over the county, the state, and probably the whole country. The town should give him some kind of medal."

"What did he do to deserve such recognition?"

"Without any hesitation at all, your husband jumped into a deep pond, clothes and all, to save a little boy that had fallen into it. The boy had already swallowed too much water and was unconscious when Mr. Davis got him out of the water. What a take-charge kind of man your husband is! He told someone to call 911, and then he proceeded to administer CPR to the ten year old boy. Mrs. Davis, it didn't look like the boy was going to make it, but your husband wouldn't give up. Not at all, he kept working on that child until he spewed out all that excess water. That's when that poor boy opened his eyes. You're married to a mighty fine man, Mrs. Davis.

"Mrs. King, where did this happen?"

"It happened behind Maynard's Sporting Goods Store. Guess who the little boy's father is?"

"I have no idea."

"It was John Maynard."

"Mrs. King, thank you for telling me this."

"You're welcome, and tell Mr. Davis that the citizens of Adamsville are mighty proud of him."

It was eleven o'clock in the morning; Joe Wilson was sitting at the breakfast table, waiting for Linda to finish cooking the sausage, scrambled eggs and grits. "Linda, guess where we're going tomorrow?"

"Where is that?"

"We're going to the mountains. I promised you a honeymoon and you're going to have one. You've only got six more days before you have to go back to work."

"Joe, you know what the doctor said about strenuous activities."

"Linda Wilson, you're my wife, I love you very, very much. It was all I could do to lay there last night and just hold my arm around your waist. I'm overdue for my honeymoon and so are you."

"I'm very excited that we're going to the mountains, but I don't intend for you to overexert yourself."

"Sweetheart, we'll just temper the honeymoon down several notches."

"You're kidding me, Joe Wilson! I've never heard of anyone tempering down their honeymoon. When people honeymoon they give it all they've got!"

"Linda, that's the funniest statement I've ever heard come from your mouth—give it all they've got!" Joe burst into laughter.

"Now, what was so funny about that?" Linda asked, smiling. "Joe, will you answer the phone?"

He picked up the phone and begun listening to the caller. Linda was placing the food onto the table. Five minutes later, Linda was sitting at the table while Joe continued talking. "Joe, your food is getting cold."

About a minute later he hung up the phone."

"Who were you talking to?"

"It was your father. You will never believe what has happened!"

"Well, tell me—what happened."

"William Davis jumped into a pond and saved a little boy from drowning. According to your father, the boy was unconscious when he got him out of the water. It seems that William administered CPR on the unconscious boy. Some bystanders thought the boy was dead, but he wouldn't quit giving him CPR. Finally, the child threw up the excess water, that's when he opened his eyes. Your father said William Davis was a town hero. What do you think about that?"

"Saving that boy's life was a wonderful thing. Joe, you already know that I am a Christian. As a Christian I've forgiven William Davis for what he did to me, but I'll never be able to forget the shame he brought on me. From what I understand, he is very remorseful for what he did. He turned himself into the law, he told his wife what he did, he drew out his savings to give to me, and he even attempted suicide, so I heard. As a Christian I believe he is entitled to another chance for happiness with his wife and children. How do you feel toward William Davis?"

"Well, at first I wanted to kill him."

"What about now?"

"I really don't know how I feel about him now. It's hard for me to forget that he had his way with you. On the other hand it does appear that he is very sorry for what he did. According to your father and mine, William Davis is deserving of another chance. Anthony told me that his wife is not in very good health and they have two young children. In fact, Mrs. Davis is physically unable to work, according to Anthony. She and those children need William Davis to take care of them. You know what makes me really mad?"

"What's that?"

"At first I wanted to bash that man's head in! Now I don't even want to do that because, in a crazy, unexplainable way I really feel sorry for him. Guess what, now our food is cold."

"That's no problem, Joe, we have a microwave. Did you enjoy watching your big screen television last night?"

"I certainly did, but we won't need a television when we get to the mountains." Joe laughed.

"You must be planning to do a lot of fishing while we're there. Are there ponds or lakes where we're going?"

"Aren't you funny?" Joe laughed. It was nearly noon when Marie Davis returned home from shopping. She had bought groceries, and stopped at Marvin Thigpen's filling station for gas. Seeing his wife's car pull into the driveway, William hurried outside and helped her bring in the groceries. Without saying a word, Marie walked over to her husband, placed her arms around him and her face against his.

"Marie, is everything alright?"

"I just want you to know how much I love you. William, you told me earlier that you helped pull someone out of a pond, but you didn't tell me that you actually saved his life with your CPR training. People are calling you the town hero. Our children will be excited when they hear this?"

"Marie, I don't feel like a town hero."

"Why don't you?"

"A lot of people in town know how I treated that service man's wife."

"William, you've made peace with God and with me concerning that situation. You need to stop torturing yourself about what has already been done. I know one thing, I'm very proud of what you did for that little child. Have you any idea whose child that was?"

"No, I haven't the slightest clue."

"William Davis, haven't you read the morning paper?"

"No, I haven't brought it in yet."

"God Almighty, William, the child you saved was none

other than John Maynard's own son! Remember, he was the very man that you went to see about a job!"

"I didn't know who the child's mother was. Now I won't be able to go back to Mr. Maynard for a job."

"Why is that?"

"I wouldn't want him thinking that he had to give me a job because I saved his child's life."

"William Davis, I should hit you over your thick head with this frozen chicken," said Marie.

"You just told me how much you love me and now you're threatening me with a dead, frozen chicken."

"Well, give me a kiss, and then I'll wait until the chicken thaws out before I hit you with it."

"I've got a much better idea."

"Okay, what is it?"

"Instead of hitting me with a thawed chicken, how about me scratching your back a little while before the kids come home."

"What kind of scratching are we talking about?"

"Just three kinds."

"What three kinds?"

"Delicate, sensitive, soothing," he laughed.

Marie started walking toward the front door.

"What are you doing?" William asked.

"I'm going to lock the front door." She had a big smile on her face.

Chapter 12

By eight o'clock the next morning, Joe Wilson and his wife were packed and ready to drive toward the mountains. They had already called their respective families and told them where they were going. "Linda, I know our car trunk is full of clothes and other things, but let's make absolutely sure that we don't leave anything behind that we may need on our trip."

"I can't think of another thing that we might need. Doris is going to save our mail until we get back."

"Speaking of your sister, how is she and Anthony getting along?"

"She told me that she really likes your brother."

"That's wonderful, Anthony is crazy about her. Well, since I'm a recuperating young man I'll let you drive us to the mountains."

"I don't mind at all, but I would bet a month's salary that

you're fully recuperated by the time we reach the cabin you've rented," said Linda, smiling.

"It always amazes me how right you can be about so many things."

*　　*　　*　　*

At ten o'clock that same morning the doorbell rang at William Davis's house. Mrs. Wilson answered the doorbell. "Are you Mrs. Davis?" The stranger asked.

"Yes, my name is Marie Davis."

"Mrs. Davis, my name is John Maynard. I would very much like to speak with your husband if he's here."

"Mr. Maynard, please come inside the house. It's a beautiful Saturday morning so William took the kids into the back yard to play some kind of ball. I'll go get him for you."

"Mrs. Davis, may I walk with you to the backyard? I would like to see your children as well as your husband."

"By all means." Marie led Mr. Maynard out the backdoor. The first thing he saw was William down on his knees hugging both his children. William stood up when he recognized the man that saved his life at the creek.

"Mr. Davis, do you remember me?"

"Sir, I will never forget your face. Marie, this is the nice gentleman that—well, the children are standing here. You know already what he did for me. Sir, I'm very glad to see you again."

"It's a real pleasure seeing you again. Mr. Davis, introduce me to your lovely children."

"This is my son, Nelson, and this is my, somewhat shy, little daughter, Heather."

Mr. Maynard leaned forward and gave each one of them a hug. "Nelson, I believe you are ten years old, is that right?"

"Yes sir, but how would you know my age?"

"Son, I know a great deal about you and your wonderful family. Nelson, did you know that your father saved my ten year old son's life?"

"Yes sir, my teacher said she read it in the paper. What is your name?"

"Son, my name is John Maynard."

"Mr. Maynard, is your son alright now?" Heather asked.

"Yes, he certainly is—thanks to your father. Mr. Davis, would you mind riding with me somewhere?"

"I'll be glad to, Mr. Maynard."

"Mrs. Davis, we'll be back in a couple hours. I hope you don't mind."

"No sir, I don't mind at all."

William Davis got into the passenger side of a brand new Mercury Grand Marquis. He immediately noticed the mileage on the odometer. The automobile only showed thirty-five miles registered on it. "I believe you like this car," said Mr. Maynard.

"It's absolutely beautiful. It sure doesn't have many miles registered on the odometer." Mr. Maynard drove out of William's yard.

"Mr. Davis, I was on a business trip the day you pulled my son out of the Koi pond. I will never be able to thank you enough for saving Timmy's life."

"Mr. Maynard, I feel the same way toward you because you surely saved my life that day at the creek. I'm ashamed to say it now, but I was ready to end my life. The shame and disgrace I felt then made life meaningless to me. I just wanted to die and end it all! It's hard for me to believe that I was so foolish at that time. For what it's worth, I've been forgiven by God, my wife, and my children for that dreadful thing I did. At first I wanted to partly blame my wife for what I did. Night after night she didn't want to make love to me, so I concocted a scheme for my personal, yet selfish satisfaction. It was not my wife's fault at all. Not once did I tell her how I really felt about her rejections. I offered all our meager savings to the lady I offended, but she declined my wife's offer. Can you believe it; she knew my wife and children needed the money more than she did. I hope one day I can, face to face, offer my sincere apology to her. Mr. Maynard, I'm sorry for telling you all this, but I just wanted you to know that I will never do anything like that again!"

"Mr. Davis, I already knew what you did to Mrs. Wilson. I, also, know that you had a perfect work record at Clemmons Pharmaceuticals until that situation at her house. From what I've found out from your former supervisors you are honest as the days are long, and that you were an outstanding manager. Mr. Davis, I'm not taking lightly what you did, but on the other hand everyone makes mistakes in life. The sad thing about most people is that they don't learn from their mistakes. In your case you have learned a great deal. You've realized your family, children, self-respect, dignity, employment and self-esteem is worth a great deal more than a few minutes of self-gratification. Anyway, we're at my Sporting Goods Store. I want to take you inside the store and introduce you to some of my personnel."

Several store employees saw Mr. Maynard and William Davis walk into the store. One of them was Roger Smith, store manager. "Good morning, Mr. Maynard, this must be the gentleman that you told me about."

"Yes, Roger, this is Mr. William Davis. He's also the man that pulled my son out of the Koi pond, and then he used his CPR skills to save his life. As you can imagine, William Davis is a very dear friend of mine. William, this is Roger Smith, my store manager."

"I'm glad to meet you, Mr. Smith."

"It's a pleasure meeting you, Mr. Davis."

"The other employees in front of you are, Cecil Matthews, George Bell, Henry Skinner, and Clark Andrews," said Mr. Maynard. Each of them shook William's hand and welcomed him to the store. William thanked the men for their nice gestures toward him.

"Roger, I want you and Mr. Davis to go with me to my office." William had no idea why Mr. Maynard was taking him to his private office. When the three men got into Mr. Maynard's very elaborate office he asked William and Roger to have a seat.

"Mr. Davis, how do you like Mr. Maynard's office?" Roger asked.

"It's beautiful."

"William, I guess you're wondering why I brought you to the store today."

"I guess I am, Mr. Maynard."

"Roger has been the manager here for ten years. He's done an outstanding job in that capacity. Roger is leaving his job here to be closer to his family. They live in South Carolina. He will still be employed with one of my companies that are located within twenty eight miles from where his new house is located. Roger, I know the movers will be at your house in a little while, so shake hands with Mr. Davis. Don't forget to brief the assistant manager again on everything before you head home."

"I'll do that, Mr. Maynard. Again, thank you for my new job in South Carolina." He shook his boss's hand and then Mr. Davis's hand. "Mr. Davis, the best of luck to you."

"Thank you very much." Roger left the room.

"William, isn't it some kind of coincidental that I saved your life, and then you saved my son's life?"

"Yes, it seems almost uncanny for something like that to happen."

"How would you like a job with me?"

"I would like that very much, Mr. Maynard." A big smile appeared on William's face.

"You're a college graduate I've learned. According to your prior employers you are a very good manager. A good manager is what I need in this store. As you might have guessed already there are millions of dollars of inventory in this one store alone. The business is located not too far from your home, making it an easy drive. How would you like to be manager of this store?"

"Mr. Maynard, I would like it more than anything! I really need a job so I can take care of my family. Our reserve funds will soon run out. When would you want me to start working for you?"

"You didn't ask me anything about salary."

"I'm confident that you will pay me fairly. Besides, I'm not making any money at all, presently."

Mr. Maynard wrote down a figure on a piece of paper. "How about we start with this salary?"

"Mr. Maynard, I've never made that much money in my entire life. Are you sure that's what you want to pay me?"

"I'm quite sure." He reached inside his desk drawer and pulled out a stack of money. "William, I want you to take this money as a bonus for accepting my job offer."

"Mr. Maynard, that looks like an awful lot of money! You don't have to pay me any bonus money!"

"I know I don't, but I want to. That's five thousand dollars, I want you to pick up the money and place it in your pocket."

"Are you sure? Are you really sure?"

"I'm quite sure. I want you to start working here not this Monday, but the following Monday. That will give you a full week to spend with your family. Maybe you can drive them to the Zoo tomorrow. I understand that it will be wonderful weather the entire weekend. Maybe you and your family would like to spend next weekend at the beach. I have three beach houses at the ocean and you could use one of them. William, you seem upset, what's the matter?"

"Mr. Maynard, so many good things is happening to me that I'm just overwhelmed." He wiped the tears from his eyes.

"I told your wife that you would be back in a couple hours, so I'll introduce you to all the other employees on your first day of work. Now, I want us to go outside to the Koi pond."

They walked around the building to where Timmy fell into the pond. "William, as the new manager of Maynard's Sporting Goods Store I want you to hire someone to build a very nice fence around this entire pond. Make sure the builders make a gate on the North, South, East, and West side of the pond. Each gate will require some kind of locking mechanism."

"What type fence would you prefer?"

"Black wrought Iron. Make sure that the fence is at least three-foot from the waters' edge. That will allow for ducks and geese to get out of the water. I never again want a child or anyone else to fall into this pond."

"I'll take care of it."

"I know you will, William. By the way, these are your keys."

Totally shocked, his hands trembling, William took the keys. "I don't understand what these keys are for?"

"That new car we came here in is yours, William. It's bought and paid for, including the insurance for a full year. The car is in your name."

"Mr. Maynard, I don't know what to say!"

"Don't say anything. My wife and I want you to be happy once again. By the way, after you start working here I want you and your family to come visit my family one day. Uh oh, I almost forgot Timmy's letter." He reached into his coat pocket and pulled out an envelope. He handed it to William. "When you get home I want you to open my son's letter that he wrote to you."

"I'll read it just as soon as I get home." He shook Mr. Maynard's hand. "Sir, I will never, ever let you down."

"I know that already, William. Now, you go home and show your family this beautiful new car."

Tears came into Mr. Maynard's eyes as he observed William drive off, fully aware that his only son's life was saved by the man he just hired.

William could hardly wait to get home. Never before had he been so excited and happy. His children were on the front porch when they noticed the brand new, shiny car pull into their driveway. Nelson opened the house door, calling for his mother. "Nelson, what is it? Why are you yelling?"

"Somebody just came into our driveway in a new looking car."

"Nelson, that looks like your father in that car!" Both children ran off the porch toward the parked vehicle.

"Daddy, whose car are you driving?" Nelson asked, excitedly.

"It's our car."

"Mommy, Daddy's got a new car!" Heather yelled.

"William, you shouldn't be teasing the children like that."

"What do you mean?"

"You know darn well this expensive car doesn't belong to you!"

"It does, Marie. Mr. Maynard gave me this car."

"You're kidding me!"

"Honest to God, we own this car."

"Why would he give you such an expensive car?"

"I don't know, Marie, but he did. The car is registered in my name. Not only that, but the insurance premiums have been paid for an entire year."

"How did your interview go?"

"Mr. Maynard gave me a job. I'm so happy I could cry! Marie, I will be the manager of that large Sporting Goods Store that Mr. Maynard owns."

Marie hugged her husband tightly around his neck. "I'm very, very proud of you, William. When do you start to work?

"He gave me off an entire week to enjoy my family and take you and the children places. How about we take the children to the Zoo tomorrow?"

"Are you sure we can afford it?"

"I really think so." William reached into his pocket and pulled out a wad of hundred dollar bills.

"Where did you get all that money?"

"Mr. Maynard gave it to me. He said he wanted me and my family to be happy."

"You shouldn't have taken his money."

"Marie, he insisted that I take the money. Besides, I'm getting you an appointment with the best doctor in this state. You're my wife and you deserve the very best medical treatment that's available."

"How much money do you have in your hand, Daddy?" Nelson asked.

"Son, you're looking at five thousand dollars. Guess where we will be next Saturday and Sunday?"

"Where will that be, Daddy?" Heather asked.

"We'll be at the beach. Mr. Maynard will let us use one of his houses that's located on the beach side of the ocean."

"Did you hear that, Nelson?" Heather asked, jumping up and down. "We're going to the beach!"

Chapter 13

At ten o'clock that night, Joe and Linda Wilson were settled in their three bedroom cabin they had rented for a week. The cabin was located in a beautiful section of the Blue Ridge Mountains. The ride to the mountains for Joe was somewhat strenuous, realizing that he was not totally healed from his surgery. "Linda, what are you doing in the kitchen?"

"I'm making us something to eat."

"What are you making?"

"I'm making pancakes and bacon."

"We just ate three hours ago."

"Yes, it was three whole hours ago, that's why I'm cooking pancakes and bacon now."

"Do we have any aspirin?"

"I've got a bottle in my handbag. Why do you need aspirin?"

"I have a slight headache."

"My pancakes and bacon will make your headache go away."

"Are you sure of that?"

"If it doesn't—two or three of my kisses will make you forget you have a headache."

"It might just take one. Anyway, I've got big plans scheduled for us later tonight."

"What sort of plans?"

"I'll let it be a surprise."

"You do remember what Dr. Starling told you about stress, don't you?"

"If you've noticed, Dr. Starling is not here. Pain or no pain I'm doing some honey-mooning tonight."

Linda sat the bacon and pancakes on the kitchen table. "Not only is my wife beautiful but she's also a wonderful cook."

"Thank you. I handle compliments extremely well."

"What the Hell!" Joe stood up; he got closer to the window.

"What's the matter?"

"There's someone standing behind that telephone pole in our yard!"

"How can you see in the dark?"

"It's not dark around that pole; it's attached with an aerial light. Look for yourself, it looks like a man and he's looking straight toward this cabin."

"I see him. It looks like he's got something in his hands."

"I see it now. I believe he's holding a rifle or a shotgun."

"Joe, what could he want?" Linda was trembling.

"I don't know, but I'm going out the backdoor and confront whoever it is."

"No, Joe, please don't do that! Please don't go out that door!"

Joe turned off the kitchen lights. He and Linda peered out the window again, but the shadowy figure had gone. "Joe, please make sure our doors are locked!"

"They are, I've already checked." They turned the kitchen lights back on so they could eat their food. "Maybe that man was just hunting." Joe suggested.

"I didn't know people hunted this time of year."

"You're right about that. Anyway, we're safe as long as we are locked up inside this cabin."

"How are your pancakes and bacon?"

"Sweetheart, they are delicious. By the way, I'll help with the dishes."

"Nonsense, there's only two dishes, two frying pans and a few utensils for me to wash. Why don't you go take your bath while I take care of the kitchen?"

"I sure do like your way of thinking. I'm going to get squeaky clean."

"How does one get squeaky clean?"

Linda washed the two plates, utensils and the pans in hot soapy water. She rinsed all the items with warm water. She used a kitchen towel to dry the items. While holding the two plates in her hands she happened to look toward a side window. Standing next to an outside window was a man with a shaggy beard. He was looking straight at her. The dishes Linda was holding fell to the floor as she ran out of the kitchen. "Joe! Joe!" She yelled.

With only a towel wrapped around him, he opened the bathroom door. "My God, Linda, you look like you've seen a ghost! What's the matter, sweetheart? What's wrong?"

It was very difficult for her to even speak. "The window! Joe, the window!" Linda was shaking all over.

"What about the window! What did you see?"

Linda was hugging Joe around his neck. "There was a man at the kitchen window! Oh, my God! He was looking at me! I'm scared, Joe! I'm scared!"

"It's okay, please don't cry! What did the man look like?"

She shook her head back and forth. "He looked horrible! His whole face was covered with hair! Joe, I don't like it here! I'm afraid something will happen to us!"

"That settles it, I'm calling the law just as soon as I get my clothes on." Joe was talking to the sheriff's office a few minutes later. A deputy informed Joe that he would be at the cabin within fifteen or twenty minutes.

"What did the law tell you?"

"A deputy will be here in a little while. Maybe he can tell us why we've got an unwanted peeping-Tom wandering around this cabin."

It was about fifteen minutes later when Linda and Joe saw car lights coming down the road toward their cabin. They waited inside until they were sure it was a deputy that exited the vehicle. They met the deputy on their front porch. "My name is Joe Wilson and this is my wife, Linda. Someone is scaring the living Hell out of my wife. We first saw a man standing in our yard. He was behind the utility pole that has the aerial light on it. I believe he was holding a rifle or shotgun in his hands."

"Is that the only time you saw him?"

"Heck no, my wife was doing some dishes in the kitchen when that nut-case stared at her through the kitchen window!

He nearly frightened her to death! She even dropped the dishes that she was holding. We didn't rent this cabin to be frightened out of our wits!"

"Mrs. Wilson, what did this man look like?"

"He was ugly!"

"That may be true, but a lot of men are ugly. Can you be more specific?"

"His face was covered with facial hair, and it was long. He looked like he was a big man. I'll never forget the way he was looking at me!" Linda shivered at that very thought.

"Officer, have you ever had any complaints before concerning this location, more specifically this cabin?"

"I believe we have had a couple complaints from prior renters, but everything must have turned out alright."

"Why did you say that?"

"Well, there were no more complaints after the renters' first night in the cabin."

"What are you telling us?"

"On those two isolated occasions the renter's just up and left after their first night here. In either one of those cases they didn't bother to come to the office for a partial refund."

"Maybe there was a reason why they didn't go after their refund."

"We have no evidence of that. We've never had any reported incidents at the other cabins in this area. This cabin happens to be in the most remote part of the forest. I'm going outside and look around."

"Is it okay for me to walk with you?" Joe asked.

"I wouldn't mind, but I'm not sure about your wife."

"Joe Wilson, you're not going to leave me alone for one second!"

"See what I mean, Mr. Wilson. You two go back into the house. I'll knock on the door when I get through checking the outside perimeter."

It was quite evident to Officer Collins that someone had been standing behind the telephone pole, and also at the kitchen window. There were cigarette butts on the ground at both locations.

About fifteen minutes later, Joe and Linda heard a knock on their door. "Who is it?" Joe asked.

"It's me, Officer Collins." Joe opened the door. "You and your wife are correct; someone was at the telephone pole and at the kitchen window. The man must be a chain-smoker because there were several cigarette butts at the telephone pole and two near the kitchen window."

"Officer, I'm going to tell you just like it is! I brought a pistol with me on this trip. It's not my desire to use it, but I'll be damned sure not to let anyone harm my wife or me!"

"Mr. Wilson, I know exactly how you feel. I would feel the same way if I was in your situation, but I must warn you about something."

"What's that?"

"You cannot shoot someone that happens to be standing in your yard. It would be a different matter if someone was breaking into an occupied house."

"You don't have any idea who the man might be?"

"I don't have a clue, unless it was Lewis Hanes. I doubt very seriously that it would be him."

"Who in thunder is Lewis Hanes? Also, why would you doubt that it wouldn't be him?"

"Lewis is a convict that escaped from Clarian Correctional Facility."

"Where is that?" Joe asked.

"It's two counties away from here. I don't see how he could have gotten this far on foot and in prison clothes. The law thinks he's somewhere in the Chicago area by now. That's where he was living before he killed his step-father and step-mother."

"How on earth did a man like that escape from prison to begin with?"

"Actually, he was being transferred to another prison when someone, most likely a friend or relative, rammed the prison van on the driver's side with his truck. The prison guard was injured in the accident, but for him things got even worse. The accomplice retrieved the keys for the handcuffs from the guard's front pocket. Upon being freed Lewis Hanes got the guards gun from his holster and then shot him between the eyes."

"How does the law know it was Lewis Hanes that fired the shot?"

"There were three witnesses on the street that saw the whole thing. One of them recognized Lewis as the shooter. Mrs. Wilson, if I were to bring you a photograph of Lewis Hanes, do you think you might be able to identify him if it was Lewis Hanes?"

"Officer, I'm not sure, but I would be willing to try."

"I'll let you folks get a good night's sleep, but I will return before noon tomorrow with a picture of Lewis."

"We both appreciate you coming out here," said Joe. "Maybe it was just someone that was hungry."

"I don't buy that at all," said Linda. "Men holding shotguns or rifles don't normally get too hungry."

"Your wife has a good point, Mr. Wilson. Anyway, tomorrow I'll bring the photographs of Lewis Hanes."

"Thank you," said Joe. "We were about to go to bed anyway before we spotted that creep out in the yard." The officer shook hands with Joe and Linda, and then he left.

Inside the house Joe looked toward Linda and smiled. "I've had my bath already."

"Joe, you must be on dope or insane if you think there's going to be any love-making tonight."

"Why do you say that?"

"For one thing—I'm scared to death that man might come back to the house! I'm going to take a bath, but I want you to stand in front of the bathroom door. My nerves are all to pieces."

"Linda, I promise not to let anyone hurt you. Now, take your bath and then we'll go to bed."

"I won't sleep at all tonight. Joe, I wish we hadn't come here!" Tears were in Linda's eyes.

"Please, Linda, don't be afraid! After you take a bath you and I will go into the bedroom and lock the doors. I got my pistol back from my father before we left. It will be lying on the table right beside our bed. Now, take your bath and we'll get a good night's sleep, even if I can't get anything else."

"Joe, I'm sorry, I didn't mean for it to be this way!"

"I know you didn't, Linda. Maybe after tomorrow everything will be back to normal."

It was about one o'clock in the morning when Linda shook Joe's shoulder. She hadn't slept one minute since getting into the bed. She shook him again, only this time much harder. Still groggy after his deep sleep, he whispered, "What's the matter?" It was all Linda could do to keep from screaming. Tears flowed down her cheeks as she snuggled closer to her husband. Joe leaned close to his wife and whispered again, "What's the matter?"

"Oh, my God, someone is in this house," she whispered.

"Are you sure?" He asked in a very low voice.

"Look at the bottom of our door. See the light moving back and forth. Someone has a flashlight in this cabin. Joe, what are we going to do?"

"Be real quiet, don't be moving around." Joe moved quietly off the bed, he picked up his pistol and then he stood, silently, about ten feet from the bedroom door. In almost near panic, Linda pulled the sheet over her head. Hearing some movement in the hallway, Joe switched the safety off his pistol; he pointed it toward the door.

There was total silence for about two minutes. All at once the door was kicked inside. Joe fired his gun until it was completely empty. A loud thud was heard as something or someone fell to the floor. Still in total darkness, Linda was under the sheet screaming as loud as she could. Anxious to turn the light on, Joe tripped over what appeared to be the form of a person. He scrambled up, found the light switch and he turned on the bedroom lights. Lying on the floor was a large bearded-man. It was obvious to Joe that the man was dead. "Joe! Joe! Please tell me you're alright!" Linda cried, still under the sheet.

"I'm just fine, Linda. I want you to take one look at this man's face and tell me if he's the one that you saw at our window."

Hesitatingly, she peeped over her sheet, but she couldn't see the man lying on the floor. "Joe, I'm scared!"

"You needn't be frightened because this man is not going to hurt you or anyone else ever again. He's dead!" She eased off the bed and then looked at the man's face. "Is this the same man?"

"Yes! That's the same man! Oh, my God, look at that man?"

"What's the matter?"

"Look at all that blood?"

"Linda, do you see what's lying on the floor beside his right hand? It's a hunting knife. Do you see what's on the floor near our bed? That's a twelve gauge shotgun. That would have been our blood if you hadn't awaked me when you did. Linda, I don't want you to see this mess any longer. Let's you and I go into the kitchen and I'll call the law. Try not to step on the blood, gun or knife. I told you before that I was not going to let anyone hurt you, and I meant it! Grab your clothes on the way out of the room. We'll be up the rest of the morning now."

"Joe, I could never sleep a minute in this cabin now."

"You won't have to, Linda. You and I will find somewhere else to stay tomorrow. Now, let's go to the kitchen so I can make the telephone call."

While Joe talked with the sheriff's office, Linda got the coffee pot percolating.

Within fifteen minutes law enforcement vehicles started arriving at the cabin. Detective Josh Langford identified the dead man as Lewis Hanes, murderer, bank robber, and kidnapper.

It was obvious to the detective that the bedroom door had been kicked open by Lewis Hanes.

Joe and Linda had been sitting on their couch for nearly an hour before Detective Langford came into the room the second time to talk with them. "Detective, how did that man get into our cabin?" Joe asked.

"Believe it or not, he had entry keys to this cabin. Not only that, but he had credit cards and other items in his pockets belonging to people who are still missing from their home towns."

"What in the world is going on here?" A stranger asked.

"Where did you come from?" Detective Langford asked.

"What do you mean, where did I come from? My name is Cyrus Owens; I own all the property around here for nearly a mile, including this cabin. I saw all the police cars headed this way so I drove here to see what was going on. Now, what is going on here?"

"Someone has been killed in this cabin."

"Lord knows, who was killed?"

"An escaped convict broke open Mr. and Mrs. Joe Wilson's bedroom door. He was shot and killed for doing so. Mr. Owens, I want you to take a good look at the deceased person and see if you recognize him."

"Sure, I'll do that." Mr. Owens followed the detective into the bedroom. "I recognize that man! He's the dad-blasted man that I saw driving Mr. Herbert Yates new car by my office."

"Mr. Owens, did you just mention the name Herbert Yates?"

"Yes, I sure did. Mr. Yates and his nice wife Tricia rented this cabin about three weeks ago. I distinctly remember that because my cleaning lady said they were gone the very next day. That's the same day that I saw this man driving their car past my office. You know, it's a funny thing."

"Why is that, Mr. Yates?"

"I would have paid them for the days they didn't use, but they never came back to my office."

"Isn't that rather unusual for them not to come back for their money?"

"It's very unusual, but it happened twice in a row."

"What do you mean?"

"The following week I rented this cabin to Donny Weeks and his wife, Velva. They were gone on their second day here. They didn't come to the office to collect their money either. That same evening I saw their car drive by the office, but I didn't see who was in the car."

Another detective that was listening to the conversation asked Detective Langford if he would step over near him. "Mr. Owens, would you do me a favor and join Mr. and Mrs. Wilson in the living room?"

"Yes, officer, I'll be glad to."

"Sgt. Peele, you wanted to talk with me?"

"Yes, did you hear who stayed here before the Wilson's?"

"I heard it loud and clear. Those are the two missing couples that were reported to us."

"Detective Langford, are you thinking what I'm thinking?"

"I believe I am. We'll need to bring the bloodhounds here in the morning. I'm sure we'll find all four of them in the woods."

"What are you going to do about Mr. Wilson?"

"Not one damn thing! Well, that's not entirely true; Mr. Wilson will be given the twenty-thousand dollars reward for the capture or apprehension of Lewis Hanes. With six bullet holes in that man's carcass you could safely say that Mr. Wilson apprehended him."

"Mrs. Wilson, I'm awfully sorry that this terrible thing happened here," said Mr. Owens. "I will be more than happy to give you your rent money back, or I'll let you move your belongings to a large cabin that's next to my office for the same amount of rent. You would love it there."

"Why is that?"

"There's a gigantic lake within forty feet of the cabin. Not only that, but there's a large fish pond located on one side of the house. Mrs. Wilson, you would be totally safe there I assure you. I didn't offer it to you to begin with because the house was built especially for honeymooners. That house has everything a newly wedded couple could ever want."

"Joe, what do you think?"

"Mr. Owens, how soon can we move our stuff into that cabin?"

"Why don't we get started right now? I'll be more than happy to help you and Mrs. Wilson take your belongings to the honeymoon cabin."

After finalizing his report pertaining to the shooting, Detective Langford told Joe that he will receive a check in the mail for the amount of twenty-thousand dollars within about thirty days.

It was almost daybreak when Joe and Linda settled down in their magnificent and spacious cabin. "Linda, you saved both our lives this morning. That man would have killed us both if you had gone to sleep as I did."

"I was too afraid to go to sleep. Joe, will it be okay if we start the honeymoon thing tomorrow?" Linda smiled.

"Yes, indeed. All I want to do now is get on that super, king-sized bed and go to sleep."

It was four o'clock that evening; Joe Wilson was looking at two mated geese swim in the lake. "Aren't those geese beautiful?" Mr. Owens asked, him walking toward Joe.

"Yes, they certainly are. By the way, Mr. Owens, did the law find those two couples they were looking for? They were supposed to bring bloodhounds to that cabin we were in."

"I'm afraid they did. There were only two graves that Lewis Hanes dug. That monster of a man buried the husband and wife in the same grave. Detective Langford stopped by my office about noon and told me they had found the missing couples."

"I wonder what Lewis Hanes did with their vehicles?" Joe asked.

"We may never have an answer to that question. Mr. Wilson, how do you like it up here in the mountains?"

"It's very beautiful, Mr. Owens."

"I'm very curious about something, Mr. Wilson."

"What's that?"

"How does one feel when they have killed someone?"

"It's not something that you ever forget, but I was justified in killing Lewis Hanes. His intention was to kill me and my wife. He would have done it too if Linda had fallen asleep like me. She saved both our lives that night."

"Well, goodness gracious there's a charming lady headed this way." said Mr. Owens. "Good evening, Mrs. Wilson."

"Good evening to you, sir. What are you two doing out here."

"We're just talking. Mr. Owens told me that the law found those four missing people buried behind the cabin we were staying in."

"That is horrible! I'm glad my husband killed that maniac!"

"I certainly am sorry that you and your husband had to experience that nightmarish ordeal."

"Joe, I'm getting hungry."

"Mr. Owens, where is a good eating place that you would recommend?"

"I highly recommend that you visit Daisy Mae's Country Kitchen. You turn left in front of my office and it's exactly three miles on your right."

"Could we bring you a plate of food back to your office?" Linda asked.

"I appreciate it, but I have already eaten an early dinner."

"How many years have you lived near the town of Corona?"

"Fifty-five years. In other words, I was born here."

"Are you married, Mr. Owens?"

"I was, Mrs. Wilson, but my wife Charlotte died three years ago with cancer."

"I'm so sorry about your wife. I shouldn't be so inquisitive."

"That's quite alright, Mrs. Wilson, I didn't mind you asking at all. It broke my heart into when she passed away. For a period of time I was very, very unhappy."

"How were you able to snap out of those feelings?" Joe asked.

"It was three days following the funeral service. I was in our home alone, holding a picture of my wife in one hand and a pistol in the other one. I guess you never get to old to cry because I was crying out loud as I gazed at Charlotte's and my wedding picture. She and I never had any children and I was feeling so alone. I was at the end of my rope, no wife, no children, no one that cared whether I lived or died—just totally alone. I kissed her picture and then I laid it down gently on the sofa. It was right then and there that I realized I was at the end of my rope. Being very rich seemed almost irrelevant at that particular time."

"Mr. Owens, you were sitting there with a loaded gun, what happened?" Linda inquired.

"That's when it happened!"

"What happened?" Joe asked.

"An unusual ray of sunlight beamed right through my picture window. It was shining right into my face. A feeling of tranquility seemed to overshadow my entire body. I laid the pistol down on my couch. I don't know how to explain it, but that memorable day changed my life. I no longer wanted to kill myself, and the loss of my wife seemed less burdensome to me. Mrs. Wilson, what do you think that beam of light represented?"

"I believe the light was straight from God. Mr. Owens, we three have something in common."

"We do?"

"Yes, each of us at one time or another has wanted to kill themselves for one reason or other, but something unexplainable happened to each of us. Mr. Owens, you seem to be a very good man. I just want you to know that Joe and I consider you as one of our friends."

"I really appreciate that, I certainly do."

"Mr. Owens, just how many cabins do you own in this vast complex?" Joe asked.

"I have seventeen cabins. Four of them have two bedrooms and the rest have from three to five bedrooms."

"Well, it looks as though they're all rented out."

"Yes, indeed. In fact, I have a six month waiting list for some of my cabins. Isn't it funny?"

"What's that, Mr. Owens?" Linda asked

"I'm fifty five years old. I own business properties in several states. I've got a lot of money, but I don't even have a girlfriend. Mrs. Wilson, money alone doesn't make someone happy."

"Mr. Owens, you're still a very handsome man. You could have all the lady friends you wanted."

"I'm well aware of that, Mrs. Wilson, but my preference in a woman is someone that thinks I'm just a hard working guy. There are hundreds of women that would go with me or marry me just to get their clutches on my money. I would like to find a woman that could and would love me as a normal man, not just because of my wealth. I've got all this money, property, prestige and no wife or children to leave it to."

"Don't you have some kin folks, Mr. Owens?"

"I'm afraid not, Mrs. Wilson. My brother died three weeks before my wife did. He never married, but he was a very successful business man. Herman and I were very, very close. In fact, I inherited his estate when he died. Most of that property is located in a town named Mountain Bluff. It's located about fifty miles from here. I've got a lawyer and a real estate agent looking after those businesses there."

"What kind of property did your brother own?" Joe asked.

"Let me see, his property included eight houses that he rented or leased, drugstore, clothing store, two service stations, hardware store, and four sizeable farms."

"Mr. Owens, how on earth are you able to manage all that property as well as the property you have here?" Joe asked.

"I have the real estate companies, two CPA firms, lawyers, and many managers that handle my properties."

"Sir, we thought you were the manager at the rental office."

"No, I've got some good workers that work in the rental office. They, also, supervise the employees' that keeps the cabins clean. I'm here quite often because I love it here by the lake, but the main reason is because my home is just a short drive from here. Well, I've talked way too much. You and your wife should head on toward Daisy Mae's Country Kitchen before they stop serving. I certainly am glad to have you two as my friends."

"Mr. Owens, Linda and I want you as a friend because we like you, not because you're very wealthy."

"Mr. Wilson, I detected that from the very beginning. Well, you two go have a nice dinner."

"I really do wish you would go with us, Mr. Owens," said Joe. "You don't have to eat anything if you don't want to, but it would be nice to have your company."

"Well, I don't see anything wrong with joining my newly acquired friends to my favorite eating place. May I drive you to the restaurant?"

"We appreciate the offer, Mr. Owens, but we will drive this time," said Linda.

Chapter 14

William Davis and his family had returned home from their trip to the state Zoo. Everyone thoroughly enjoyed their visit, especially Nelson and Heather. The Davis children had never attended a Zoo before. The family was in their living room discussing their trip. "Daddy, why were the giraffes neck so long?" Nelson asked.

"Well, that's how God made giraffes."

"I still don't know why God made their necks so long."

"Nelson, the reason giraffes necks are so long is simple," said Marie. "A great deal of their food is leaves. Most leaves are high from the ground, and God made them with long necks so they could reach those leaves."

"God must be awfully smart," commented Heather.

"Darling, God created everything that crawls, swims, fly or walks. He created the moon, sun, mountains, stars, oceans, mountains and millions of other things. Yes, Heather, God is very, very smart."

"Mother, how do you know all these things?"

"Heather, do you see that book lying on the coffee table?"

"Yes."

"Well, that is a Bible. That book tells how the world was created and how everything got to be as it is."

"I liked the elephants more than anything," said Nelson. "I didn't know elephants could grow so big."

"There are elephants that are much bigger than the ones we saw," said his father.

"How could they be bigger than what we saw?"

"The elephants that we saw were Asian elephants. Some people call them Indian elephants. They were big alright, but the African elephants grow much bigger. In fact, the biggest land animal in the world is an African bull elephant. They can be as tall as thirteen feet and weigh up to thirteen thousand pounds."

"Goodness gracious, Daddy, how can they stand up?"

"They've got enormous sized legs to support their weight."

"How can they grow so big?" Nelson asked, shaking his head back and forth.

"Elephants can eat up to four hundred pounds of food each day."

"Daddy, what do they eat?" Heather asked.

"They eat grass, leaves, roots, bark, hay, fruit and a lot of salt whenever they can find some."

"Okay, it's time for you two kids to go to bed," said Marie.

"Mother, Daddy, we sure did have fun at the Zoo," said Nelson. Heather and I will always remember the day that our parents took us to the state Zoo." Marie hugged Nelson's neck, and then Heather's.

"Don't you two run off yet," said William. "I want to give each of you a hug."

"We love you too, Daddy."

"I know you do, Heather. I've always known that."

* * * *

"Mark, it's been three days now since Joe and Linda left for the mountains. I wonder how they're getting along."

"Sarah, Joe was away from Linda for months, how do you think they're getting along?"

"For land sakes, is sex all men ever think about?"

"I didn't say one thing about sex."

"Well, that was your implication."

"It may have been, but is sex such a bad thing? It's the best way I know to bring children into the world. Besides, I remember our honeymoon. What a time that was. You and I didn't come out of our rented cabin for three days straight."

"Mark Wilson, you know darn well that we were not in bed that whole time!"

"That's true. We did take time to shower and for me to shave," he laughed.

"You're a naughty old man!"

"You didn't think I was naughty then, so what's different now?"

"We're just getting old."

"You may have that perception, but I don't think that way."

"Why don't you?"

"It's simple; I've got myself a new friend."

"What new friend are you talking about?"

"His name is Mr. Viagra." Mark burst into laughter. "Now you know why I don't feel so old."

"I didn't know you took those fool things!"

"Now you know why about once a month you say things at night like, 'Mark! Oh, my God, Mark! Don't stop, Mark, and stuff like that!' I see you're blushing. Yes, yes, let me see that smile on your face. That's it, let that smile come on out."

"Mark Wilson, if I didn't love you so much I would crown you with that broom handle near the kitchen counter."

"You might as well admit it, Sarah, aren't you glad that I introduced you to my new friend?"

"If you say so, Mark, if you say so."

"What on earth are you two laughing about?" Joan asked, entering the room.

"We were just having some fun, weren't we Sarah?"

"Yes, I suppose were."

"Mother, I drove here from my house to ask your advice on something."

"What is it that you want to know?"

"A very handsome man saw me at Clayton's restaurant yesterday. I was having lunch with Doris Thigpen and Louise Potter when this man came to the table and asked what our names were and where we worked. Without thinking too much about it I told him our names and that we worked at Hudson's Clothing Store. The man thanked me and then he walked back to his table. Later that day the same man called me at the office and asked me if I would have lunch with him one day."

"What did you tell him?"

"I told him that I was sorry, but I didn't date or have lunch with total strangers."

"What happened then?"

"He told me his name again, where he worked, his telephone number, and who his parents were."

"Who are his parents?" Mark asked.

"He said their names were Simon and Marie Oakland."

"Joan, I know Simon Oakland very well. In fact, I've played golf with him several times. Simon is a very wealthy man. I've been told that he owns several sizeable companies and at least four large farms. What is his son's name?"

"His name is Gary Oakland. I don't know if he has any sisters or brothers."

"I think he only has one son, but I didn't know what his name is. What kind of work does Gary do?"

"He said he worked for one of his father's companies."

"Joan, same as my original question, what is it that you want to know from us?"

"Mother, I was wondering if you and father would mind having him over for dinner or something, that way I could meet him here."

"Joan, we don't mind having him over for dinner, but who's going to invite him to come?"

"I will, Mother."

"You hardly know Gary, why are you interested in him?"

"I know that, Mother, but I've got very good eyesight. Gary is more than handsome, he's extremely handsome! I've never had a male friend as good looking as he is."

"I hate to put a sour note on your excitement, but looks is not everything," said Mark. "What really matters is the qualities, goodness, trustworthiness, and purity in ones' heart."

"Well, Father, I'm hopeful that Gary will have something

going for him other than his good looks. Mother, would Sunday evening be okay for dinner?"

"Yes, but on one condition."

"What condition?"

"You help me with the dinner, not just show up after all the work has been done."

"That's fine; I'll be here early Sunday afternoon. Now, all I've got to do is call Gary back."

After Joan left the house, Mark noticed a smile on Sarah's face as she looked through the kitchen window. "What are you thinking, Sarah?"

"With Joe and Linda on their second honeymoon, and Joan interested in a new boyfriend we're going to have some grandchildren before you know it."

"Good Lord, Sarah, Joan hasn't gone on her first date and you're talking about grandchildren!"

"Everything happens in due time," she said, smiling. "Guess what, Anthony is thinking about buying Doris an engagement ring?"

"You've got to be kidding me! They haven't been dating all that long!"

"That's true, but they've known each other since they were young teenagers. Won't it be wonderful when we have some grandchildren that we can love and spend money on?"

"Sarah Wilson, you will spoil them rotten," he said, smiling.

"Only a little bit, Mark. Only a little bit."

* * * *

"Joe, this is our fourth morning in the mountains, and I want to know one thing."

He turned toward her as they lay in bed. "What would that be?"

"Have I made you happy on our second honeymoon?"

"Yes, Linda, you have fulfilled your duties as a loving wife. I could not have asked for more.

In fact, I discovered that Dr. Starling sure does know what he's talking about."

"What do you mean?"

"Let me put it this way, I need to spend more time fishing in the trout lake than I do in this bed."

"I'm sorry, Joe, I didn't realize you were having any kind of problem."

"Linda, I'm just fine, I just need a couple days of inactivity."

"I thought you were going trout fishing, that's an activity," she grinned.

"That's not the kind of activity I was talking about." He burst into laughter.

"Joe, I'm the happiest woman in the whole world."

"Now, now, why are you crying? Linda, what's wrong?"

She wiped her eyes with a tissue. "I can't tell you!"

"Linda, what is it that you can't tell me? Please! I've got to know!"

Tears streamed down her face as she looked toward her husband. "The day after you saw me in bed with William Davis I opened a whole bottle full of pills. I wanted to die! The humiliation that I felt was so overbearing I couldn't stand it! In my mind I knew you would never love me again! I turned the bottle up to my mouth and that's when it happened."

"What happened?"

"You won't believe me if I tell you." She sniffed back her tears.

"I will! I will believe you, Linda! Please—tell me what happened!"

"There was a voice in my head, it was loud and clear."

"What did the voice say?"

"As I said, it was loud and clear. It said, 'Linda, don't do that, you need to live!' I was so shook up by the voice that I dropped the bottle of pills onto the floor. Joe, I'm telling you the truth, I swear it!"

"I believe you, Linda. As a matter of fact I almost killed myself after seeing you in the bed with William Davis. I got my pistol down off my closet shelf. My intentions were to kill myself because life without you was not worth living."

"Joe, what happened?"

"Just before I was ready to pull the trigger, my phone rang. Can you believe that, the phone rang?"

"Who was calling you?"

"It was my mother calling me. She invited me to her house for dinner. I realized after talking with my mother that killing me would be the most selfish thing I could possibly do."

"What did you do?"

"What I should have, I went to my mother's house and ate the best food I had eaten in months. Now clear your eyes, sweetheart, our breakfast should be on the way here."

"Where is our breakfast coming from?"

"It's coming from Pete Strand's Diner. I ordered it twenty minutes ago."

"What did you order?"

"I ordered bacon, ham, grits, eggs, toast, jelly, orange juice and milk, uh-oh that must be our food now. I'll slip on my trousers real quick." Joe paid the delivery man a twenty dollar tip for bringing the food.

"How in the world are we going to eat all this food?" Linda asked.

"After breakfast we'll start eating more modestly, but for now I plan to gorge myself soon as I wash my face and hands."

"I was going to cook your breakfast."

"Linda, for the rest of this trip you're not going to do any work at all, except maybe help me fix our bed. After we eat we're going to catch a couple trout for lunch."

"Who's going to cook them?"

"It will be your husband's job to cook the fish."

"What if we don't catch any fish?"

"In that case we'll drive into town and eat at a very nice restaurant. While we're in town we'll find a nice jewelry store."

"Joe, why would we stop at a jewelry store?"

"How else can I buy you a nice necklace and a beautiful set of ear rings?" A smile overshadowed Linda's face.

"I was just thinking," said Linda.

"What were you thinking?"

"I was thinking how much a hook would hurt those trout's mouth if we were to hang them on a sharp hook. It makes my mouth hurt just thinking about it."

"Are you suggesting that we go into town for lunch, instead of me cooking fish for dinner?" He smiled.

"If you must insist—that's what we'll do." Linda started giggling.

Joe shook his head back and forth; he placed his arms around his wife. "Linda, will you ever forgive me if I spoil you rotten?"

"My forgiveness will be totally assured."

Chapter 15

It was Saturday morning, the last weekend before William Davis had to start working at Maynard's Sporting Goods Store. William had already contacted Mr. Maynard concerning the beach house that they were to stay in during the weekend. Nelson and Heather were very excited about the beach trip. "Marie, do we have everything loaded in the car that we need for the weekend?"

"I believe we do. I can't think of another thing that we might need."

"Daddy, why aren't we driving our new car?" Nelson asked.

"Son, we wouldn't want to mess up our new car with all that beach sand, would we?"

"No sir, I guess not."

"Mother, did you get my little bucket and my shovel?"

"Yes, Heather, it's in the trunk of Daddy's car."

"Marie, take the children to the car so I can make sure the

water and lights are turned off. I need to make sure all the doors are locked, also."

The Davis family was headed toward the beach about five minutes later. "Daddy, do you know what my teacher told our class?"

"No, Nelson, what did your teacher say?"

"She said that you were a real genuine hero for saving that little boys life."

"She said all that?"

"Yes sir, she sure did! Everyone at school treats me sort of special now."

"Why is that?"

"Well, Butch Johnson told all the boys in my class that he would clean their plow if anyone bothered me."

"Who's Butch Johnson?" Marie asked.

"He's the biggest boy in our class. Butch is not afraid of anybody. He likes me because my daddy is a hero."

"William, what does it mean when you might clean someone's plow?" Marie asked.

"That's sort of a country term meaning I'll whip you good if you do this or don't do that."

"Nelson, we wouldn't want Butch to inflict injury on the other boys' in your class."

"Mother, had you rather for the other boys to clean my plow?"

"No, Nelson, I guess not."

"Marie, we'll stop at a restaurant before we get to the beach," said William. "Be on the lookout for a nice place to eat."

*   *   *   *

Melvin Jones was sitting in a lounge chair at home. He hadn't been feeling good for the last few days. "Melvin, I don't understand why you don't get a doctor's appointment."

"Grace, I'll be okay in a day or two. I'll go to a doctor when I need to."

"Why does Daddy need to see a doctor?" Doris asked, coming into the room.

"Dear, I didn't hear you drive up."

"Mother, that's because I've got a very quiet running car. Daddy, why do you need to see a doctor?"

"I'll be okay, Doris. Old people sometimes have rather bad days."

"That's true, Daddy, but you're not that old. Mother, how long has he been like this?"

"It's been several days now. I've tried to get him to see a doctor."

"Daddy, are you hurting somewhere?"

"I'm hurting in the lower part of my body."

"Doris, your daddy has to go urinate several times during the night."

"Daddy, that's not normal, you must see a doctor!"

"I promise to go next week. Anyway, today is Saturday and my doctor's office is closed on the weekend. I thought Linda and Joe would be back from the mountains by now."

"Melvin, she told us they wouldn't be back before tomorrow evening."

"Guess where Anthony and I are going tonight?"

"I have no idea," said her mother. "Where are you going?"

"We're going dining and dancing at the Palomino Steakhouse and Dance Hall."

"Doris, I've heard that place is very expensive."

"Mother, I didn't pick out the location, Anthony did."

"You like him a lot, don't you?"

"Yes, Mother, I like him very, very much."

"I'm surprised he hadn't given you an engagement ring by now," said Melvin. "You two have known each other since you were children."

"Melvin, for Heaven sakes—don't rush Doris into anything!"

"He's not rushing me, Mother. I'm hoping I get something that glitters tonight."

"If you ask me, Anthony's eyes glitters every time he looks at you."

"Melvin Jones, that's not the kind of glitter that Doris is talking about! She's talking about an engagement ring!"

"Don't you think I know that? I'm sick, but I'm not stupid. Doris, I believe Anthony is a fine young man. I would be proud to have him as a son-in-law if it comes to that. Doggone it, I miss Linda and Joe. I'll be glad when they get back from their trip."

"You mean honeymoon, don't you dear?"

"Grace, you know as well as I do that Joe was in no condition for a darn honeymoon."

"That may be true, but as the old saying goes—where there's a will there's a way." She and Doris started laughing. Melvin just sat there, shaking his head back and forth.

*   *   *   *

William Davis and his family arrived at the beach at noon. They unpacked their belongings, and then they spent most of the day on the beach. Marie used plenty of suntan lotion on herself and her children so they wouldn't get blistered. "Daddy, we sure did have fun today."

"I'm glad you did, Nelson."

"Did my little eight year old daughter have fun?"

"I sure did, Daddy. Mother, will you help me pick up some pretty shells tomorrow?"

"Of course I will, Heather, what will we put them in?"

"We'll put them in my sand bucket."

"Daddy, why can't I see the other side of the ocean?"

"That's because it's a very longs ways to the other side of the ocean."

At six o'clock that evening William and his family ate seafood at the Fisherman's Wharf.

"Marie, how do you like the beach house that we're staying in?"

"It's beautiful, William. I know it cost a lot of money to build that large house. It's hard to believe that a single house would have five bathrooms in it."

"Daddy, what time tomorrow do we have to leave for home?" Nelson asked.

"We should leave by four o'clock in the evening. Why are you asking?"

"I want to see Elsie again."

"Now, who might Elsie be?"

"She's a pretty girl that I met on the beach today."

"Let me get this straight, you're ten years old and you like girls already."

"Yes, he sure does, Daddy," said Heather. "He held that girl's hand until her daddy came along."

"What happened then, Heather?"

"Nelson pretended that he was looking for shells."

"How about that, Marie, we have a lover in our midst."

"William Davis, you quit teasing Nelson. Sweetheart, was she very pretty?"

"Mother, she was real pretty!" A big smile overshadowed his face.

At eight o'clock the next morning, Nelson and Heather Davis were anxious to be on the beach. "Listen, both of you, no breakfast, no beach," said Marie. "It's as simple as that."

"Mother, I'm not really hungry," said Nelson.

"I've cooked bacon, eggs, and rice, I expect you to eat something before we go outside. Look how well your father is eating."

"That's because Daddy is bigger than us," said Heather. "When we get big we'll eat a lot too."

"No one said a thing about you having to eat a lot. I said you needed to eat something."

"Let's hurry up and eat something Heather," said Nelson. "I need to get to the beach before Elsie leaves for home."

William helped Marie wash the dishes and straighten up the kitchen. Nelson hurried down the steps that led from the house to the beach. He was very excited as he started looking in opposite directions trying to spot Elsie. William walked down the steps carrying Heather on his back. Marie followed closely behind them.

Marie was carrying Heather's plastic bucket so she and her daughter could pick up some sea shells. They were not concerned with just any kind of shell; they had to be beautiful and perfectly formed. William stood underneath an overhead fishing pier as he observed Nelson walking along the beach, attentively looking for the young girl he met the prior day. Marie and Heather walked farther and farther from the pier as they selectively picked the shells that they placed into their bucket. Nelson was about two hundred yards in the opposite direction from his mother and sister when he spotted Elsie. William smiled when he saw his son running toward her and two adults that she was with.

"Hello, Elsie," said Nelson. "I was afraid you had gone home already."

"Hi, Nelson, this is my mother and father."

"Nelson, my name is Carl Hetherington and this is my wife, Patricia. Elsie said you were a nice looking boy, and I agree with her."

"Thank you, sir. Where do you live?"

"We live in Asheville, North Carolina. Where do you live?"

"Adamsville, North Carolina."

"Elsie, would you like to walk along the beach?" Nelson asked.

"Daddy, is it okay?"

"Yes, but don't walk too far from where your mother and I are sitting."

Nelson's father was still underneath the pier observing his wife and daughter pick up sea shells along the water's edge. Occasionally, he noticed Nelson and Elsie as they walked along the beach in the opposite direction.

It was about thirty minutes later when William saw several men and women pointing out toward the ocean. They seemed very excited as they walked closer to the beach, but still pointing. Curiosity got the best of William; he had to see what all the commotion was about. He walked hurriedly toward the small group of people that were acting very strange.

"What's all the excitement about?" William asked.

One of the men pointed straight out toward the ocean. "That swimmer is much too far out in the water and appears to be in some kind of trouble!" The man answered, excitedly. Without hesitation, William ran toward the water. He waded waist deep into the surf, and then begun swimming toward the distressed swimmer. William realized quickly that he was in a riptide, same as the other individual. "Help me! Help me!" A teen age boy yelled.

"I'm coming to help you! What's your name?"

"My name is Brian! Please, mister—no matter how hard I swim I keep going farther and farther in the ocean. I'm going to die! Oh, God, I don't want to die!"

William was still about twenty five yards from Brian. "Brian, you're doing everything wrong! Listen to me! Don't try to swim straight into the beach! Start swimming parallel to the beach!"

"I don't understand what you're telling me to do!"

"Watch the direction I'm swimming! We've got to get out of this riptide!

"Mister, please don't let me die!"

"Brian, do as I say and you will not die! That's it—you're swimming in the right direction now."

"Mister, I'm very, very tired!"

"You forget about being tired! Do you hear me? You've got to keep swimming if you want to live! You're doing great,

Brian! Keep swimming, we should be out of this current in a little while!"

"I don't think I can make it!"

"The Hell you can't make it! What am I supposed to tell your father and mother? Am I to tell them that you just gave up and drowned?"

"Mister, I'm tired!"

"You think I'm not tired? I came out here to save your life, and by golly that's what I'm going to do; now you keep swimming!"

A large crowd was following along the beach as William and Brian got farther and farther from the pier, but now they were swimming parallel with the beach. Marie Davis and her children were among the group observing the swimmers, but she had no idea that her husband was one of them.

"Brian, we're out of the riptide now! Start swimming straight toward the shore!"

"Mister, I don't know whether I can make it or not!"

"Keep swimming like you are, I'm coming to meet you!" William didn't tell Brian how tired he was, but he knew their only option was to keep swimming.

Within five more minutes William and Brian were swimming alongside each other. "Brian, you're doing very well. We're getting closer and closer to the beach."

Nearly out of breath, Brian asked, "Mister, what is your name?"

"William Davis."

"Mr. Davis, I was a goner for sure if you hadn't come to help me. I would never have made it."

"Brian, we're about to get some help."

"What do you mean?"

"We're almost to the breakers. Those waves will help carry us toward the shore."

Marie recognized that one of the swimmers was her husband when William and Brian got within fifty yards of the beach. She and several of the men ran waist-deep into the water to offer assistance to the swimmers as they got closer and closer to the beach.

Within twenty five yards of the beach, Brian could swim no more. William grabbed him with one hand, struggling to keep his and Brian's head above water. All at once a huge wave picked them up and moved them a considerable ways inward. Standing in shoulder-depth water, two men grabbed Brian and they helped him to the beach. With tears streaming down her face, Marie grabbed William and helped escort him to the beach. Both William and Brian were lying on the wet beach trying to get their wind back. Nelson and Heather got down on their knees beside their father. They were both crying as they placed their hands against their father's face.

Three different people were using their cameras to take pictures of Brian and William by the time they stood up. Still on wobbly legs, Brian walked over to William, he placed his arms around his neck and whispered, "Thank you. Thank you from the bottom of my heart." Tears filled Brian's eyes. "Mr. Davis, how on earth will I ever be able to repay you for what you did?"

"Son, you don't owe me a thing. By the way, how old are you?"

"I'm fifteen years old."

"Are you alone at the beach?"

"No sir, my parents went shopping. They'll be back after awhile. Mr. Davis, I've got to know something, why did you do it?"

"Why did I do what?" People gathered close by to hear what William's answer was going to be.

"I was wondering why you risked your own life to save mine. Out of all these people standing on the beach you were the only one that came to my rescue. Some of the other people knew I was in serious trouble, but all they did was point and shout. That's why my question is still this, why did you do it?"

"First of all, what is your last name and where do you live?"

"My last name is Hayward. My father's name is John Hayward, my mother is Laura Hayward. Mr. Davis, we live in La Grange, Georgia."

"Answering your question, I knew you were in trouble and I didn't want you to die."

"Mr. Davis, I'll never forget what you did for me. What are your two children's names, Mrs. Davis?"

Marie wiped her watery eyes. "My daughter here is Heather and my son is Nelson."

Brian got town on his knees and said to them, "Your father just saved my life. There is no doubt about it; I was going to drown before he came to my rescue. Always remember this—if your father had not come after me when he did I would still be in that ocean—dead! Heather, Nelson, your father is a real genuine hero!" Brian turned toward Marie. "Lady, you've got yourself a mighty fine man." With tears in his eyes, Brian shook William's hand; he then headed toward the beach house.

A woman walked up to William and started asking him questions about the incident, asking him where he was from. With his permission she snapped two more pictures of him.

"William, the children and me are ready to pack up and head home. Is that okay with you?"

"Yes, Marie, I'm ready."

As they walked toward their parked car, Nelson held onto his father's left hand, Heather the right one. "Mother, my father is a hero."

Marie placed her hand on William's shoulder. "Yes, Heather, he surely is."

Chapter 16

By noon that same day, Joe and Linda Wilson had already packed all their belongings in their car. Joe was feeling much better now from being in the hospital. "Joe, why are you staring at that bed?" Linda asked. A slight grin appeared on his face, but he didn't say anything. "Joe Wilson, what on earth are you thinking about?"

"I was just thinking about the great time we had on this bed," he smiled.

"Are you sure I made you happy?"

"Yes, indeed you did."

"Let's stop by Mr. Cyrus Owens office and say bye to him. He's such a nice man. I sure do feel sorry for him. Can you imagine how lonely he must be not having a single relative to turn to?"

"Let's invite him to visit with us sometime for a week or two."

"Joe, that's a great idea."

They drove their car to the rental office which was only about two-hundred yards from their rented cabin. Mr. Owens was sitting in a chair under a mimosa tree. He was observing several ducks swimming in the lake. "Hello, Mr. Owens," said Linda.

"Good afternoon to you, Mrs. Wilson." He looked at his wrist watch. "Yes, it is afternoon.

It's quarter past twelve. I see you and Joe are all packed and ready to go."

"Yes sir, Joe has to be back on his job tomorrow. Mr. Owens, have you had lunch?"

"Well, no I haven't, why do you ask?"

"Would you do Joe and me a great big favor?"

"I surely will if I can. What would you have me to do?"

"Joe and I would consider it an honor if you would ride with us to Daisy Mae's Country Kitchen and have lunch with us."

"Is it all that important that I have lunch with you?"

"Yes, Mr. Owens, it really is. Besides, it's only a short ways there, the very place that you recommended to us earlier."

"Alright, I'll be delighted to go with you."

A few minutes later Mr. Owens, Joe and Linda were seated at the restaurant. As they waited for the waitress to bring their orders, Mr. Owens seemed a little bit concerned about something. He shook his head back and forth a couple times. "Mr. Owens, is something wrong?"

"I hope not, Joe, but something is bothering me. I didn't want to worry you about it, but I guess I should tell you what occurred in my office this morning."

"What happened?"

"Two men came to my office about ten o'clock this morning and started asking me a lot of questions concerning Lewis Hanes' death."

"Were they the law?"

"Certainly not, they looked more like hoodlums."

"What kind of questions were they asking?"

"They were asking all kinds of questions. They wanted to know where you lived. I told them that I didn't know where you lived. Also, they wanted to know if the police found a lot of money that Lewis may have had hidden. I told them that I didn't know anything about what happened in that cabin. It looked like they were about to get rough with me, but Deputy Sheriff Charlie Harris happened to park outside the office to look at six Canadian Geese that had landed on the lake. The two men hurried out of my office, and they drove off. The reason I was sitting under that mimosa tree was so I could be on the lookout for those two men. I have my cell phone in my pocket to call the law if they came back. Joe, it appeared to me that they were angry that you killed Lewis Hanes. I don't know if they were friends of his or not."

"Mr. Owens, are you thinking they might come back and harm you?"

"I really don't think so, but I'm not sure about it. Joe, it would grieve me terribly if something were to happen to you or Linda. You both have been here only a few days, but I have taken a liking to each of you. In a weird sort of way it's like having some family again."

"Mr. Owens, you can always consider us as your friends, and your family."

"I appreciate that, Linda. You two are the nicest people that I have ever met."

"I wouldn't be overly concerned about those two men, Mr. Owens," said Joe. "They might just think that Lewis Hanes had some money stashed away someplace. Anyway, here comes our food."

Tears were in Linda's eyes an hour later as she hugged Mr. Owens neck in front of the rental office. It was very obvious that he didn't want them to go. "Mr. Owens, Linda and I will be back here next year about this same time. We'll call a few weeks ahead of time to reserve the same cabin that we just stayed in. By the way, we cleaned the cabin up so good you would never know that we stayed in it."

"Thank you."

"Mr. Owens waved to them as they drove out of his parking lot. Silent, alone, he stood there as tears filled his eyes.

*   *   *   *

It was two o'clock that same day when Sarah Wilson picked up the phone and called her daughter. "Joan, there's no need for you to come here today to help with dinner."

"Mother, why not, I promised to help you?"

"I know you did, but this will be your first date with your new boyfriend. You need to be at my house before Gary Oakland gets here. Dinner will be served at six o'clock this evening, but remember this—Gary will be here about thirty minutes earlier than that. You've got all afternoon to get yourself ready for yours and his meeting."

"Mother, are you sure you don't need my help?"

"I'm quite sure. By the way, which one of your outfits will you wear this evening?"

"Mother, I'm so excited I don't know what I will be wearing. I've got three outfits lying on my bed now."

"Quit worrying so much, no matter what you wear you will look gorgeous."

"Thank you for saying that."

"I've got to go now, but make sure you get here this evening before some stranger rings my doorbell."

Sarah walked into the living room; Mark was sitting in his favorite lounge chair. "Sarah, who were you talking to?"

"It was Joan. She's so excited about having dinner with Gary Oakland this evening. I do hope they have compatible chemistry."

"You hope they have what?"

"I said I hope they have compatible chemistry."

"Are you sure there's not an element of ugliness in what you just said?"

"Mark Wilson, I can't believe you just said that! This comes about through interpersonal attraction."

"Uh oh, it's getting worse by the minute," Mark laughed.

"Don't you understand anything? The attraction I was talking about comes from simple things, such as the way someone smiles, talks, acts, color of their eyes, hair, or the perfection in their teeth. The list goes on and on."

"Well, I'm glad I don't have to worry about compatible chemistry," said Mark, smiling.

"Why do you say that?"

"Because I've got all those good qualities that you were just talking about," he laughed.

"Well, there's one thing that I can say about you, Mark."

"What would that be?"

"I can see that you're not conceited one bit," Sarah smiled.

Joan arrived at her parent's house at five o'clock. "Mark, look at our beautiful daughter, isn't she gorgeous?"

"She most certainly is! Have you noticed her distinct resemblance of me?"

"Joan, don't pay any attention to him, he's been a comedian all day."

"Well, Mother, you've got to admit that Daddy is quite handsome for his age."

"See there, Sarah, she took her smarts after me as well as her looks." Mark winked at his daughter. "Uh oh, this is the moment you've been waiting for, Joan,"

"Why is that?"

"I just heard someone drive into our yard."

"Oh, my goodness, Mother, do I look okay?"

"Yes, you look just fine. Now, be ready to answer the door when the doorbell rings."

A big smile overshadowed Joan's face when the doorbell rang. She walked gracefully toward the door. She opened it; she was shocked when she saw two strangers standing on the porch. "Is this the Joe Wilson residence?" One of the men asked?

"I'm sorry, but it isn't."

"Joan, who are you talking to?" Mark asked, getting up from his chair. He walked to the doorway. "Who are you men looking for?"

"We're trying to get up with Joe Wilson," said the larger of the two men.

"First of all, who are you men?"

"My name Lester Hanes and this big guy here is Harry Saunders. We happen to be friends with Joe Wilson."

"May I ask why you would like to see my son?"

"Listen here you old goat—!"

"Harry, keep a civil tongue in your head!" Lester warned. "Since you're Joe's father you should know where he lives."

"Yes, I know exactly where he lives, but I'm not going to tell you. Something doesn't seem right with you two!"

"Let's go, Lester!" Harry advised.

"Are you crazy? We need to find out where that murdering scoundrel is?"

"I'm going to ask you one more time, where is that gutless son of yours?"

"If you men don't leave now I'll be forced to call the law!" Mark warned.

Joan was shocked when she saw Gary Oakland drive into the driveway. Lester Hanes watched Gary as he exited his car. "Hey you, is your name Joe Wilson?" Lester asked.

"No, my name is Gary Oakland."

"For the last time—you men must leave my house right now!"

"Mr. Wilson, what seems to be the trouble?" Gary asked.

"I've asked these two trouble makers to leave, but I reckon I'll have to call the law to get them gone."

"Mr. Wilson wants you men gone right now, so beat it! Hit the road! Vamoose!"

"Listen pretty boy, who do you think you're talking to?" Lester Hanes asked.

"You men are about to spoil my dinner with a beautiful lady, I won't allow that. Go now, or you will be awfully sorrow!"

"Since you said that, pretty boy, we're not going anywhere?" Lester vowed. "The first thing we're going to do is beat you to a pulp."

Before Mark could even turn around to go phone the law, at lightning speed Gary struck Lester three times knocking him down and out. Harry Saunders reached for a hidden pistol underneath is coat, but Gary jumped into the air, kicking him a crunching blow to his head. The pistol fell onto the porch. With three hard blows from Gary's fist—Harry fell on top of Lester, unconscious. "Mr. Wilson, if I were you I would contact the police and let them come get these trouble makers." Mark just stood there, momentarily, totally astonished as to what he just witnessed. Joan had both her hands up to her face. She was in total disbelief that her dinner date had just knocked out two men larger than he was.

"Mr. Wilson, you should call the police before they come to."

"Yes, Gary, I'll do it now." He hurried toward the phone.

Joan, still in a daze from what she saw, walked to the doorway. Gary used a napkin from his coat pocket to pick up the loaded gun. A little bit of blood was oozing out of his knuckles from hitting the larger man. Without saying a word, Joan led Gary into the house. "I'm sorry for what I did at your house, Joan."

"I'm not sorry at all, Gary. That was the bravest, most courageous thing I've ever seen! How were you able to do that? How?"

"I have a black belt in karate. I, also, noticed that at least one of the men had a pistol underneath his coat."

"How were you able to see a pistol?"

"Actually, what I saw was the outline of a gun underneath the big guy's coat."

The dinner meal was put on hold for a while. Police Lieutenant Frank Jenkins let two more officers take Harry

Saunders and Lester Hanes to jail. He stayed back at Mark's house to fill him and his family on some details that he knew about, but they didn't.

"Mr. Wilson, I'm glad you've got most of your family together in your living room. I'm going to tell you something that's going to shock each of you."

"My God, Lieutenant, is it all that bad?"

"I'm afraid it might be."

"Fortunately for you and your family, Mr. Oakland here may have saved your lives. Those two men that came here are killers. They're wanted in three states for robbery and murder. The worst one of the two was Lester Hanes. Mr. Wilson, Lester Hanes came here to Adamsville to kill your son, Joe."

Sarah almost fainted. "Mother! Mother, are you okay?"

"Yes, Joan, I'll be alright. Go ahead, Lieutenant, tell us everything."

"Lester Hanes was going to kill Joe because Joe killed his brother up in the mountains."

"Lieutenant, this is hard to believe! Joe doesn't just go around killing people! Besides, we haven't heard a word about my son killing anyone!"

"Mr. Wilson, Joe is not in any kind of trouble. The man he shot was named Lewis Hanes. He was an escaped murderer that had already killed seven people that we know about. Sometime after midnight, armed with a shotgun and a hunting knife he broke open the door to your son's bedroom. His intention was nothing less than to kill your son and his wife. Unfortunately for Lewis, Joe shot him six times before he could accomplish his evil deed. Not only is Joe in the clear, but he is going to receive a twenty thousand dollar award for the apprehension of that murdering scoundrel."

"Lieutenant, why on earth didn't my son let us know about this?" Sarah asked.

"Mrs. Wilson, Joe didn't want to worry you about what happened." He turned toward Gary Oakland. "Mr. Oakland, this may come as a surprise to you, but you earned yourself fifty thousand dollars by whipping those two men and keeping them nice and tidy until we got here."

"I don't understand. Why would I get money for beating those men?"

"It's simple, there's a thirty thousand dollar reward for Lester Hanes and a twenty thousand dollar reward for the Harry Saunders. You should be getting the money in about thirty days."

"Lieutenant, how did you know about Joe killing that man?" Mark asked.

"The news came over our wire right after it happened. In fact, your son, Joe called the station sometime in the evening for us to be on the lookout for two suspicious looking men. We've had Joe's house staked out since he called the station. We had no idea that those men would come to your house. Mr. Oakland, what are you going to do with all that money?"

"I'm going to try to make a good first impression with Joan by giving her half the money."

"That would certainly have to be your second impression for me. I was extremely pleased this evening with my first impression of you. I was so shocked by what you did that you could have knocked me over with a feather."

"Mrs. Wilson, are we still having dinner this evening?"

"Yes, Gary, we certainly are. Lieutenant, would you care to eat with us?"

"I appreciate it, but my wife has cooked a turkey, and we're having potatoes, green beans and some dressing for my dinner."

"Lieutenant, just one last question—are we to be concerned now that Lester Hanes or the other man will ever come back and bother Joe or anyone else in this town?"

"No, Mr. Wilson you have absolutely nothing to worry about. Those two will never get out of prison again."

Chapter 17

The first place Joe Wilson and Linda stopped when they got back to Adamsville was his parent's home. His father, mother and sister gave Joe and Linda big hugs. Excitement of their return was quite evident. "Joe, we've already eaten, but there's plenty of food still left on the table. You and Linda go help yourselves."

"Mother, I believe we will. Linda, you're not going to let me eat all by myself are you?"

"No, I'll join you."

"Joan, this handsome looking man must be your friend?"

"Please forgive my manners! Joe, Linda, this is Gary Oakland." They shook hands with Gary.

"Joe, we'll retire to the den while you and Linda eat your food, but when you finish we have a lot to talk about," said Mark.

"It must be about work."

"It's not about work, but we'll talk in a little while. You and

Linda enjoy some of that good food that your mother cooked."
Everyone but Joe and Linda went into the den.

"I don't even know where to start," said Linda.

"Why is that?"

"There's so much good food here. Does your mother cook like this each meal?"

"No, she doesn't. It must be for a special occasion, probably for Gary and Joan."

"Joe, have you ever seen Gary before tonight?"

"No, but he seems very nice. Maybe my sister has found herself a keeper this time."

"What in the world do you mean by that?"

"Well, whenever someone is fishing and they catch a little fish or ugly fish they normally throw them back into the water. When they catch a nice looking, sizeable fish they generally hang on to that one."

"Is that why you held on to me because I look like a fish?" Linda laughed.

"No silly, the reason I held on to you is because you are curvaceous, good looking, have beautiful teeth, broad smile, great disposition, blue eyes and radiant blonde hair."

"I'm shocked to the core," said Linda, smiling.

"Why are you shocked?"

"If I had known I was all that good looking with all those virtues I might have married Chester Sloan."

"That one hundred and four pound weasel! He reminds me of a bantam rooster suffering from malnutrition." He and Linda burst into laughter.

"I couldn't help overhearing your laughter," said Sarah. "What in the world was so funny?"

"Mother, Linda just implied that her marriage was between me and Chester Sloan."

"Joe, Linda was just pulling your chain. She's been in love with you from the first moment she laid eyes on you. Linda, there's ice cream in the freezer and there's an apple pie sitting on top of the stove."

"Mrs. Wilson, I've already got more in my plate now than I'll be able to eat. I hope someday that I will be able to cook as well as you."

"Linda, there's not one thing wrong with your cooking," said Joe.

"I appreciate the compliment, but your mother is heads and shoulders above me when it comes to cooking."

Joe and Linda entered the den about fifteen minutes later. "Joe, you and Linda have a seat. I need to tell you what happened here a little earlier this evening, "said Mark. "Our doorbell rang before we had dinner this evening. We all thought it was Gary ringing the doorbell, but it wasn't. It was two men and they were looking for you."

"Did they say why they were looking for me?"

"Let me finish telling my story. First of all, they didn't look like anyone that I thought you would associate with. I kept asking why they wanted to see you, but each time I asked the madder they seemed to get. Finally, I told them that they would have to leave or I would call the law. About that time Gary showed up and inquired if I was having some trouble with these two men. I told him that I had asked them to leave, but they didn't offer to go. Gary asked them nicely to leave and that's when they got confrontational. We didn't know it at the time, but Gary is trained in martial arts, holding a tenth degree black belt. Lester Hanes was one of the men. He was going to whip Gary, but he's the first one that got knocked out cold. The other man was carrying a gun underneath his coat. I didn't realize it, but Gary noticed it right away. After Lester fell down the other man reached for the gun, but that turned out to be a very bad mistake for him. Like a flash of lightning, Gary leaped into the air and kicked that man side of his head. With three more blows from Gary's fist he fell on top of Lester Hanes. At that point I called the law."

"Daddy, who were these men, and furthermore what did they want?"

"Both men were wanted in three states for murder, bank robbery, extortion and a host of other illegal activities. Their names are Lester Hanes and Harry Saunders. Does either one of their names ring a bell to you?"

"You said, Lester Hanes, I wonder if he was any kin to Lewis Hanes?"

"Yes, Joe, he was Lewis Hanes brother."

"What did he want with me?"

"He was going to shoot you on sight for killing his brother."

"Joe, what are you going to do?" Linda asked, nervously.

"He doesn't have to do a single thing, Linda. Both men are in jail and that's where they will remain for the rest of their lives. Joe, we didn't know a single thing about your run in with Lewis Hanes until an Adamsville police detective told us earlier this evening. Why on earth didn't you tell us that you and Linda were in danger of being killed?"

"Daddy, we didn't know we were in any danger until Lewis Hanes burst our door open in the wee hours of the morning.

Linda saved both our lives that night by not falling asleep. She awoke me just in time for me to get my gun. We both knew then that an intruder was in our cabin. When he burst the door open I unloaded my gun toward the doorway. Afterwards, I found out that he had been hit six times. Lewis Hanes had a hunting knife and a loaded shotgun when he broke into our bedroom. There's something else, he had already killed two different couples that had rented the cabin before us."

"Well, there's one thing for sure, Gary solved your problem with those two men."

Joe stood up; he shook Gary's hand for doing what he did. "Joan, what do you think about Gary's heroic encounter with those two ruffians?"

"Not only am I still in shock, but I'm amazed that Gary could do what he did. By the way, Joe, it didn't take him long at all to put their lights out."

"I just want all of you to know that I'm no bully, nor will I ever be. The reason I acted as quickly as I did is because one of the men was going to reach for his gun. Under normal circumstances, I'm as docile as a cat."

"Just remember folks," said Mark, smiling. "There are all kinds of cats, large and small, some not too docile."

"Mother, where is Anthony?"

"Joe, your brother is on a date with Linda's sister. It's such a sweet thing to watch them hold hands and smile toward each other. Linda, I'm afraid I do have some unpleasant news for you."

"What is that, Mrs. Wilson?"

"Your father has been sick for a few days."

"Do you know what's wrong with him?"

"No, I really don't, but your mother said he was going to have some tests performed on him tomorrow."

"Joe, will you take me by my parent's house before we go home?"

"Sure I will. In fact we'll go there now. Gary, you probably saved my life by what you did to those men. I really appreciate it. Mother, the food was delicious, as always it is. Daddy, I'm ready to start to work tomorrow morning. Where should I meet you in the morning?"

"No, Joe, I distinctly remember the doctor saying that you shouldn't go back to work for two weeks. You've got another week to rest up and give your stitches time to heal."

"Well, Daddy, I could work in the office shuffling paper or something. I need to be doing something."

"Okay, I know what you can do. I'll be at our main office about eight o'clock in the morning. You can sit in my office and order building supplies, but you're not to do anything more physical than use the telephone for the entire week."

"I'll be there at eight o'clock," said Joe.

Joe and Linda were standing on her parent's porch twenty minutes later. Doris Jones answered the doorbell. "I thought you and Anthony was on a date." Linda commented.

"We were supposed to be, but father is sick. Anthony is in the house with Daddy, Mother and Reverend Levi Olson. How was yours and Joe's vacation?"

"It was very exciting to say the least, but we did manage to have a good time. I'll tell you all about it sometime."

Doris led them into her parent's bedroom, Reverend Olson was pleading for Melvin to go to the hospital. He didn't want to go to the emergency room on Sunday night, especially since he had an appointment to see the doctor the next day. "Melvin, I'm your minister, but more importantly I'm your friend. You need to be in the hospital. Prayer, for which I've done, is very important, but even more important when it's done along with a trained physician. For goodness sakes, look at Grace—she's got tears in her eyes and she wants you to see a doctor tonight. Please, Melvin, we'll call an ambulance right now!"

"Okay, Reverend Olson I'll go to the hospital, but no ambulance."

"Daddy, what's wrong with you?" Linda asked, tears in her eyes.

"Linda, sweetheart, when did you and Joe get home?"

"We got home this evening, Daddy. What seems to be the trouble with you? Where do you hurt?"

"I hurt almost everywhere, but especially in my head and lower part of my back and stomach."

"Mother, how long has Daddy been like this?" Linda asked.

"For several days now I've tried and tried to get him to see a doctor, but he wouldn't go. He just wanted to take some pain pills. Doris, you and Linda step outside so Joe and Anthony can help your father off the bed. Reverend Olson, I greatly appreciate you coming here and praying for Melvin."

"That's quite alright, Mrs. Jones I was pleased to do it. I'm going now, but I will see him in the hospital tomorrow. Melvin, I'll be praying for you."

"Thank you, I really appreciate that."

Linda walked nervously back and forth in the living room. "Doris, I can't believe I was off having fun while Daddy lay sick in his bed."

"That's nonsense, Linda you didn't know that he was sick."

"Someone could have called me!"

"That's crazy! Why spoil yours and Joe's well-earned vacation just so you could drive all the way back here. Linda, Joe needed that time with you! It was his right to have that vacation with you!"

"You're right, Doris, it seems that you're always right about things. That's why I love you so very much." Linda hugged her neck.

"I love you too, Linda—I always have."

Melvin Jones arrived at the hospital twenty five minutes later by ambulance. His breathing had become more erratic. The emergency room doctor on call was Dr. Charles Langley, a highly trained physician with thirty one years of medical experience. Grace Jones remained in the room with her husband as Dr. Langley checked Melvin's vital signs. Linda, Doris, Joe, and Anthony remained in the waiting room. "Mrs. Jones, how long has your husband been like this?"

"Dr. Langley, he's been sick for nearly a week, but not quite this bad."

"Mrs. Wilson, based on my initial observation your husband is a very sick man. I'm going to schedule a series of tests for him, but I can tell you now that his blood pressure is through the roof. I'll give him something right away to bring it down, but that doesn't address the root of his problem. You can be with him for a few more minutes until he's taken to MRI."

A nurse came for Melvin fifteen minutes later. Grace walked a few feet down the hallway as the nurse pushed his bed slowly forward. Grace grabbed his hand, and then hurriedly kissed him on his cheeks.

"Nurse, wait up a minute," said Melvin. "I want to tell my wife something. Grace, please don't cry! No matter what happens, I just want you to know that I love you with all my heart. You've been the best wife any man could ever hope for. If God calls me home, please don't go through the rest of your life unhappy." The nurse turned her head to the side as tears flowed down Grace Jones's face. "Tell Linda and Doris that they have always been the love of my life. I'm not forgetting Joe; he's like a son to me. Let him know that, Grace. Also, let Doris know that Anthony Wilson is a swell guy. I think he would make her a nice companion."

Barely able to control her voice Grace said, "Melvin, life without you would be no good." Tears flowed down her face.

"Grace Jones, don't say stuff like that, please! There are two wonderful daughters to consider. Nurse, let's move along."

"Melvin, I love you." Grace stood still as the bed started moving forward.

It was then that Melvin replied, "I know that, Grace, I always have."

Everyone in the waiting room stood up when Grace opened the waiting room door. Tears were clearly visible in her eyes. Linda and Doris helped their mother to a chair.

"Mother, what did the doctor say about Daddy?" Doris asked.

Grace wiped her eyes, and then she answered, "Dr. Langley said he was very sick!"

"What did he say was wrong with him?"

"He didn't say. The doctor checked his vital signs and that's when he told me that he was very sick. I think it had something to do with his blood pressure and possibly an irregular heartbeat. I'm so worried I don't know what to do." Tears were now obvious in Grace's eyes, as well as her daughters.

Joe placed his arms around Linda. "I'm sorry about your father's condition. Is there anything that I can do for you or your mother?"

"Joe, I'm scared, I don't ever remember seeing my father sick like this!"

"I know, sweetheart, I wish there was something that I could say or do that would make things better."

"Joe, there is something that we can all do?" Anthony whispered.

"What would that be?"

"Let's all hold hands and I will pray that Mr. Jones gets well." Anthony held Doris's hand and then the others joined in. "Lord, we come to you openly and humbly to ask that you heal Mr. Melvin Jones from whatever his health abnormalities are. Mr. Jones is a good, decent, and loving husband and parent. We, also, ask your blessings for his family during this time of uncertainty and heartbreaking experience. Lord, these two sisters very much need their father. Mrs. Jones is a loving and faithful mother that almost never misses going to church on Sundays. As long as I have known her she would always tell you that Sunday was the Lord's day. If it be your will, Lord, heal Mr. Jones from his ailments so he can go home and be with his family. Amen."

Doris still held onto Anthony's hand for a few seconds. "Anthony that was the most beautiful prayer I have ever heard. I want to thank you from the bottom of my heart for what you just did."

"Doris, I meant every word of it."

"We all want to thank you, Anthony," said Linda. "Like Doris said, it was a beautiful prayer."

"Mrs. Jones, may I get you something to drink or eat?"

"I don't care for anything, Joe, but I appreciate it anyway."

"Doris, Linda, may I get you all something to eat or drink?" They declined Joe's offer.

"I want all four of you to do something for me," said Grace.

"We'll be glad to, Mother, what is it?"

"All four of you need to be at work tomorrow. I'm the only one that doesn't have to be on a job. If there's any change at all I'll call each of you."

"Mother, each of us needs to be at work tomorrow, but I'm not leaving here until the doctor comes into this waiting room and tells us what is going on with my daddy!" Doris said.

It was two hours later before Dr. Charles Langley came into the waiting room. He looked toward Mrs. Jones. "I apologize for taking so long to get back with you and your daughters, but I had to call a heart specialist in to check over our tests. His name is Dr. Cecil Murphy, and without a doubt one of the best heart doctors that I have ever known."

"Are you saying my husband has a heart disease?"

"No, Mrs. Jones, I'm not saying that, but your husband does have a clogged artery going to his heart."

"What does that mean? Will he be able to get over it?" Grace asked, tearfully.

"Mrs. Jones, there are never any 'absolutely sure' answers when it comes to treatment or prescribed medicines, but it is my professional opinion that your husband will do just fine when Dr. Murphy does his magic."

"What is this magic you're talking about?" Doris asked.

"Mr. Jones is scheduled for a stent to be placed into his clogged artery at one o'clock tomorrow. That's as early as he can get to him. Mrs. Jones, your husband is being moved to the fourth floor, room 426. You're welcome to sit with your husband all night or you can go home and get a restful night of sleep."

"I'll sit with my husband. Doris, will you and Anthony run by my house and get me a few things. You already know what I might need."

"We'll go to your house right now."

"Dr. Langley, thank you for what you've done for Melvin."

"You're more than welcome, Mrs. Jones. Your husband will still be in good hands with Dr. Murphy treating him. Well, I've got three more patients that I need to check on. I'm hoping everything will turn out good for your husband and your family."

"Thank you, Dr. Langley." The doctor left the room.

"Linda, you and Joe go home so you can unpack your clothes and stuff from your vacation. I want both of you to report to work tomorrow. Maybe one or both of you might be able to leave work a little early and be here when Dr. Murphy inserts the stent into Melvin's artery."

"Mother, are you really sure it will be okay for me to leave?"

"Yes, dear, I'm quite sure. I don't want you to lose your job where you work. Joe, I know for a fact that your father needs you on the job. He has a lot of projects going on and you need to relieve him from some of that pressure."

"Okay, Mother, we're going, but I intend to be here tomorrow afternoon when they put that stent in my daddy's artery," said Linda.

Doris and Anthony were back to the hospital within an hour. Doris had her mother's clothes and other personal things packed inside a suit case. "I appreciate you and Anthony bringing me my clothes."

"You're welcome, Mother. I think I'll stay at the hospital with you."

"Doris, you'll do no such thing! You need to go home and get some rest. I'm afraid you might lose your job if you don't go to work tomorrow. You've already missed several days of work this month for one reason or another."

"Mother, I'm worried about my daddy!"

"I know you are, sweetheart, but you can come here tomorrow after you get off work. Now, give your mother a big hug so Anthony can take you home." Grace waved bye to Doris as she and Anthony walked out of the room.

Chapter 18

It was Monday morning, William Davis's first day on the job. He was a little nervous when he entered Maynard's Sporting Goods Store. Scott Sanderson, a store employee escorted William to Mr. Maynard's private office. "Welcome aboard, William. Did you and your family have a pleasurable week?"

"Yes sir, we certainly did. My wife and children asked me to tell you thanks for your generosity. We went to the Zoo during the week and to the beach during the weekend. Mr. Maynard, your beach house that we stayed in is a very, very nice place. Thanks again for us being able to use the house."

"You're quite welcome. Speaking of the beach, how did everything go down there? Did you eat some good seafood while you were there?"

"We sure did, Mr. Maynard. Seafood always seems to taste better at the ocean."

"What was the biggest excitement you encountered at the beach?"

"I guess the biggest excitement was when a young boy got caught in a rip tide, but he finally got to the shore."

Mr. Maynard reached into his desk drawer and pulled out a national newspaper. He turned to page three and then placed the newspaper in front of William. It was two photographs of William and Brian Hayward at the beach. One of them showed William tugging Brian toward the shore. The other one showed Brian hugging and thanking William for saving his life. The full article stated that even though there were several men on the beach, William Davis didn't hesitate one second when he realized that a person was being swept out to sea by a strong riptide.

The article further stated that Mr. Davis risked his own life to save someone that he had never met. The article went on to describe William as a real hero.

Tears came into Mr. Maynard's eyes as he reached for the paper that William had glanced at.

"William, without a doubt—you're the most modest man I have ever met. You saved my only son's life after he fell into my own pond. Now you've saved someone's life that you didn't even know. I guess you're wondering why I became a little tearful a couple seconds ago when I reached for the paper. Do you have any idea whose life you saved at the ocean?"

"Mr. Maynard, I believe he said his name was Brian Hayward. He was a very nice young man."

"Yes, he's a very nice person."

"Mr. Maynard, are you saying you know Brian Hayward?"

"Yes, William, that's what I'm saying. In fact Brian and

his parents were using one of my other houses located at the beach."

"That sure is a coincidence," said William.

"It's a greater coincidence than you realize, William."

"Why is that, Mr. Maynard?"

"William, Brian's mother is my niece. Her name is Laura Hayward, and her husband's name is John Hayward. You've saved my son's life and my great-nephew's life in the short time I've known you. I'm thankful to God that I was at that bridge the day you were prepared to end your life. William, you are needed in this world, please don't ever think about taking your life again."

"I promise you that I won't, Mr. Maynard. I thought Gary said that he and his parents live in La Grange, Georgia."

"That's exactly right, they do live there, but each year, sometimes two or three times they use my beach house for their vacation. William, there's something in my desk drawer that I want you to have."

"What is it, Mr. Maynard?"

"It's a five thousand dollar check from my niece. She wants you to have it for saving her son's life."

"Mr. Maynard, outside of my own family you are the nicest person that I have ever met. Please tell your niece that I can't accept the check."

"William, my niece is very wealthy, why wouldn't you accept her check?"

"Mr. Maynard, it's hard for me to explain, but I'll try. I jumped into the ocean to save whoever it was because God has given me another chance in life. There's only one more thing that I need to do to cleanse my body and soul."

"What is that?"

"To tell Mrs. Linda Wilson, face to face, that I'm sorry. I've asked my God for forgiveness, and I honestly believe I have been forgiven by Him. Yet, there is this lingering desire to tell her in person that I'm a changed man and that I'm sorry for what I did."

"William, you wouldn't want my niece to be sad, would you?"

"No, I surely wouldn't, Mr. Maynard."

"Well, do me a big favor and put this check inside your wallet. This money will come in good when your children enter college. Go ahead, take the check." Still reluctant to have the check, he finally picked it up and placed it inside his wallet. "Now, let's go into the store so I can introduce my new manager to the store employees."

*   *   *   *

Doris Jones was getting out of her automobile in the hospital parking lot when her sister, Linda stopped her vehicle three parking spaces from her car. It was one o'clock in the afternoon, an hour before their father's planned surgery. "What a coincidence we both arriving here at the same time," said Doris.

"Yes, it certainly is. I told my supervisor that I just had to be at the hospital this afternoon when my father had his surgery. Doris, I'm scared to death that something will go wrong with that stent procedure."

"I'm very scared, myself. I hope Mother is doing okay this afternoon."

Linda and Doris were shocked when they entered their

father's room and found their mother crying hysterically. Grace's preacher, Levi Olson and his wife Margie were trying to console her. "Mother, what's the matter? What's wrong?" Linda asked. With tears flowing down her cheek Grace embraced both her daughters. Reverend Olson and Margie lowered their heads as tears emerged from Linda's and Doris's eyes.

Doris gently raised her mother's head up a little. "Mother, tell Linda and me what's the matter." Grace couldn't answer; she fell across her husband's empty bed and cried uncontrollably.

Fearing the absolute worst, Linda looked toward Reverend Olson. "Linda, I've known you and Doris since you were both born. Oh God, it saddens me to tell you this, but your father passed away thirty minutes ago. He had a massive heart attack." Hearing the awful news Doris became weak in her knees. Mrs. Olson helped her to a chair. Linda dropped to her knees; she pounded her fists against the floor as tears slid down her face. Mrs. Olson knelt down beside her, placing her arms around Linda's neck. The room door opened quietly, Joe Wilson entered the room. He knew instantly that something terrible had happened to Mr. Jones. Seeing Joe standing there, Mrs. Olson stood up. Joe knelt down beside his wife. She was shaking her head back and forth as tears spattered against the tile floor.

"Linda, it's me, Joe—what's wrong?"

Linda looked toward him with her watery eyes. "Joe, my father is dead! Oh Lord, how could this happen to our family?"

Joe helped her up from the floor, and into a nearby chair. "Reverend Olson, do you know what happened with Mr. Jones?"

"Dr. Cecil Murphy told Mrs. Jones a half hour ago that her husband suffered a massive heart attack before they even started with his surgery. It happened in the operating room while the doctor and nurses were getting prepared for Mr. Jones's surgery. He said that it happened so quickly that there was nothing that he could do."

"Mrs. Jones, may I take you home now?" Joe asked. "Linda, you and Doris help your mother up. This is no place for her to be now. She needs to be at her home."

"Joe, you're absolutely right," said Reverend Olson. "She will be much more comfortable there. Before we go our separate ways I would like to pray for Mrs. Jones and her daughters."

Everyone bowed their heads. Lord, we were hoping that Mr. Melvin Jones would be just fine as soon as the stent was placed into his blocked artery, but it seems that you had different plans for him. Lord, we will never question your wisdom or the reason that things don't always go our way. Mr. Jones was a very religious man that attended church regularly and always did good things for people less fortunate than him. I'm asking you now as a preacher and a man of God to bless this grieving wife and her two daughters that have lost their father. Lessen their heartaches and the sadness from each of them. Let them know that Melvin Jones is in a much better place now than he was here on earth. Lord, this family needs your blessing in order for them to find any peace concerning the tragedy that they have just experienced. In all circumstances, you Lord knows what is best for each of us. Amen."

Grace contacted the funeral home before leaving the hospital. She rode in Joe's car as they headed toward her home. Extremely saddened, but not crying anymore, she looked straight ahead as they neared her home. Linda and Doris followed behind them in their cars.

The first thing Grace did when she got inside her house was to go to Melvin's closet. She took down his favorite shirt and placed it against her face. Still holding the shirt she shook her head back and forth realizing that her husband would never come home again. Her grief was more than she could bear as she cried openly, still holding the shirt she fell across her bed. Both in tears, Doris and Linda observed their mother as she pounded her fists against her pillow.

"Mother, I'm going to get you something to drink," said Doris. "Mother, please—you've got to drink something."

"I wonder if she's had anything to eat or drink in the last few hours," remarked Linda.

Grace sat up in the bed; she looked toward Joe as he stood in the doorway of her bedroom. He had tears in his eyes as he looked downward. "Joe, I want you to come over here near me."

He wiped his eyes, and then he walked near Grace as she, too, wiped her eyes. "Yes, Mrs. Jones, what can I do for you?"

"I want you to know something about my husband. Melvin loved you as though you were his own son. He prayed night after night for months that you would come home alive. He has told me fifty times at least that if anything should ever happen to him that he wanted you to have what was in his miniature safe that has been locked and sealed since you were sixteen years old. According to his wishes the safe may not be opened until his Last Will and Testament has been read."

Joe placed his arms around grace. "Mrs. Jones, I loved your husband more than I know how to say. As long as I can remember he was always nice to me, he encouraged me at a young age to always do well, and treat everyone else like I would like to be treated." Joe backed away a short distance so Linda and Doris could get to their mother.

"Mother, I'm going to make you a bowl of soup," said Linda. "You've got to eat something! We don't want to lose you, too." With tears in her eyes, Linda pleaded, "Will you eat some soup?"

"I guess I will. Joe, help me to my chair in the living room. Doris, please stop crying now. Every time I see you and Linda crying I start crying all over again."

"Mother, I love you a lot!"

"I know you do, Doris, and that's another reason that I've got to be strong. More than ever, we need each other to lean on during this stressful, heartbreaking period that we're going through." Joe helped ease her into her special chair. "Linda, before you start making the soup I want all of you to sit down for a few minutes." Grace wiped her eyes with a tissue from a nearby box. Any time after three o'clock tomorrow evening we will be allowed to view your father at Lauren Funeral Home. I recommend that we all go together at six o'clock. His funeral service will be the next day at seven o'clock at the same funeral home."

"Mother, don't you have to pick out his casket, vault, and whatever else is required for a funeral?"

"No, Doris, I don't have to do a thing. Melvin and I made all our burial arrangements at Lauren Funeral Home many years ago. We did this so the longest one to live or our children would not have to go through the ordeal of purchasing those items that you just mentioned during a most stressful time for the family. Joe, you are part of our family, would you like to join us for the viewing?"

"Yes, Mrs. Jones, I certainly would."

It was almost four o'clock that afternoon when Grace Jones doorbell rang. Doris answered the door. "Mr. and Mrs. Wilson, please come inside. Here, let me help you with some of that food you are carrying."

"Doris, I can't tell you how sorry I was to hear the news concerning your father. It was a terrible shock to both of us."

Mark, Sarah and Doris sat the food on the kitchen table. Sarah went into the living room; Grace was still sitting in her chair. This time she was looking at an old photograph of Melvin.

Sarah walked over to Grace and gave her a hug. Sarah whispered softly into Grace's ear telling her how sorry she was about Melvin's untimely passing.

"Grace, we brought some food so you and your daughters won't have to concern yourselves with cooking."

"Thank you, Sarah. I guess you already know that you and Mark are our very best friends."

"Grace, have you decided when and where the funeral will be?"

"It will be at Lauren Funeral Home at seven o'clock, day after tomorrow. Graveside service will be at eleven o'clock the following morning at Maplewood Cemetery."

"Grace, is there anything at all that Mark and I can do for you, anything at all?"

"Just being my friend for all these years is more than enough. Sarah, what on earth am I to do now that Melvin is gone?" Tears came into her eyes.

"Grace, I'm not about to say that I know how you feel because I don't. What I do know is this, you have your wonderful memories of Melvin, and you have two precious, wonderful daughters. In time your broken heart will mend because no matter what—life continues on.

As long as Mark and I live you will be able to count on us, no matter what. I'll tell you something else; Linda and Doris are taking their father's death extremely hard. They need your strength to carry them through the next few days."

"Sarah, would you mind singing Melvin's two favorite songs during the funeral service. He always enjoyed hearing you sing those songs."

"I would be happy to do that. I believe you are talking about these two songs, Lord, I'm Coming Home, and In the Sweet Bye and Bye."

"Yes, those were his two favorites."

"Grace, don't even think about cooking tomorrow because women from our church are going to bring a lot of food here."

"Where is Mark?"

"He's in the kitchen talking with Linda, Joe and Doris. Why don't we join them in the kitchen? Besides, I brought you your favorite treat."

"You mean you brought me some of your homemade nut bread?"

"I mean I did. Let's go to the kitchen and you and I will have some coffee along with my super delicious nut bread."

Anthony arrived at the Jones residence at 6:15 that evening. He stopped momentarily on the porch and gazed at the funeral wreath on the front door. As he stood there for a couple minutes he thought about Mr. Jones family and how much they would miss him. Doris happened to notice him through the living room window as he stood on the porch holding his work cap in his hand. She went to the front door, opened it and then stepped out on the porch. Anthony noticed that she had tears in her eyes. "Doris, I heard the bad news a good while ago, but I couldn't leave the job area at that time, please forgive me!" Anthony lowered his head as though he was ashamed for him not being with her when her father died.

"Anthony, I've known you most of my life, but we've only been dating for a short while. You don't have to apologize for not being with me when Father died. In fact, he died before I arrived at the hospital for the stent to be inserted into his artery." She placed her hand on his.

He was about to speak, but she spoke first. "Anthony, I'm in love with you, I believe I have always been in love with you."

Tears emerged from Anthony's eyes. "That is the most wonderful news that I have ever heard." He placed his arms around her, and then he kissed her on her cheek. "Doris, I can't believe that I let all those years go by and not ask you for a date. It was always like we were just good friends as we grew up, almost like cousins. Well, you're not a cousin and I love you more than I can express in words. Again, I'm so sorry about your father passing away. Is there anything that I can do for you?"

"Yes, let's go into the house and see how my mother is doing. Your parents and your brother are here."

Inside the kitchen, Anthony walked over to Grace and hugged her neck, "Miss Jones, I came here straight from work. I'm sorry I couldn't come earlier."

"I know you were busy as a bee trying to keep things going at your father's company."

"Yes, he certainly was," said Mark. "We seem to have more work now than we know how to handle."

By eleven o'clock that night everyone had left Grace Jones's house. Her daughters informed their mother that they would spend the night with her, but Grace told them to go their homes. Her point to them was that she might as well get used to being home alone. Grace did as she always did before going to bed; she brushed her teeth and then took a hot shower. Afterwards, she slipped into her night gown and then went to bed. After thirty minutes on her bed and unable to fall asleep Grace got up and retrieved Melvin's favorite shirt, she laid it on the pillow next to hers. Thoughts of her husband ran rampant through her mind as she clenched the sleeve of the cotton shirt. Unable to hold her composure any longer she burst into tears. Never before had she experienced such loneliness or been so sad.

Two hours later, Melvin's shirt pulled next to her body, Grace was in a deep sleep. It was sometime before three o'clock in the morning when she started having a nightmare. In her nightmare, Grace was sitting in her couch when she saw what appeared to be an apparition forming right before her eyes. Intense fear permeated her entire body! She wanted to run out of the house, but her legs would not move! Her eyes bulged as the apparition continued to form a human-looking form. Grace tried to scream, but her mouth wouldn't open. All at once she closed her eyes in horror, thinking it was a monster that came to get her. "Grace, Grace, open your eyes," sounded a voice. To Grace it was a familiar voice. Still extremely scared, she opened her eyes to see standing before her a recognizable apparition.

She slowly leaned forward in her chair. "Melvin, is that you? Is that really you?" Tears flowed down her face as she saw the smile on Melvin's face.

"Yes, Grace, it's me. I only have about a minute or two, but I just had to come here and tell you goodbye. Grace, I never ever want you to be unhappy again. Look, even now you're crying."

"I'm crying because I miss you so much."

"I know that, but I'm leaving you with something that no one can ever take away."

"What is it? Melvin, please tell me—what are you leaving me?"

"I'm leaving you with fond memories of our life together, and the love that we shared together for so many years."

"Melvin I want you back! I want you home with me!" Grace cried.

"Grace, you know that it doesn't work like that. I'll never come to you in a nightmare again, so listen to me good! I want you to get on with your life because you and I will meet again one day in Heaven."

"Melvin, how on earth can I get on with my life without you?"

"After your mourning runs its course and in due time I want you to find yourself a companion. Grace, for God sakes don't waste the remainder of your life crying, being unhappy, and worrying about me. I know where I will be. Someday you and I will meet again."

"Melvin, are you remotely suggesting that I marry another man?"

"You're not the kind of woman that can live alone and be

happy. You were good to me, Grace, very good. From now on all I can be to you is a memory. When the time is right, find yourself a good man that will love you and keep you safe. I was just informed that my time is up. Grace, tell my daughters that I love them and that I said goodbye. Also, tell Joe that I left him something in my miniature safe." Grace reached for the apparition, but in the twinkle of an eye it was gone. All at once Grace awoke; her face was covered in sweat. To her the dream was so real. She immediately got out of bed and turned on the bedroom light. She wasted no time dialing Linda's home telephone number as she sat on the edge of her bed. It seemed that Linda would never pick up the phone. She wanted to tell her about her nightmare and her visit with Melvin. She knew that it was just a dream, but she wanted to share that dream with her daughter.

"Mother, is this you? Is everything alright?"

"Linda, I'm sorry for bothering you, but I—."

"Mother, is something wrong?" A wonderful, but shocking feeling overshadowed Grace's body as she stared toward her closet door. "Mother, I'll come right over!"

"No dear, I wouldn't want you to do that. I just called to tell you that I'm doing just fine and I don't want you worrying about me. Now, try to go back to sleep." Grace was still staring toward the closet door. She wiped away her tears; she started smiling as she continuing looking in the same direction. On the door knob was a hanger holding Melvin Jones favorite shirt on it, the very one that she had in her bed earlier. Grace knew exactly what this meant; it was his final goodbye, and her release from the man she had loved for so many years.

Chapter 19

Grace Jones, her two daughters, Joe Wilson and his brother Anthony arrived at Lauren Funeral Home about six o'clock the next evening. Once inside the funeral home, Grace stopped at the doorway leading into the room where an opened casket was on display. She lowered her head for a few seconds, tears emerged from her eyes. Linda and Doris placed their hands on her back.

Joe and Anthony were deeply saddened as they witnessed all three of the women crying.

"Mother, let's go see Daddy," said Doris. Linda handed her mother a couple tissues as they moved forward. Joe held Linda's right hand when they stopped at the coffin where Melvin's body lay on display. As tears slid down Grace Jones's face she expressed a peaceful smile as she gently placed her hand on his face. She knew that Melvin's ghost or spirit had come to her in the dead of night to say goodbye and to wish her well. Linda and Doris burst into tears when they saw their mother lean over and kiss their father on his forehead. Anthony walked quietly out of the room. Joe followed behind him to see if he was alright.

Anthony wiped his watery eyes with a tissue. "It makes me very sad to see Mrs. Jones and her daughters grieving like they are. Mr. Jones was a very good man."

"Yes, Anthony, he certainly was."

Grace, Linda and Doris were still standing by Melvin's casket. "Isn't that a beautiful suit that your Daddy has on?"

"Yes, Mother, it's very beautiful," Linda answered. Doris and Linda couldn't help but notice a peaceful looking smile on their mother's face. She no longer had tears in her eyes. Grace was remembering Melvin's last visit with her even though it was in her dream. Grace nodded her head up and down, acknowledging that she need not cry anymore. More than ever she realized that Melvin wanted her to have peace of mind, not continued sorrow for the rest of her life. She also realized that she would have to make significant adjustments in her life; he would never be a part of her life again, except in her memory. She placed her hand against his face once again as a gesture of thanks for him coming to her in a dream to say goodbye. How could it have been a dream, she thought remembering his shirt hanging neatly on the doorknob? A feeling of tranquility overshadowed her body as she looked toward her daughters.

"Mother, what are you thinking?" Linda asked.

"I'm thinking that it's time for us to go home."

By 6:30 the next night Lauren Funeral Home was filled nearly to capacity. People in the chapel were overwhelmed with sadness as Joe Wilson escorted Grace Jones and her two daughters to the casket for a final viewing of Melvin Jones.

Linda and Doris were very emotional. Anthony Wilson could stand it no longer seeing Doris crying as if she were a child. He got up from his seat and went to Doris, placing his arms around her neck. Joe held Linda tightly as tears slid down her face. Even though enormously saddened as she looked down at her husband, Grace didn't shed a tear. Melvin coming to her in the dead of night had given her peace, understanding, and a form of closure to their marriage. Joe and Anthony escorted the ladies back to their seats.

Sitting middle way of the chapel was Mark and Sarah Wilson. Joan and her new boyfriend, Gary Oakland was sitting beside them. Sarah and Joan were both in tears as they looked toward the Jones family sitting on the front row. Gary reached over and placed his hand on Joan's. Mark handed his handkerchief to his wife so she could get prepared to sing in a little while.

There was complete silence in the sanctuary as the funeral director and his assistant walked down the aisle to close the casket. Grace could hold her composure no longer, tears slid down her face. Joe and Anthony were also overwhelmed as they noticed Linda and Doris crying.

Following the closing of the casket, Reverend Levi Olson stood up. "For most everyone in this room—today is saddened by the passing of our good friend and neighbor, Melvin Jones." He turned toward the Jones family. "Not only was Melvin Jones an honest, hard-working man you could count on in any kind of crisis, but he was a faithful husband and a model father. Melvin Jones was the kind of man that would give you the shirt off his back if you needed it more than him. He and his wife, for years and years, were truly faithful to their God and to their church. I know a great deal of sadness is with us all today, but here me out—Melvin Jones is in a much better place today because he was not only a good man, an honest man, but he practiced what he preached! He was a man of God!"

Reverend Olson talked and preached for twenty minutes. Not only did he talk about the good things that Melvin did, but what God can and will do if you follow the teachings of the bible. Finally, he motioned for Sarah Wilson to come forward to sing her songs. "Ladies and gentlemen, Mrs. Sarah Wilson is going to sing two of Melvin Jones's favorite songs, Lord, I'm Coming Home and In The Sweet Bye and Bye." Reverend Olson took a seat; Sarah got up from her seat, and then she walked to the podium. The piano player started playing the first song. The sound of Sarah Wilson's melodious voice brought smiles to some, and tears to others. She quite often had sung in front of her own church. Mark Wilson shook his head back and forth in absolute approval of his wife's singing.

It was 9:20 that night when Grace Jones and her daughters were able to leave the funeral home. They were accompanied by Joe and Anthony Wilson. About three hundred and twenty people had waited in line to give their condolences to the Jones family. It had been a long night for everyone, especially for Grace, Linda and Doris.

"Mother, did you enjoy hearing Mrs. Wilson sing?" Linda asked as they were getting into Joe's car.

"I sure did. She's the best singing woman that I've ever heard. You should hear her sing in her church sometime. Not only can she sing, but she's also a wonderful lady."

"Mrs. Jones, are you sure you will be okay at your home tonight?"

"Yes, Joe, I'll be just fine. Even though I miss Melvin awfully bad I have a feeling that I can't explain."

"Mother, what kind of feeling are you talking about?" Linda asked.

"Let me just say this—I have a feeling of peace and acceptance of your father's death. He came to me in a dream and told me not to be sad, not to worry, and to get on with my life. I love the memory of your father more now than I could ever explain. He came to me in my dream to say goodbye and to wish me well. I'm glad your father did that. I'm very glad, indeed!"

*   *   *   *

Two days later, four o'clock in the evening everyone that would be involved with Melvin Jones's Will being read was at Grace Jones's house, including Mr. Graham Tidwell, the family attorney. "I see we have everyone here so we'll get started with the reading of the will." He opened up his attaché' case, pulled out a document and then said, "The Will reads as follows, 'Item A. I, Melvin Allen Jones, being of sound mind and body do hereby leave to my faithful and loving wife, Grace Jones, the house we shared with each other, all my business properties, all vehicles that are in my name, all monies in my checking and savings accounts, all stock options, and my bearer bonds. I, also, leave a two hundred and fifty thousand dollar life insurance policy to my wife, Grace Jones. To my wonderful, kind-hearted, beautiful daughter, Linda Jones Wilson I leave her a one hundred thousand dollar life insurance policy. For my other beautiful daughter Doris Jones I leave her a one hundred thousand dollar life insurance policy. Item B. To my very good friend Joe Wilson, a man of honor, courage, and trust-worthiness as any man can be, I leave him my miniature safe and its contents. As clearly stated in Item A, I leave any and all property, tangible and intangible, to my wife Grace Jones, except for what is mentioned inside the miniature safe. Linda and Doris, I hope each of you the very best that any father can hope for.' Well, folks, there you have it," said Mr. Tidwell.

"Mr. Tidwell, why would Daddy want to leave us so much money?" Doris asked.

"Miss Jones, your father loved you and your sister as I've never known another father to do so. He could never mention either one of your names without smiling. The same went for his wife when her name was mentioned. By the way, your mother has yours and Linda's life insurance policies in that big safe that Melvin owned. Joe, inside the big safe is the miniature safe that was mentioned in the will. Mrs. Jones will turn over that miniature safe to you this very day."

"Mr. Tidwell, thank you very, very much for coming to my house in order to read Melvin's will."

"You're quite welcome, Mrs. Jones. If there's nothing else I'll be on my way."

After Mr. Tidwell left, Mrs. Jones went to the large safe and opened it up. She took out Linda's and Doris's life insurance policies. She handed them to her daughters. "Doris, Linda, as soon as I get Melvin's death certificates I'll give each of you a copy so you can collect the insurance money." Next, she handed Joe the 1-foot square safe.

"Mrs. Jones, I wonder what's in this safe."

"Joe, I haven't the slightest idea, but whatever is in there Melvin wanted it to be yours and his secret. Why don't you open it when you get home?"

"My own wife should know what's in that safe."

"Joe, you weren't married to Linda at the time he placed something inside this safe. Of course it's okay for her to see what's inside it."

Joe and Linda arrived home an hour later. They had brought the safe with them. "Now that we've got the safe home I don't know how to open it," said Joe. He looked on the top and sides of the safe to see if the combination was marked or written on it.

"Have you looked underneath the bottom of the safe?"

"No, Linda, but I will."

"Well, how about that—there it is, thirty to the left, forty one to the right, ten to the left."

Joe and Linda were very excited as he opened the little door on the safe. Inside the safe was a manila envelope. Joe opened the flap on the envelope and retrieved two handwritten sheets of paper. Linda looked on curiously as Joe began to read silently, 'Joe, you're a sixteen year old boy at the time I wrote this letter. I've known you for most of your life and I have always admired you for being the kind of person that you are. You have many qualities that most teenagers do not have. You respect everyone, young or old. You never curse, smoke, do drugs or any other thing that would bring ridicule or shame to you or your parents. I see nothing but genuine goodness in you, and that's why I hope and pray that one day, especially after you finish school, that you might take a greater interest in one of my daughters. I love the idea of you being my son-in-law one of these days. You may not know this, Joe, but Linda already has her eye on you. I just hope that when you get a little older you will notice that interest of hers.' Joe laid the paper down momentarily and hugged his wife. "Linda, why didn't you tell me that you were interested in me when I was sixteen?"

"I had to let you find out for yourself. Joe, I had a crush on you when I was twelve years old."

"Doggone it—I must have been pretty dumb to not have noticed that." Joe kissed her tenderly on her lips.

"Joe, finish reading the paper."

He picked the paper up and begun reading again. 'Well, if it works out that you are not my son-in-law I'm accepting you as a son that Grace and I will never have. Doris was the last child that she will ever have. Joe, either as a future son-in-law or as my adopted son I want to give you some things. I have arranged with my wife and attorney that you are to get my miniature safe in one of three ways. One, you marry either of my daughters and when the first baby is born. Two, when you reach the age of thirty. Three, you are to be given the safe within three days of my death. You might wonder why one of the options was your age. Well, it's quite simple; by the time you get that old I won't have any further use for some of the things that I'm giving you. I was always a great planner. Joe, I want you to know that I love you just like you were my own son. In doing so, I have left you an insurance policy for one hundred thousand dollars. You're to take this letter to my attorney, Graham Tidwell, and he will retrieve your policy from a safety deposit box from my bank.' Tears emerged from Joe's eyes. Linda placed her arms around his neck. Joe could not hold his emotions any longer. Still holding the papers in his hand he cried like a young child. Linda handed him some tissue.

"Linda, I don't know what to say! I shouldn't get that much money!"

"Joe, my father loved you very much. After he saw me in bed with William Davis he cried off and on for three days. He couldn't stand the thought of you being hurt. If it hadn't been for my mother he was going to shoot William Davis with his shotgun. Joe, you do deserve the money. Now, finish reading the letter."

He started reading where he had left off. 'Not only will you get the insurance money, Joe, but you now own my fishing boat and trailer, all my fishing equipment, my golf bag and its contents, and all of my guns. I have three rifles, two shotguns and four pistols. Grace and I both decided that you should have the things that I just mentioned so it will not come as a surprise to her. What Grace doesn't know is what is written on the second sheet of paper.' Joe flipped the first page over and he began reading. Linda was looking over his shoulders. 'Joe, if I should die, especially when you're older, I don't want Grace going through the rest of her life sad and unhappy. I love her more than words can say. After a reasonable time of mourning has passed I want you to do everything in your power to get her interested in someone else. Grace is the type of person that cannot and will not be happy living alone, especially without companionship. You're a very smart person and I know you will be able to get her interested in another man. I realize that this is not a normal thing that a husband would be asking someone to do for them, but I love my wife and I want her happy. Remember Joe, I'm counting on you!'

"Linda, now I know why your daddy always had a smile on his face when he saw me. He really did love me."

"Yes, Joe, he always did. My father was a very wonderful and remarkable man. I don't believe my mother would ever get interested in another man."

"In about a year we'll see about that. I have a man in mind already."

"You've got to be kidding me!"

"No, sweetheart, I have the perfect man in mind."

"Who in the world is it?"

"You will know yourself when you see him."

Three weeks have passed since Melvin Jones was laid to rest at Maplewood Cemetery. Grace Jones was no longer crying over the loss of her husband, but she was extremely lonely with him gone. She was sitting in her favorite chair when her doorbell rang. She had a big smile on her face when she answered the door and saw Joe and Linda standing on the porch. "Joe, I see you didn't have to work this Saturday."

"No, Mrs. Jones, Linda and I decided to keep you company for a little while."

"Splendid! Come inside the house. I've got a fresh pot of coffee ready to drink."

All three of them went into the kitchen. Grace poured them, and herself coffee.

"Linda, I'm your mother and I know you like a book that I've read three times. You've got something on your mind, so let's have it!"

"Mother, how do you know that I have something on my mind?" She smiled.

"It's a dead giveaway. I can see it in your eyes, expression, and your nervousness. Am I getting warm?"

Linda stood up; she could no longer keep her secret. "Joe, I'm pregnant!"

"You are! Linda, don't kid with me! Are you really pregnant?"

"Yes! Yes, we're going to have a baby!" Joe hugged Linda, and then he kissed her passionately on her lips.

"How about that, Grandmother-to-be, I'm going to be a daddy!" Joe was so excited he could hardly control his emotions. He held Linda in his arms, and then he kissed her.

"Joe, you have tears in your eyes, why come?" Linda asked.

"It's because I'm so darn happy! Mrs. Jones, your daughter is giving you the grandchild that you've always wanted."

"Joe, it takes two to tango. You and Linda are giving me my long awaited grandchild."

Chapter 20

Today was the third month that William Davis has been working at Maynard's Sporting Goods Store. He thoroughly enjoys his work and has gained the respect of all the store's employees. William was working on some paperwork when he looked up and saw Mr. John Maynard and his son, Timmy coming into his office. William quickly stood up. "William, I brought my son here today to thank you again for saving his life."

"No further thanks are necessary, but I'm very glad to see you Timmy. How have you been?"

"I've been just fine, sir. I do want to thank you again for saving my life."

"Well, Timmy I'm just glad that I happened to be at your father's pond the day you fell into it."

"Timmy, go in the store and look around a little while I talk with Mr. Davis."

"Sure, Father. Mr. Davis, my mother told me to say hello for her."

"That was very nice of your mother, Timmy. Tell her that I really appreciate her saying that."

"Now that Timmy is gone I want to talk with you, William."

"Mr. Maynard, is everything alright here at the store?"

"Yes, William, everything is just fine here. Our profits are up since you've been here these last three months, and all the employees here seem to like you a lot. In fact, you've done such a fantastic job here I've come to offer you another job."

"You're offering me another job?"

"Yes, William, I want you to manage another sporting goods store that I have in Siler City.

That store is much bigger than this one, with twice the number of employees. Did I mention that the salary will be greater also?"

"Mr. Maynard, when would you like me to start working at this new job?"

"You could start in about three months from now. My present manager, Mr. Robert Ellis will retire in about three months and you are the perfect man to fill that position. Of course, it will mean about a thirty five minute drive to Siler City from Adamsville. It probably takes you about eight to ten minutes now."

"Mr. Maynard, the driving part doesn't bother me one bit. I am overjoyed that you are offering me this job. You know as well as I do that you're the only reason that I'm alive. I really do like you, Mr. Maynard. I never dreamed that a wealthy man like you could be so kind and generous."

"There is just one thing, William."

"What is that?"

"You have three months to get your assistant manager up to speed to take over your job, that is—if you think he's up to the task."

"Mr. Maynard, I really do believe that Jonathan Elmore will do just fine as the store manager. I rely on Jonathan a great deal right now, but I will fine tune his managerial skills over the next three months."

"That sounds good. Oh, before I forget it—here's a gas card with your name on it. Stop using your money when you purchase gas. Let's just say it's my appreciation to you for doing such a great job."

"Mr. Maynard, I just don't know what to say!"

"Now, now, I don't want my store manager all teary eyed. The card was my wife's idea.

That being the case, I don't want to hear about you using your own money for gas again," Mr. Maynard smiled.

"Everything I have ever wanted has come true—well, except for one thing."

"William, what is that one thing?"

"I would like to tell Joe Wilson's wife how sorry I am for what I did. There isn't a single night of my life that I don't punish myself for treating her the way I did."

"It's been months since that happened, William; you should be over that now."

"That is the only bad thing that I have ever done! I can't seem to have any kind of closure to my despicable act. If only I could tell her and her husband that I am truly sorry, I believe I could get over it. On the other hand, Mr. Maynard,

I have never let it interfere with my doing a good job for you."

"I know that. Well, I'm glad you are accepting my new job offer. I need to go find Timmy now and head for home. William, I'm very proud to have you in my employment."

"Thank you, sir. I really do appreciate hearing you say that."

*   *   *   *

It was Saturday afternoon, Joe and Linda Wilson had just come back from shopping for baby clothes. Linda is now seven months pregnant. It's difficult to determine who's the happiest, Joe or Linda. "Linda, did you know you've got a big belly?" Joe laughed.

"Guess who made me this big?" She smiled. "Joe, I'm hoping our first baby is a boy."

"Linda, I know you said that for my benefit, but I really don't care whether it's a boy or girl. All I've prayed for is a healthy child."

"Joe, someone just drove into our yard."

"You sure can hear a lot better than me. I'll go see who it is." Joe opened his front door and saw a distinguished looking man exiting a brand new car. Joe waited on the porch while the man walked toward him."

"Sir, is your name Joe Wilson?"

"Yes, it certainly is."

"My name is John Maynard. In fact, I own a business or two here in your hometown of Adamsville. You may be familiar with the Maynard Sporting Goods Store."

"Mr. Maynard, I recognize you now. I've seen you on

television several times. What brings a famous business man like you to a poor working man's home?"

"Mr. Wilson, the happiest individuals that I have ever known were just ordinary, hard-working folks. Money and prestige is not worth two cents unless you have friends and your own self-respect. I've come here today to talk with you and your wife concerning a subject that has bothered me for months. May I please go into your home and talk with you and Mrs. Wilson?"

"Of course you can. Please come inside and I'll introduce you to my wife."

Mr. John Maynard came back to his sporting goods store exactly one week later. He and William Davis were in the manager's office discussing a new line of boating equipment when a worker knocked on William's office, and then he walked inside. "Excuse me Mr. Maynard, but there's a couple people outside that would like to come into Mr. Davis's office."

"That's quite alright, Darryl. Did they say who they were?"

"No, Mr. Maynard, they said it was very important that they see Mr. Davis."

"Tell whomever it is to come into William's office." William Davis stood up; he was totally shocked seeing Joe and Linda Wilson walking toward him. Mr. Maynard observed very carefully as Joe Wilson, a much bigger man than William Davis, walked up to the man that had taken advantage of his wife.

"Are you William Davis?"

"Yes, Mr. Wilson my name is William Davis. I have been expecting you for a very long time."

"Why were you expecting me?"

"I've been waiting for you to beat the living Hell out of me! I wish you would go ahead and beat me real good for what I did to your wife. Mrs. Wilson, I know you will never forgive me for the shame I brought on you and your family, but I am truly sorry for what I did! Go ahead, Mr. Wilson, beat me up real good! I believe I will have some relief after you've taken your hatred out on me."

"Sit down, William," said Mr. Maynard. "Mrs. Wilson, you and Joe have a seat next to me."

William looked totally confused as he lowered his head. "Mr. Wilson, you didn't come here to beat me up?"

"No, William, I didn't come here to beat you up. My wife and I came here to say that we've moved beyond that awful day when I arrived home from the military. It's time for you to move on with your life."

Tears slid down William's face. "Linda, I mean Mrs. Wilson, I wish you could know how truly sorry I am for doing what I did. I just wish there was something I could do to make things right for you, but I can't! I can't undo what's already been done!"

"Mr. Davis, as my husband said a little while ago, we've moved beyond that situation involving you and me. I understand that you go to church regularly now."

"Yes, Mrs. Wilson, I go to church with my family each Sunday."

"From a very reliable source I was told that you tried to commit suicide because of what you did to me."

"That's correct, I was going to take the cowardly way out, but God intervened and that's why I have a good job with Mr. Maynard."

"Joe and I found out that you've saved two people from drowning. What really prompted you to jump into the ocean against a very bad riptide to save a stranger's life?"

"Mrs. Wilson, I guess the truth is that I was trying to make up for the pain I had caused you and Mr. Wilson. Mr. Wilson, I really don't know why you didn't kill me that day at your house. I sure enough deserved it."

"William, Mr. Maynard has told us a great deal about you. You've turned out to be a model husband and father. You're going to church and you've done some remarkable things for other people. I think it's time for us three to put this thing behind us."

"Mr. Wilson, I appreciate that more than you'll ever know. Mrs. Wilson, do you think you will ever forgive me for what I did?"

"Mr. Davis, I'm a Christian woman, I've already forgiven you. Sometimes individuals make very bad decisions, but in your case I truly believe that you are sorry for what you did. Fully realizing your bad conduct that day you've become a much better person. Mr. Maynard sure does believe that, and now so do we." Linda got up and extended her hand to William.

With tears flowing down his cheeks, he said, "Thank you from the bottom of my heart, Mrs. Wilson."

"William, how well do you like Mr. Maynard?"

"Mr. Wilson, I owe my very life to him, he's like a father to me!"

Joe shook William's hand, and then Joe and Linda left the office. William sat down next to his boss. "Mr. Maynard."

"Yes, William."

"I greatly appreciate what you did for me concerning Mr. and Mrs. Wilson. I'll never forget this day and what just happened here. For the first time in months—I feel really free of my guilt! I'm so happy I don't know what to do!"

"I know what you can do, William? Take the day off tomorrow and enjoy your family."

"Mr. Maynard, I have a question?"

"What is the question?"

"Why on earth are you so good to me?"

"William, after three years of marriage I cheated on my wife. Afterwards, I had a feeling of guilt that I could not shake. My wife didn't know about it, but that didn't seem to matter. I knew what I did was wrong, but as time went on the guilt got stronger and stronger. I wanted to tell Gloria, but I couldn't get up enough nerve. Well, it turned out that I was set up for blackmail. Twenty four days after the affair that same woman came to me with photographs of us in bed. I don't know who took the pictures, but they were authentic."

"Good Lord, Mr. Maynard, what did you do?"

"Well, at that very time I was willing to pay a reasonable amount, but she wanted more, much more! That woman demanded that I pay her five hundred thousand dollars or she would turn the photographs over to my wife. I had that much money, but I wasn't about to pay her that much money for fifteen minutes of sexual pleasure."

"What did you do?"

"The first thing I did was tell my wife, and then I went to the police. The woman was arrested for trying to extort money from me. My wife asked me to leave the house. For three days I stayed in a downtown motel trying to drink my worries away.

Similar to you, I became a little suicidal. I bought an illegal firearm and a box of bullets."

"Oh my goodness, Mr. Maynard, you were aiming to shoot yourself?"

"Yes, William, I had made up my mind that Gloria would never let me move back into my home. I was deeply in love with Gloria; I couldn't go through the rest of my life without her. William, I couldn't believe that I had an affair with that two-bit whore! The mistake was of my own doing. There was no one else to blame but me."

"What happened with the gun you bought?"

"I drove down to Logan's creek which was about four miles from my house. I got out of my car with my loaded pistol, and then I walked to a large oak tree not far from the creek. I sat down under the tree, leaned my back against it and then raised the pistol to my temple."

"Mr. Maynard, this is terrible!"

"Tears came into my eyes as I placed my finger against the trigger, and that's when it happened!"

"Happened? What happened, Mr. Maynard?"

"A teen-aged boy walked in front of me with a fishing pole in one hand and a can of worms in the other. He asked, 'Mister, why do you have that gun pointed at your head?' I lowered the gun, stood up, placed the gun inside my belt, and then asked him where his father was. He told me that he didn't have a father. I asked him why he didn't have a father and he said, 'My father killed himself with a shotgun four years ago.' I asked him why his father did a fool thing like that. He told me that his father lost his job at the saw mill and he couldn't find another job. He said that's when his father started drinking whiskey, getting drunk, and feeling sorry for himself. It was then that I followed the boy to the creek bank. I sat and talked with him for a very long time. Never in my life had I felt so sorry for someone. At that moment I realized what an idiot I had been a short time earlier with that gun pointed toward my head."

"What else did you find out from the boy?"

"He had no brothers or sisters, and his mother was poor. John was the young boy's name; he was at the creek to catch some fish so he and his mother would have something to eat for lunch. John was sixteen years old."

"What happened to that boy, Mr. Owens?

"William, from that day forward I made sure that he and his mother had everything they needed to live on."

"What about your wife, what made her take you back?"

"I went to her begging and pleading for her to take me back. She wasn't going to do that until I told her what happened at Logan's creek. I promised her that I would never do anything to undermine her trust again."

"Mr. Maynard, John would be all grown up now after all those years. Do you know what happened to him?"

"Yes, William, I know exactly what happened to him. You know, you never asked me what John's last name was."

"What was his last name?"

"It was Hayward."

"For some reason that name sounds familiar."

"It should, you saved John Hayward's son from drowning."

William's eyes grew larger as he contemplated what his boss just said.

"That's incredible," said William.

"After John got grown I introduced him to my niece one

day. They hit it off very well together. I even started referring to him as my own cousin. Anyway, John is a successful business man now and doing extremely well. I love him and his family a great deal. John saved my life a long time ago down at Logan's creek."

"Now everything makes a lot of sense to me, Mr. Maynard. You're a very good man, and thanks for sharing your story with me. You know, Mr. Maynard, I rather not take off from work tomorrow."

"Why is that?"

"I'm already as happy as any man can ever expect to be!"

Chapter 21

"Sarah Wilson, you've been grinning all evening. What do you have on that clever little brain of yours?"

"Mark, I believe Gary Oakland is going to ask Joan to marry him tonight. Guess where he's taken her for dinner?"

"How many guesses do I get?" He laughed.

"Okay, silly, I'll tell you. He's taking her to the internationally famous Ritz's Steakhouse."

"Do you know why it's internationally famous?"

"No, do you?"

"Sure I know why, it has that label because it is internationally famous for being very expensive. A hundred dollar bill there is pocket change."

"Mark, I'm so excited I hardly know what to do! If that happens we'll have our third grandchild on the way before you know it! Anthony and Doris were married three months ago and Doris is already two months pregnant. They sure didn't waste any time getting down to business. Just think Mark, Linda will soon have hers and Joe's baby, followed in a few more months with Doris's baby, and then Joan's baby. We'll have grandchildren crawling all over our carpet."

"Sarah Wilson, Joan is not even married yet! Do you know what that would imply?"

"It would imply the exact same thing for any couple just married and romping around on their bed somewhere."

"Romping! Gee whiz—you're getting more liberal by the day! I can't even think about what happens after Joan is married and goes on her honeymoon."

"I'm going to let you in on a little secret, Mr. Naive. The same thing will happen with our daughter as it did with us when we were on our honeymoon. Remember, hour after hour of love-making." Sarah smiled.

"Oh, my God, you don't mean to say—!"

"Uh huh, the exact same thing goes on in their bedroom!"

"Sarah, that's terrible!"

"You didn't think it was so terrible for us at the time."

"Yes, but our own daughter?"

"Honeymoons are for getting to know your spouse real well."

"Sarah, all kidding aside, how was I on our honeymoon?"

"Well, that all depends."

"Good heavens, what does that mean? I mean, did I meet your expectations? That's not exactly what I'm asking?"

"Just what are you asking?"

"Doggone it; I'm ashamed to ask you."

"Well, let me put it this way, Mark. If you had been anymore masculine I don't think I could have dealt with it."

A big smile was expressed across Mark's face. "Sarah, whether that was true or not I sure do appreciate you saying it."

"Mark, I wasn't kidding at all. You fulfilled every womanly desire that I had in my body. The only question remaining is this; did I make you happy on our honeymoon?"

"Lord yes, I was so happy I thought I had died and gone to Heaven. Does that answer your question?"

"Yes, I believe it does."

Gary Oakland and Joan have been dating for several months now. He has taken her to the famous Ritz Steakhouse tonight for a special evening of dining and dancing. He has a special ring inside his coat pocket that he is eager to show her tonight. He gave Joan a friendship ring months ago. "Are you sure we're in the right place, Gary? This place looks very expensive."

"Joan, I want this to be a special night for both of us. I don't care how expensive this place is." They were escorted to their reserved table. Gary and Joan ordered their food. "While we're waiting to get our food would you dance with me?"

"Yes, you know I will." Gary and Joan joined the other two couples on the dance floor. The song being played by a four-piece band was a beautiful Waltz. The young lady playing the violin made it sound like an Angel from Heaven was playing it.

"I didn't know you could dance so well."

"I guess you bring out the best in me, Joan." They danced to two songs before going back to their table. Shortly afterwards they were brought their orders. After the waiter left Gary remarked, "They might charge a lot, but they sure don't give you a lot of food. My steak is no bigger than a fried egg," he laughed. "I'll have to use a miniature fork to eat salad from that incredibly small bowl," He smiled.

"Gary Oakland, you had better not embarrass me in front of all these people."

"I won't, I was just kidding about the egg, but no wonder all the people eating here is skinny, but you and me. Oh Lord, I wish I hadn't said that! Joan, I didn't mean to imply that you were fat or anything. In fact, I wish I had left my mouth home."

"That's okay, Gary, I like your sense of humor."

"You do?"

"Of course I do. I'm glad that you're not some old stuff shirt like many men are."

"I guess now is the right time."

"It's the right time for what, Gary?"

"Joan, I've always been just a little bit bashful, but I'm going to try my best tonight. Oh God, I hope it comes out alright!"

"Gary, for Pete sakes, what are you trying to tell me?"

"Joan, we've been dating for months now. I've enjoyed every minute that we've been together. We've been places and done things together that I will remember the rest of my life. Every time I look at you I get goose bumps!"

"Gary, my steak is getting cold. If you keep beating around the bush so you can propose to me the answer is yes, yes I will marry you."

Gary jumped up, knocking his glass of tea onto the floor. "Joan, you're not joking with me, are you?"

"No, Gary, I wasn't joking." He hugged her neck and then kissed her passionately on her lips.

"Sir, is there something the matter here?" A waiter asked. "No, my good man, everything here is great! Gary looked toward the other customers. "Listen everyone; this beautiful woman next to me is going to be my wife!" He gave out a loud cowboy yell!"

"Gary, please sit down before they run us out of here!"

"I'm the happiest man that ever lived! How soon can we get married?"

"On second thought we may not be able to get married."

"Joan, I had your promise!"

"Well, I haven't seen an engagement ring," she smiled.

"I can't believe it, I forgot about the ring!" He reached nervously into his coat pocket for the small box he had brought with him. He opened it and showed Joan its contents.

"Oh my, it is the most beautiful ring I've ever seen!" She slipped it on her finger. "We'll get married in thirty days, is that okay?"

"That's great! Joan, please don't ever scare me like that again! I was about ready to keel over."

"Not only will I be marrying a handsome man, but a comedian as well."

*　*　*　*

Mr. Cyrus Owens was sitting in his office when Clay Maxwell came into his office. Clay had rented one of Mr. Owens cabins twice each year for nine years in a row. "Looks like you're reading a letter, Mr. Owens."

"I sure am, Clay. It's a letter from two of my good friends in Adamsville. Since Joe and Linda Wilson rented a cabin from me about eight months ago they have written letters to me two or three times each month since then. They are two very nice people."

"Mr. Owens, you are a very nice man, you should have lots of friends."

"Yes, that's true, I do have a lot of friends, but these two are very special to me. These friends in Adamsville are about to have a new baby. Joe mentioned in his letter that he and Linda would be coming back here after their baby is born. He said he's bringing one of his dearest friends with him. He said he was pretty sure that I would like this friend of his. I wonder who that might be."

"I can't believe you haven't remarried by now. You're still a handsome looking man. From what I hear you are incredibly rich and you're not an old man. Mr. Owens, just how old are you?"

"I'll soon be fifty six years old."

"You're a long ways from being considered old."

"I know I'm not old, but I'm far from being a young man. Anyway, how can I help you, Clay?"

"My grandson, Jeffery wants to fish in your lake, but I didn't bring any fishing gear."

Mr. Owens walked to a closet door and withdrew a fishing pole and a tackle box. "That's no problem at all, here's my tackle box and my rod and reel. Furthermore, I've got a cup of worms in my office refrigerator. I'll get them out and then you can take your grandson fishing."

"Thanks, Mr. Owens. No wonder I keep coming back year after year. By the way, you could be in one of your corporate offices or just doing some world traveling. Why is it that you're here most of your time?"

"This is a very special place for me, Clay. My mother and father are buried within a mile from here, and I very much enjoy the scenery here. I, especially, like the lake and meeting new people all the time. Maybe one of these days I might meet a nice lady that may develop some interest in me."

"There are thousands of women that would like to get their grips on you."

"I'm well aware of that. Most of those women you are referring to would just be seeing dollar signs when they look at me. If I ever marry another woman it will be someone that has almost no interest in my bank account. I would love to have a family that loves and respects me for who I am, not because I'm wealthy.

*   *   *   *

It was one o'clock in the morning; Joe and Linda Wilson were wide awake. Linda was in labor. Joe had been timing her contractions for over an hour. "Linda, it's time for me to take you to the hospital. Your contractions are coming about every four or five minutes and they're lasting between sixty to eighty seconds." Joe picked up the phone and dialed Grace Jones, Linda's mother. He told her about Linda's condition and for her to call Doris and Anthony to let them know that Linda was going to have her baby. "Joe, I'm hurting awfully bad!"

"I know you are, sweetheart. Your hospital bag is already packed, I'll slip on my trousers and shoes and I'll have you at the hospital in a matter of minutes."

"Please hurry, Joe I don't want my water to break before I get to the hospital. Oh, my God, I'm hurting awfully bad!"

Every step Linda took toward the car was extremely painful, even with her husband's assistance. Joe was emotionally upset, hearing the painful groans and moans from his pregnant wife.

"Hang in there, Linda; we'll be at the hospital in about twelve more minutes."

"Joe, I believe the baby is coming!"

"Please! Please, Linda, keep the baby where it is until we get to the hospital."

"Joe, I hate to say it, but that was about the dumbest thing I've ever heard you say!"

They arrived at the hospital a few minutes later. Excitedly, Joe hurried inside the emergency room to summon help. He led the way as a nurse rolled a wheelchair to Joe's car. She and he helped Linda into the wheelchair. "Nurse, where will my wife be taken from here?"

"She will be taken to the birthing center of the hospital. It will be a very nice room with some of the conveniences you would have at home. It's a private room and the actual birth takes place there. You can be in her room until she's ready for delivery, or as the husband you can observe the proceedings."

"I rather not be in the room when she gives birth. I might have a heart attack or worse."

"In that case you may wait in the nearby waiting room during delivery."

Dr. Stephen Mallard, Obstetrician checked Linda shortly after she was situated in the birthing center. "Dr. Mallard, Linda is having awful pains, can't you do something?"

"Mr. Wilson, I understand your concern, but all women experience pain when they're about to have a child. Mrs. Wilson, on a scale from one to ten, how much are you hurting?"

"A good fourteen and a half," she answered.

"Where are you hurting?"

"Almost everywhere, but in my back and the lower part of my stomach mostly."

"Your best solution for your pain is to utilize the breathing techniques you learned during your pregnancy. However, if it's absolutely necessary we can always consider epidural or spinal anesthesia."

"No! No! Sally Johnson told me that either one of those ways are very painful! Joe, don't let them do either one of those, please!"

"Mrs. Wilson, neither of those procedures can be used without your permission. Mr. Wilson, help your wife with her breathing techniques while I check her."

"Well, Mrs. Wilson, your baby is only a few minutes from being born. You're almost fully dilated now, nearly ten centimeters. Nurse, I'll be back in about five minutes. Mr. Wilson, it's time for you to go or stay. Your wife's baby is about ready to come out." The doctor left the room."

Joe bent over and kissed his wife on the cheek. Tears were visible in his eyes as he observed her grimacing from her pain. "Linda, I'm going to the waiting room outside. Your mother and sister will be anxious to know what's going on. Nurse, you take good care of my wife, she's all that I've got!"

"I will, Mr. Wilson. It will be all over with in a little while. Your wife is doing extraordinarily well." Reluctantly, Joe left Linda's room.

Joe had only been in the waiting room five minutes before Grace Jones and her daughter, Doris came into the room. "Joe, how soon do you think Linda will have the baby?"

"Dr. Mallard said that the baby was heading south right

now. To me south means down, so he must be looking for an exit right now."

"Mother, Joe has never been accused of not having a way with words," said Doris, smiling.

"Doris, how is married life?"

"Married life is great, Joe. I married a very, very good man."

"She may be exaggerating a little," said Anthony, coming into the room. "Doris thinks I'm some kind of superman or even greater. Boy, I didn't think I would ever find a parking spot. Joe, will it be a girl or boy?"

"I'm not sure, Anthony, I'm only hoping for a normal child."

"Joe, has Doris told you hers and Anthony's good news?"

"No, Mrs. Jones, I don't believe she has. Doris, what is the good news?"

"I'm pregnant; Anthony and I are going to have a baby."

Joe hugged Doris's neck, and then he shook his brother's hand. "Congratulations to both of you. Mrs. Jones, what do you think about all these forthcoming grandchildren?"

"It's great news to me. I just wish Melvin was here to see them when they're born."

"Oh, my goodness, I forgot to call my parents!" Joe said. He used his cell phone to call and let his parents know that Linda was about to have a baby.

It was several minutes before anyone answered. Mark Wilson noticed it was 3:00 AM when he got out of bed.

"This had better be some good news or I'm going to clean somebody's plow!"

"Mark, why are you going to clean someone's plow when

you haven't answered the phone yet?" Sarah asked. "Now, pick up the phone!"

"Daddy, this is Joe, Linda's in the hospital! She's about to have our baby!"

"We're on our way!" He hung the phone. "Sarah, get up! Get up!"

"You look like you've seen a ghost! Who was that?"

"It was Joe! Linda is having our grandchild!"

"Oh, my Lord, I'm so excited I don't know what to do!"

"For starters, get dressed so we can head toward the hospital!"

Mark and Sarah Wilson arrived at the hospital just in time to hear the obstetrician tell their son that Linda Wilson had just delivered a healthy, eight-pound baby boy. "Mr. Wilson, your wife is waiting for you in her room," said Dr. Mallard. I believe she wants you to come into her room alone at first."

"Thank you very, very much, Dr. Mallard. Everyone else, I'll come back for you in just a little while." Joe followed Dr. Mallard out of the room. "Oh, Dr. Mallard, have you any idea why Linda wants to talk privately with me? I mean—there's nothing wrong with her or our baby is there?"

"Mr. Wilson, I assure you that nothing is wrong with either one of them." Dr. Mallard continued down the hall. Joe hurried toward his wife's room.

Linda saw her room door open quietly. Joe had a big smile on his face as he entered the room. Linda was holding their just-born little boy. Joe's eyes gleamed with joy as he placed his little finger side of his son's face. "Linda, I'm the proudest father in the whole world! You've given me something that I have always wanted, a son. I love you more than anything in the whole world! Guess what, your folks and mine are waiting anxiously to see you and our baby."

"Linda, you're crying! What's wrong, sweetheart? Are you hurting somewhere?"

"No, I'm not hurting."

"Well then, why are you crying?"

"Joe, I'm crying because—!"

"Because what?"

"You'll hate me when I tell you!"

"Not ever again will I hate you! I love you no matter what! Now tell me why you are crying!"

She closed her eyes and then said, "Joe, I'm not sure whose baby this is."

"What?"

"It's either yours or William Davis's baby. I swear to you that I don't know which it is! I have never told you this because I was afraid you would leave me! Joe, please don't hate me! I'll agree to have a DNA test performed on the baby to see whose baby it is, if that's what you want."

Joe Wilson dropped to his knees, he started crying. With tears streaming down her face, Linda Wilson acknowledged that their marriage might be over. For months and months she had worried that this day of revelation would come. Finally, Joe Wilson stood up; he wiped his eyes with his shirtsleeve, and then looked down at the little baby. "There will not be a DNA test performed on this baby! I'm accepting this baby as is—my own flesh and blood. There will never be any future talk among us or to anyone else concerning this matter."

"Joe, you have made me the happiest woman in the whole

world. I thought you were going to leave me! Joe, I will always love and respect you for your decision."

"Linda, what name will we give to my new son?"

"I would very much like for this little tyke to be named after you."

"That would make me a senior and him a junior. I really like that. Linda, there is one little thing that I would like for you to do for me before I call everyone into your room."

"I've already said I would do anything for you."

"I want a juicy kiss from those pretty lips of yours."

"You already know what shape I'm in, how juicy do you want it?"

"In that case, how about a regular kiss?"

"Joe Wilson, you should have been a comedian," she laughed.

"Darn it, I thought I was. Anyway, I'll go bring everyone to see my new baby boy!"

Chapter 22

Joe escorted his and Linda's family to Linda's room. There was standing room only as each of the family members took their turns congratulating Joe and Linda for their new baby boy. It was difficult to determine who was more excited, Sarah or Grace. "Son, that is a mighty fine boy that you fathered," said Mark. "I know for sure now that you're a chip off the old block." He winked at Joe.

"Yes, Daddy, he is a very fine boy. I'm as happy as any father can be."

Linda had listened attentively at Joe's response to his father. "Mr. Wilson, you should be very proud of Joe because he is the very best husband in the whole world."

"Did you hear that, Sarah? Not only is my daughter-in-law beautiful, but she recognizes the male quality in we Wilsons."

"I guess no one has to toot my husband's horn," said Sarah. "They don't come any better tooter than him," she laughed.

"Linda, your baby is beautiful. Grace, look at what we'll be holding in a few days from now. Isn't it wonderful?"

"It certainly is. Well, we've got one down and another one on the way. Sarah, we'll be quite busy after Doris has her baby, won't we?"

"We most certainly will. I'm so excited I don't know what to do!"

"Mother, my baby only has about four hairs on the back of his head."

"That won't be a problem at all. His hair will grow out in due time. The little fellow has the bluest eyes I've ever seen on a baby. Joe, you've got to admit that he got those blue eyes from his mother."

"Yes, I suppose he did." Linda looked toward her husband knowing full well that his eyes were dark brown.

"Joe, don't concern you with the color of his eyes," said Anthony. "All the rest of him looks like you." Everyone laughed at Anthony's remark.

"Linda, since I've got to go through the same thing you did, how much pain did you experience?" Doris asked.

"It's funny that you asked that question because I don't remember the pain being as severe now as it was at the time. There is no question about it—you will experience some very hurting pains, but it is truly worth the pain and discomfort."

"Anthony, we may only have this one child that I'm carrying. However, if we can divvy up the pain I might consider another baby."

"Would hitting my big toe with a hammer do the trick?" He laughed.

"Well, it won't be my big toe that will be hurting." Everyone burst into laughter. Mark Wilson had to sit down to control himself.

Linda was back in her home two days later, but Joe had to go back to work. He and Anthony were looking over blueprints on an, in-progress, construction site for a new mall that their father's company was building. Mark Wilson's superintendent, Clayton Melbourne was with Joe and Anthony. "Joe, I understand that you are a proud new father."

"Yes sir, Linda and I have the prettiest little boy I've ever seen."

"Mr. Melbourne, he favors Joe a lot, except for his eyes," said Anthony.

"What's wrong with his eyes?" Joe asked.

"Nothing, Joe, I just meant they're blue and your eyes are brown, like mine."

"Anthony, I'm sorry! I don't know why I asked you that question."

"It's alright; I've heard that new fathers get a little irrational at times. The same thing will probably happen to me when I become a father."

"Joe, I've written down all the materials that we will need for the next two weeks," said Mr. Melbourne. "Go do your magic and get us some good deals on the materials. Try to get most of it delivered to the site within twenty four hours. Anthony, if you don't mind, I want you to closely supervise the interior construction of the mall. That especially includes the ceiling construction. Make sure that all of our workers are earning their pay. I've got a short fuse when it comes to loafers on the job."

"Mr. Melbourne, now I know why my father pays you so well, and likes you so well."

"Just who do you think trained me to be like I am? It was your father, that's who! Now, you two earn those big bucks that your father is paying you," he smiled.

Anthony walked inside of the large complex that will have forty seven individual businesses when built and fully leased. He couldn't help but notice George Summers, a skilled carpenter sitting on a large spool of wire holding a paper in his hands. "George, what's going on? You don't look very happy?"

"To tell you the truth, Mr. Anthony, I'm not happy at all."

"George, what seems to be the trouble?"

"I found this letter on the kitchen table when I got home yesterday evening. I guess you would call it a Dear John letter. Debra moved all her clothes out of our house yesterday while I was working. She said in the letter that she didn't love me anymore." Tears came into George's eyes.

"Did she say why she didn't love you anymore?"

"Yes, she sure did!"

"What did she say?"

"She said my brother was better looking than me and that he was a much better lover."

"Of all the nerve, you mean your own brother?"

"Yes, my own brother."

"George, how did this happen?"

"He was out of work for a while. I let him move into our house until he could get on his feet. I didn't ask him to pay a penny for food or shelter. I even paid his car payments for five months. It seems that he was having an affair with my wife the whole time he was living free at my home. Mr. Anthony, I feel like a fool for letting him move into my house!"

"George, why don't you take a couple days off? I wouldn't

want Mr. Melbourne to see you in this condition. You are a great carpenter and my father needs your talent with his company."

"I appreciate you doing this. It will be best if I take off a couple days to get my mind properly focused."

"George, I don't think your brother is the entire problem. Your wife shares the lion's share of the blame. She could have nipped the whole thing in the bud from the beginning. Do you and she have any children?"

"No, thank God for that."

"I'm not all that good in giving advice, but you are a young man with your whole life ahead of you. There are millions of women that you can choose from, but you must chose wisely. Don't waste weeks, months or years fretting about a wife that was deceptive, unfaithful, and downright inconsiderate of your feelings! George, you're a good man, you deserve much better than a cheating wife."

"Mr. Anthony, I really appreciate you talking with me. It's meant a great deal to me. Now, I want to ask a favor from you."

"Sure, George, what is the favor?"

"Forget about me taking off two days. After talking to you—I don't need to take any time off from work." He crumbled the letter from his wife, and then threw it into a trash can.

"Thank you, George, you are definitely needed here." George stood up, pulled out his ruler and then started measuring for a proposed doorway.

Anthony was surprised to see Mr. Clayton Melbourne standing nearby in the hallway. "I may have been wrong about you, Anthony."

"Why is that Mr. Melbourne?"

"Whatever your father is paying you is not enough.

I happened to follow you inside the building to tell you something. I heard everything said between you and George Summers. In a matter of minutes you were able to do something that absolutely astounded me. In fact, I just learned a good lesson from you, Anthony. "

"What did you learn, Mr. Melbourne?"

"I learned to be more considerate of employee's feelings. Not only is our very best carpenter back on the job, but you caused him to feel good about himself again. Anthony, your father would be proud to know what you just did."

"Thank you, Mr. Melbourne. That means a lot to me coming from you. Well, I had better be on my way to see how everyone else is doing."

Mr. Melbourne walked over to where George Summers was working. "George, how is it going?"

"Everything is just fine, Mr. Melbourne."

"Did Mr. Anthony Wilson come by here?"

"Yes sir, he sure did. He left a little while ago. I have a lot of respect for that man."

"Why is that, George?"

"He's more than a foreman or someone's boss man. He genuinely cares about other people's feelings. A man like that can get the very best performance from employees. He sure did solve a personal problem for me."

"George, I just want you to know that you're a tremendous asset to our company. You have a job with this company as long as you want it."

"Gee thanks, Mr. Melbourne, I never thought I would run into two great people in the same day."

Clayton Melbourne walked down the hallway realizing

that you never get to old to learn. He knew already that he should temper his emotions some when dealing with personnel problems.

*   *   *   *

"Linda, it's hard to believe that our baby is three months old now. Each day he looks more and more like you."

"Well, babies are supposed to favor their mother some. What are you going to do on this beautiful Saturday morning?"

"I thought I would take my boat down to the river. I haven't been fishing in a very long time."

"Why not ask Anthony to go fishing with you?"

"I would, but he and Doris have gone out of town for the weekend. Would you like to go fishing with me?"

"No thanks, I've got too much housework to do."

"I don't have to go fishing. I could stay here and help with the housework."

"Nonsense, what good is that boat Mr. Jones left you if you never use it?"

"I won't argue with you because most of the times your ideas are better than mine."

"I wouldn't necessarily agree on that, but I appreciate you saying it. I want you to go fishing and enjoy yourself. Do you want me to fix you some sandwiches to take with you?"

"No thanks, I have some potted meat and Vienna sausage already."

"That's another reason I don't do a lot of fishing."

Joe had been gone over an hour when her doorbell rang. Linda recognized the visitor through the peep hole in her door.

She opened her door, and invited her mother inside. "Where is my precious little darling?"

"He's lying quietly in his crib."

"Well, I might just change that situation rather hurriedly because I'm dying to hold little Joe!" They walked into the living room. "There's my little grandchild," said Grace. "Isn't that sweet, he opened those big blue eyes just for me? Linda, your baby is beautiful. One day he will melt some girl's heart with those peepers of his." Grace sat on the couch with the baby in her arms.

"Mother, what happens when a person has a secret, but that same person doesn't know the answer to that secret?"

"Linda, not only am I a woman, but I'm also your mother. Women quite often observe things that men are likely to overlook. I think I know what your secret is. Would you like for me to tell you what that secret is?"

"Mother, I'm not sure I want to hear it!"

"Well, you're going to hear it anyway! You don't know whether the father of this child is Joe Wilson or William Davis!" Linda burst into tears. "Linda, I didn't just come up with this idea, I've thought it from the time you announced your pregnancy. You didn't go to the hospital the same day that Joe came home to eliminate any possibility of you getting pregnant. You and he made up in a reasonable time. Linda, you couldn't possibly know whose father this child is! Have you told Joe about your secret?"

"I told him in the hospital right after the baby was born."

"How did he react?"

"He was devastated at first, but then he seemed to come to grips that the baby might not be his. That's when he said there would not be a DNA test. Right then and there, Joe accepted the baby as his own child. Mother, Joe loves our baby, but every time he looks at him he sees those blue eyes. William Davis has blue eyes, but Joe has brown eyes. I, definitely, feel like Joe is hurting inside even though he doesn't say anything. I don't know what I should do!" Tears flowed down Linda's face.

"It doesn't make any sense at all for both of you to spend the rest of your lives not knowing the truth! So what if William Davis is the father, Joe Wilson is going to love this child no matter what, but at least each of you will know the truth! The truth can and will set you free from your suspicion and guilt. Your father and his father had brown eyes, so did a lot more of his family. This child could just as easily be Joe's son as he could be the son of William Davis."

"Mother, will you help me find out which one it is?"

"Linda, I love Joe as if he were my own son. I don't want to do anything to jeopardize our relationship. You don't need me in order for you to find out the answer."

"I wouldn't know how to go about getting a DNA test on my baby."

"Linda, getting a DNA from the baby is no problem at all. The problem will be getting a DNA sample from Joe, without him knowing about it."

"How could I do that?"

"There are many ways I'm sure, but one absolutely sure way."

"What way is that?"

"If he should ever scratch himself shaving or nick his finger or leg, try to get access to the tissue or the cloth that he used to stop the bleeding. You then would go to a reliable DNA

Paternity Testing Center with the baby and the blood sample from Joe. They would determine whether Joe is the biological father or not for around three or four hundred dollars. If he's not the biological father then William Davis would have to be the father of your child, unless."

"Mother, what do you mean by this 'unless'?"

"Unless there's another man involved."

"Mother, I swear to God Almighty that only two men has ever had sex with me! One of them was without my consent, meaning William Davis!"

"Linda, I've never known you to tell a lie, I believe you're telling me the truth. Well, what are you going to do?"

"I'm ashamed to admit it, but I'm just waiting for Joe to bleed a little bit around me. Goodness, I sound like a vampire or something!"

Chapter 23

Joe was on the river to do some fishing, and to try out his boat and motor that Mr. Melvin Jones left him when he died. Joe's 25 horse power Evinrude motor was performing flawlessly as he cruised downstream, observing the beautiful scenery and trying to spot an animal of some kind. All at once he saw several wild turkeys, he grabbed for his camera, but the elusive birds hurried behind some undergrowth. It was a beautiful sight seeing a tom turkey leading his flock.

Joe was wondering why he hadn't used his boat more often as he guided the boat farther and farther downstream. Finally, he saw a perfect place in the river to fish. He slowed his engine as he headed for an area along the river bank where the water seemed to be moving very slowly because of a fallen log lying in the river. He used a short section of his anchor rope to tie his boat to a protruding limb. He was filled with excitement as he reached for his rod and reel. He already had it rigged with a cork, lead and hook for fishing with worms or crickets. He decided he would use a fishing worm first. No sooner than his hook settled down in the water his cork went under the water. The fish felt like a giant against the ultra-light reel and rod that Joe was using. The fish pulled the line outward, and then Joe would wind the line inward. Finally, he got the fish alongside the boat. It was an enormous largemouth bass. Joe used his dip net to bring the fish into the boat. It was the largest bass he had ever caught. He was determined to take a picture of the fish before releasing it. He got out his camera and pointed it toward the fish lying in the bottom of his boat. Joe eased him back into the water after snapping two pictures of the fish. It was at that very moment that he noticed something two or three inches underneath the water and small tree limbs. At first it looked like a torn red shirt, but something didn't add up to Joe. He untied the anchor rope. He paddled his boat about ten feet alongside the tree brush to get a better look at whatever it was submerged a little ways underneath the water. His eyes bulged, he gasped for breath, seeing what appeared to be a dead man. That's when it occurred to him that the peculiar smell he detected earlier was that of a decaying body. His left arm scraped across a jagged limb as he used his paddle to push the boat away from the body. Without any thought to the blood oozing from his arm, Joe used the paddle to push the boat farther and farther from the fallen log. He cranked his boat motor fast as he could, and then guided the boat to the opposite side of the river. After tying his boat to a small tree next to the riverbank he took out his cell phone and called 911. He told the dispatcher that he was downstream several miles from Tucker's Boat Landing. He promised the dispatcher that he would wait in that area for the authorities to arrive. They told him to anchor his boat in the middle of the river and keep his cell phone turned on. Joe used the bottom of his undershirt to stop his arm from bleeding.

In less than an hour, Joe heard the roar of several boat engines coming downstream toward him. Finally, the lead boat stopped beside Joe's boat. "Apparently you're the 911 caller," said Detective Bill Woodard.

"Yes, my name is Joe Wilson, and sure as you're born there's a dead body across the river under that fallen tree top. You'll be able to see him fairly good because he's wearing a red plaid shirt."

"Mr. Wilson, if you don't mind, please stay anchored where you're at until I come back to you."

"That's no problem, officer." Detective Woodard was a homicide detective with the Felton County Sheriff's Department. He and five more sheriff deputies guided their three boats across the river to the fallen tree.

Joe watched curiously as the officers retrieved the body from underneath the underbrush. He could easily tell that the body was placed inside a body bag.

Detective Woodard guided his boat across the river to where Joe was still anchored. "Mr. Wilson, you were absolutely right, it was a body, but we don't know whose body it is at this time. What is your telephone number in case I need to get up with you?" Joe gave him his home and cell phone numbers. "I thank you for calling 911 and reporting your discovery, and I want to thank you for waiting while we retrieved the body. The body will be taken from here to the coroner's office for forensics and body-identification. I guess you'll go back to fishing now."

"I'll go alright, but it will be upstream. I don't have the stomach for anymore fishing today."

The boats the authorities were using had much greater horsepower motors than Joe's motor.

In a matter of minutes those boats were out of hearing range. Joe pulled in his anchor, cranked his engine, and guided his boat upstream. He noticed that his wound was still oozing a little blood. Again, he used the bottom of his undershirt to press against his wound.

It was nearly two hours later when Joe backed his boat trailer and boat to the back of his lot. He used a garden hose to wash his boat. Afterwards, he gathered all his fishing tackle and placed it neatly inside his garage.

Linda was watching television when Joe entered the house. "For goodness sakes, Joe, what happened? You've got blood all over your tee shirt! My goodness, you've got a bad scrape on your left arm! Sit down on the couch and I'll get something to clean your wound."

"I didn't have a good time at all."

"Why is that?"

"I found a dead body under a tree that was lying in the river."

"Body, what kind of body was it?"

"It was the body of a man. It was awful!"

"What did you do?"

"I called 911 and had the law come retrieve the corpse."

"Oh, my God!"

"Linda, what is it?"

"I bet I know who the man is that you found!"

"How would you know that?"

"I'll bet anything it was Mr. Jim Turner that was in that river! Let me ask you this, did he have on a red shirt?"

"The body did have a red shirt on it, but how would you possibly know that? How?"

"Mr. and Mrs. Turner operated a small convenience store about a half mile past Tucker's Boat Landing. I've seen it on the local news about three times now, stating that Mr. Turner was missing, along with his cash register, thirty cartons of cigarettes, and about twelve cases of beer.

His wife reported him missing about three or four days ago. That poor, poor man."

"Linda, you should have been a detective."

She cleaned his wound with soapy water, applied a healing agent, and then wrapped the scraped area with gauze. Joe stood up; he removed his bloody tee shirt. "Will you place my tee shirt into the garbage can?"

"I'll take care of everything. Why don't you go into the bathroom and get cleaned up a little."

"Linda, is little Joe asleep?"

"Yes, but don't try to wake him up. It took me a good while to get him to sleep. By the way, you received another letter from Mr. Cyrus Owens today. He thanked you for sending him little Joe's pictures. Mr. Cyrus said he's anxious to see you, me and the baby soon as we can get back to the mountains. He mentioned that you were bringing a friend with us on our next trip."

"That's right; I want your mother to ride with us so she can see the beautiful scenery, especially that picture-perfect lake behind Mr. Owens office."

Joe went into the bathroom. Linda hurried to the kitchen with the bloody tee shirt. She placed it carefully into a large plastic bag, and then she took the bag and shirt to her closet.

She placed the bag as far back on her closet shelf as she could. She now had everything she needed for a DNA test."

* * * *

It was Sunday afternoon; Grace Jones drove to Maplewood Cemetery after attending church services. Lying on the seat beside her was a beautiful wreath of flowers. It has been months since her husband passed away. She visits his grave a little less frequent, but when she does she brings flowers to show her respect. Grace parked her car a few yards from the cemetery gate. Normally, there were other people at the cemetery when she visited, but today she didn't see anyone. Somewhat apprehensive, she carried her wreath to Melvin's resting place. Grace was glad she brought the wreath because the live flowers she brought the last time were becoming unsightly. She bent over and removed dead flowers from one of the vases, laying them on the ground. When she leaned over to get flowers from the other vase she heard a noise in the nearby woods. She rose up, but she didn't see anything. Assuming it was a limb falling to the ground she removed flowers from the other vase. With care and reverence, she placed the wreath next to Melvin's tombstone. With tears in each of her eyes she looked straight at her husband's tombstone. "Melvin, I don't know if you can hear me or not, but I'll say it anyway.

Linda and Joe's baby is growing like a weed. I've wished and prayed that you could be here to see their child grow up." Tears slid down Grace's face. "Joan will be getting married soon to Gary Oakland. Personally, I'm doing okay, but I do miss you a lot. Melvin, we had a lot of wonderful years together. You always made me feel like I was very, very special. I really did appreciate that. I would be lying if I told you that I wasn't lonely, but I'm glad that you released me the night you came to me in my dream. Melvin, I'm not so sure it was a dream. Your shirt got hung on the doorknob, but I didn't hang it there. I figured you did it to show me that I had to get on with my life. Melvin, no matter what path I take you will be in my cherished memory until the day I die."

Suddenly, Grace Jones was horrified when she looked toward the cemetery gate. Standing near the entrance of the cemetery were three young men. She easily identified them as gang members with their over-sized tee shirts, emblazed with a picture of a dragon. She had never been more scared in her whole life. Her hands started trembling; she didn't know what to do.

"Hey lady, what idiot would be talking to a tombstone?" Chuck Snyder, a notorious gang leader yelled. Grace turned back facing her husband's tombstone. She was almost paralyzed with fear. "You better come out of the cemetery or we're going in there after you!"

"Why don't you go away and leave me alone! Don't you realize that this is a cemetery?"

"Sure we do, lady," said Chuck. "In fact, we helped put a few of these people in here!" He laughed loudly.

Grace's legs trembled as she headed toward the gate, not knowing what they were going to do to her. She was about halfway to the gate when she saw a familiar car drive up. She stopped dead in her tracks when she saw Gary Oakland and Joan exiting their car.

"Gary, these hoodlums have been threatening me!" Grace cried out.

"Joan, go back to the car," said Gary. She did as he asked.

"Well, guys we've got three people to rob now instead of one," said Chuck.

"Don't you morons have anything better to do than to pick on a defenseless woman?" Gary asked.

"Chuck, he called us a moron!" said Pete Lawson. "Let me pound his head a little!"

"Go ahead, Pete, show that dude what you're made of!" Pete ran toward Gary with brass knuckles on his right hand. As quick as the eye can register, Gary jumped into the air and kicked Pete Lawson under his chin with a thunderous blow causing him to fall to the ground unconscious.

"I see you've got a little karate experience, tough guy," said Chuck. "Let's see you kick this! He pulled out an eight inch knife from its sheaf. Chuck moved the knife back and forth as he walked slowly toward Gary. Joan started crying, fearing that Gary would be seriously hurt. Grace held her hands to her mouth as the gang leader got closer and closer to him.

"Gary, please be careful!" Grace yelled.

"You're about as despicable as they come you overgrown nit wit!" Gary said, standing his ground.

"No one calls me a nit wit!" Chuck was within ten feet of Gary.

"I just did, you piece of slime! The best thing you can do is pick up that varmint from the ground and take him back to your cardboard shelter! If you don't, I'm going to put a real hurting on you!"

"I'm going to kill you for talking to me like that!"

"Well, come on—get at it! I've got things to do later this evening!"

Chuck lunged toward Gary with the knife. Gary turned sideways, and then he grabbed Chuck's arm, twisted it behind Chuck's back until it snapped.

"You broke my damn arm! You broke my arm!"

"Well that's not good enough. You frightened my future mother-in-law out of her wits. I can't let you get away with that!"

"Billie, get this bastard!" Billie ran toward the road. "Billie, you little worm! I'll kill you for running off like that!"

"You must be the ring leader of this mop squad," said Gary. "Do you have any idea what I'm about to do to you for bothering Mrs. Jones?"

With his good arm, Chuck reached for his knife lying on the ground. Gary punched him hard against his mouth, knocking him down. Blood oozed from his mouth. "You broke my teeth, you bastard." He grabbed the knife and then stood on his feet. "I'm going to cut your head clear off your shoulder." He jumped toward Gary with the knife, but Gary was prepared. He kicked Chuck side of his head with a crushing blow. Chuck fell to the ground, knocked completely out.

"Mrs. Jones, are you ready to go home?"

"Yes, Gary, I'm quite ready. Are those two dead?"

"No, they're just taking peaceful naps."

"Gary, I was afraid they were going to hurt you!" Joan yelled, running toward him.

"What are you going to do about these two?" Grace asked.

"Well, I see two hound dogs coming toward us. Maybe they'll lick them on their faces until they wake up."

"Gary, aren't you afraid they will get even with you?"

"No, Mrs. Jones, I'm not afraid. Hoodlums like these normally prey on people that can't defend themselves. That ring leader may even decide that being a gang member is not his cup of tea," he said, smiling.

"Gary, I was scared to death that they were going to hurt you!" Joan said, hugging him tightly. "Mother, are you okay?"

"Yes, but this will be my last time coming to this cemetery alone."

Chapter 24

It was Monday morning. Linda was holding little Joseph Edward Wilson, Jr. in her arms.

"I've got me a big Joe and a little Joe now," said Linda. "Smile at your daddy, sweetheart. Look,Daddy, little Joe is smiling real big."

"I don't know what's in his baby food, but he's growing like a wild weed."

"Did you hear that, little Joe? Your father said you were a weed."

"I did no such thing, little Joe! Your mother fibs a little here and there."

"Little Joe, ask your father when he might start planning for you a brother or sister."

"Little Joe is only three months old now. It's way too soon to think about another child now. Linda, are you sure you'll be alright for the next three days?"

"I'm very sure, Joe. Besides, your father wants you to go to this seminar very badly."

"I know he does, but I hate to leave you here all by yourself."

"I won't be here by myself. I've got little Joe to protect me." Linda smiled.

"As much as I love our baby, I don't think he's going to offer very much help if there's any kind of problem while I'm gone."

"What hotel will you be staying in?"

"I'll be staying at the Radisson Hotel. I will call you when I arrive and let you know my room telephone number."

"How long a trip is it?" Linda asked.

"I guess about four hours. I'll bring you and little Joe a present when I return."

"I'm not going to give you a hint or anything, but my necklace broke about two weeks ago."

"Are you suggesting that I—?"

"Not at all." Linda smiled.

Joe had only been gone on his trip for a half hour when Linda picked up the phone and dialed a DNA testing center, located about an hour's drive from her house. They asked her a few questions, and then she told them that she would be there tomorrow with her baby and the bloody shirt. After hanging up the phone a feeling of guilt and deception overshadowed Linda's body. Now she wasn't sure that she was doing the right thing. She wondered what Joe's reaction would be when he found out that she had a DNA test done on their child.

Grace Jones was sitting in her living room when her phone

rang. She picked it up and heard a familiar voice. "Linda, what are you doing this morning?"

"Mother, I've got to make a decision and I don't know what to do!"

"What kind of decision?"

"I've got everything I need for the DNA test. Should I go ahead with it or not?"

"Linda, I'm your mother, but I'm not God. However, I do have my own opinion about what you should do."

"What is your opinion?"

"Like I told you before, if I were you I wouldn't want to go through the rest of my life without knowing who little Joe's father was. If you're asking me for my opinion, that's what it is. Has Joe left on his trip yet?"

"Yes, he left about a half hour ago. Mother, I've got to go now, but I'll let you know what I decide."

It was three o'clock in the afternoon when Linda's doorbell rang. She answered it to see an elderly woman standing on the porch. "May I help you?" Linda asked softly.

"I'm hoping so. Is this where Mr. Joe Wilson lives?"

"Yes, it certainly is. My name is Linda Wilson, I'm Joe's wife. Please come inside."

"Mrs. Wilson, my name is Grace Turner."

"Oh, my goodness, I recognize you now from a segment on television, you're Mr. Jim Turner's wife."

"Widow is more like it."

"Please have a seat Mrs. Turner. May I get you something to drink?"

"No thank you, I'm not a bit thirsty. Mrs. Wilson, the sheriff's office told me that your husband discovered my husband's body in the river."

"Yes, Mrs. Turner, I'm afraid he did. I'm so sorry about your husband's death."

"I appreciate that, Mrs. Wilson. Is your husband at home?"

"No, he won't be back for three or four more days. He's attending some kind of meeting for his company. Is there something that I can tell him for you?"

"I brought over his check."

"Check! What kind of check, Mrs. Turner?"

"I was offering a three thousand dollar award for anyone that found him. I was hoping he wouldn't be dead when he was found."

"Mrs. Turner, as much as I appreciate the offer there is absolutely no way that my husband would accept any reward money for finding your husband."

Tears came into Mrs. Turner's eyes. "They got those dirty rascals that killed my husband! They deserve the same punishment they gave to Jim."

"Mrs. Turner, please have a seat." She sat down alongside Linda.

"Mrs. Turner, what actually took place the day of the robbery?"

"It was eight o'clock at night, I had just gone into the back of our building where our apartment is located. Jim had closed the front door to the store. He was removing money from his cash drawer when a cement block was thrown through a store window. At this time I was inside my kitchen. I heard the window crash, and I started looking at our surveillance monitor. I could see everything that was going on."

"What did you see?"

"A man standing outside the broken window with a shotgun made Jim open the front door. Three men came into the store, one had a shotgun and the other two had some kind of pistols. The one with the shotgun stuffed the cash back into the cash register. He told one of the men to get the cash register. He asked Jim if there was any more money in the house. He said that was all the money we had, except for what was in the bank. They were about to come into my apartment when a car pulled into the parking lot. Seeing that the store was closed the car drove off. Those men made my husband take out his car keys, and then they fled out the store, taking Jim with them."

"Mrs. Turner, please let me get you something to drink. I have orange juice, ice tea, milk and bottled water."

"I'll have a bottle of water."

Linda hurried back with the water for Mrs. Turner. "Did the law tell you how your husband was killed?"

"Yes, I'm afraid they did. They shot my poor husband five times before throwing his body into the river." Mrs. Turner broke down and started crying. Linda placed her arms around her shoulder. The heart-broken woman looked up at Linda with great sadness. "Jim is gone, I have no children, no relatives, no one that cares whether I live or die! I don't know what I'm going to do!"

"Mrs. Turner, my husband and I will always be your friend. You can visit with us anytime you want to."

She wiped her eyes with her handkerchief. "Mrs. Wilson, you don't know how much I appreciate you saying that. Now I've got to sell that business of mine. I don't ever intend to open it up again. I paid Ronnie Davenport to board up the broken window."

"Mrs. Turner, if you sell your business that will include your apartment as well. Do you have another house that you can live in?"

"No, Mrs. Wilson, I really don't. As a matter of fact, I hadn't thought about that."

"How about just calling me Linda? I tell you what, Mrs. Turner after you sell your business Joe and I will help you find an apartment somewhere close to our house. That way it won't be inconvenient for you and us to visit each other. Since we're friends now, I guarantee you that Joe will never let anyone scare you again."

"Uh oh, I hear a baby crying."

"Yes, we have a little boy named Joseph Edward Wilson, Jr. Do you love children, Mrs. Turner?"

"I love children!"

"Perhaps when we go on some of our trips you might like to come along with us."

"Yes, Linda, I would be thrilled to go with you and your family. Well, I do have to be going. You're about the nicest and most gracious person that I have ever met. I can go home now knowing that someone really cares about me. I don't feel so alone anymore."

Linda Wilson left little Joe with her mother the next morning. She was on her way to a DNA testing location. The only way she could get a blood sample from her baby was to prick his finger with a small needle. She cried when she placed a ball of cotton against his tiny finger. Joe's bloody shirt was in the trunk of her car along with the cotton ball. Her intention was to find out once and for all who her baby's father was. She was hoping and praying that Joe wouldn't call and ask what she was doing. Linda tried to stay under the speed limit, fearing that she might have to explain everything to her husband if she got a speeding ticket.

Finding Morganton Genetics would not be a problem for Linda. She programmed the address into her GPS prior to leaving home. Her only concern now is whether a paternity test is the right thing to do. Linda is already experiencing a sense of guilt and betrayal by doing something behind Joe's back. Her mind starts to wander, what if William Davis is the father? Would it be fair to let him know, she was thinking? What about Joe, should I tell him the truth if it's William's child? All at once she pulled off to the side of the road; she turned off her engine. She reached for her cell phone and dialed her mother's number. "Mother, I'm halfway to Morganton Genetics, but I'm confused about what I should do."

"What do you mean—confused?"

"I'm thinking about turning around and coming home."

"Linda Wilson, don't you dare come home until you do what's necessary to find out who the father of my grandchild is! You pricked his little finger to get a sample of blood! Now, do what you're supposed to do and quit thinking about consequences of knowing the truth!" Grace turned off her phone.

"Mother, who were you talking to?" Doris asked, walking into the room.

"I didn't hear you drive up."

"That's because I have a quiet running car. You sounded upset a little while ago, who were you talking to?"

"I was talking to your sister."

"Why are you mad with Linda?"

"Doris, it's something rather personal between me and your sister."

"Well, if it involves my sister I think I have a right to know what it is!"

"Linda went somewhere to get a paternity test! You insisted that I tell you! Linda didn't want me to tell anyone! Doris, you must not tell anyone about this!"

"She doesn't know who the father of her child is?"

"The child's father is William Davis or Joe Wilson; it's no one else's."

"Mother, does Joe know about this situation?"

"Linda told him that she wasn't sure whose baby it was. Joe accepted that fact at the time she told him, and said he didn't want a paternity test. He was willing to love little Joe whether he was the father or not."

"Then why is she getting a paternity test? Why not leave the situation status quo?"

"Doris, it doesn't make a lick of sense for Linda and Joe to go through the rest of their lives not knowing who little Joe's father is! It's not fair for little Joe, either! Later in life there could be potential health issues for little Joe, depending on who his father is. I'm talking about inherited traits. Linda is doing the right thing."

"What will Joe say about all this?"

"We'll have to wait and see about that."

It was a welcomed relief for Linda when she parked her car in the Morganton Genetics parking lot. She opened the trunk of her car and removed the two plastic bags containing the blood samples. After closing her trunk she headed toward the front door of the building.

Once inside the building, she walked to the counter where a lady was working with her computer. "May I help you?"

"Yes, I want a paternity test accomplished to see if one particular man is the father of a baby."

"Please have a seat. Is this your baby that we're talking about?"

"Yes, it's my baby. His name is Joseph Edward Wilson, Jr."

"Did you bring the baby with you?"

"No, but I have a sample of his blood on a cotton ball."

"Is this particular man you mentioned with you?"

"No, he's not with me, but I have his tee shirt that has blood on it?" She handed one of the bags to the receptionist.

"This is getting interesting by the second. Who is the man that owned this bloody tee shirt?"

"He's my husband."

"If I may ask, how did he happen to get blood on his tee shirt?"

"It happened on a fishing trip. Lady, please don't make me sorry for coming here!"

"What is your name?"

"Linda Wilson."

"Is that Miss or Mrs.?"

"It's Mrs."

"Mrs. Wilson, I'm sorry for asking so many questions, but it's the law that we ask them. Where is the blood sample for the baby?"

"It's on a cotton ball in this other plastic bag." Linda handed the bag to her. "Remember, the tee shirt has my husband's blood, and the cotton ball has my baby's blood on it."

"You don't have any other blood samples?"

"No, I only have these two. All I want to know is one thing—is Joe Wilson the father of my baby? I don't want to, or need to know anything else." Linda handed the lady the two plastic bags.

"I'll need for you to fill out these forms so we'll know where to send the test results."

"How much is this going to cost me?"

"The cost is three hundred and fifty dollars." Linda counted out three hundred and fifty dollars. She handed it to the lady. "By the time you get through filling out those forms I'll have your receipt prepared."

Ten minutes later Linda was back at the counter with the forms filled out. The lady at the counter handed her the payment receipt. "I only have one question, how long before I will receive the test results in my mail?"

"Maybe between seven to ten days."

Linda headed for home. She felt like a heavy burden had been lifted off her shoulders.

Chapter 25

"**M**r. Cyrus, I see you're reading another letter," said Bill Whitley, one of his renters.

"Yes, it's from my good friend Joe Wilson. He lives in Adamsville, along with his wife and baby. I receive two or three letters each month from Joe and Linda. They're mighty fine people. They were here a little over a year ago. He says in the letter here that he's going to some kind of seminar in a couple days. He and his family are coming here at the end of the month. I'm very anxious to see them and their baby! Joe is bringing a very special friend that he wants me to meet. I have no idea who the friend might be."

"I see you don't have the honeymoon cabin for rent."

"I'm holding it open for Joe and his family."

"Mr. Cyrus, I see a twinkle in your eye each time you mention the name Joe Wilson. Why is he so special to you?"

"Well, it's quite simple."

"How is that?"

"He reminds me of someone that I've never known."

"Mr. Cyrus, if you're trying to confuse me, you just did."

"I'll make it simple for you. Joe Wilson is like the son that I never had. I see in him all the qualities that I would want in my own son. In fact, his wife is just as nice as he is. I like them both an awful lot."

*   *   *   *

Linda was in her wash room doing laundry when Joe peeped into the room and yelled, "I'm home!"

"Good lord, Joe Wilson! You scared me half to death! When did you get back from your trip?"

He looked at his watch, and then said, "One and a half minutes ago," he answered, smiling.

"I see you're still a comedian."

"Well, you wouldn't have it any other way. How about giving me a big, juicy, sloppy kiss?"

"Maybe we should defer the sloppy part." Joe placed his arms around her neck. He kissed her gently on her lips. "Perhaps a little sloppiness might be in order, kiss me like you're glad to be home." He gave it all he had with the next kiss.

"Was that better?"

"Yes, it certainly was. Now go get my shoes."

"What happened to your shoes?"

"That last kiss blew them off my feet," she laughed.

"Now, who is the comedian—you or me?" Joe smiled.

"Joe, guess how old little Joe is today?"

"Let me think, —he's three months old."

"No, no, no, he's three and a half months old today. We're going to celebrate his birthday tonight."

"Linda, the celebration sounds real good, but he lacks eight and a half months from having a real birthday."

"We won't let a little formality like that hinder us from giving little Joe a birthday party."

"Alright, let's go see my little buckaroo!" They went into the living room. Little Joe started smiling when he saw his parents. A big smile overshadowed Joe's face as he looked down at his little son.

"Little Joe, say dada to your father," said Linda. Little Joe smiled, but that was all. Joe made a few funny faces at his son trying to get him to laugh.

"Daddy, did you hear what little Joe said?"

"No, I don't believe I did."

"You must not have been listening. He said, 'Hello, daddy.'

"He did?"

"Of course, he did," said Linda, teasing her husband.

"Well, I'll have to get one of those things."

"What things are you talking about, Joe?"

"A hearing aid," they burst into laughter.

"He's got the bluest eyes I've ever seen on a baby," said Linda. Moments later she realized what she just said. It was very evident to her that her husband was no longer smiling. "Joe, I'm sorry. I shouldn't have said that."

He wiped a tear from his right eye, and then he remarked, "Little Joe does have pretty eyes."

He reached down and picked up the baby. "Little Joe, you've got a pretty little smile as well as pretty eyes."

"Joe, he sure does like to play with that little rubber ball you bought him. I'm glad it's not any smaller though."

"Why is that?"

"Sometimes, little Joe thinks it's a hamburger or something. He wants to eat it."

"Linda, we're going to the mountains at the end of the month. You haven't forgotten about that, have you?"

"Of course not."

"What did your mother say when you asked her to come along?"

"She didn't seem to be interested at first, but I told her how important it was for you that she go with us. She finally said that she would go. Are you sure your father is going to let you off from work for a whole week?"

"Yes, I'm quite sure. We'll have a great time. Besides, Mr. Cyrus is letting us stay in the honeymoon cabin. Every time I think about us staying there I get real excited!"

"How excited do you get?"

"Tonight I'll explain it to you in much greater detail," he laughed.

It was the last Saturday of the month. Joe and Linda's car was packed with luggage, including everything needed for Little Joe. Linda and Little Joe were in the backseat as Joe drove toward Grace Jones's house. Linda smiled at Little Joe as he lay in his car seat. The baby smiled back at her. "Linda, what did you do while I was gone?" Joe asked.

"What do you mean?" Linda asked, suspiciously.

"Well, did you go shopping? Did you visit with your mother, or whatever?"

"I just did my normal routine, take care of the baby, wash clothes, and watch a little television."

"How was your trip?"

"It was rather boring for me since I don't drink, gamble or flirt with wild women," he laughed.

"There are three words you just said that I don't like."

"What three words?"

"Flirt, wild women," she smiled.

"Linda Wilson, you know you're the only woman that interests me."

"Joe, do you know what I like about what you just said?"

"No, what?"

"Everything!"

Joe drove his car into Grace's yard. Linda and the baby stayed in the car. Joe rang the doorbell. Grace answered the door. "I see you have your luggage ready to go. I'll carry it to the trunk of my car."

"Thank you Joe. I'll be to the car as soon as I ensure all the electricity has been turned off."

"Mother, you look very pretty today," said Linda, as her mother got into the front seat of the car.

"Thank you. Joe, how long does this trip take?"

"About four hours, but we'll stop for lunch, so it could take a little longer. Mrs. Jones, I'm thrilled that you're going with us to the mountains."

"Why is that, Joe?"

"Mrs. Jones, it is one of the most beautiful places that I have ever seen. Right behind our cabin is a gigantic lake. There are ducks, geese and some other kind of water birds that you can see on the lake."

"Mother, there's a large fish pond there, too. You can actually see the fish swimming in the pond."

"Well, I'm sure it's quite nice there. I'm looking forward to seeing all that beautiful scenery that you two have told me about."

"Joe, we've been on the road for two hours now," said Linda. "It's bathroom time, and while we're stopped we'll have lunch."

"Mrs. Jones, what kind of food do you like?"

"As long as it's not snake, turtle, alligator, shark, sushi, catfish, or frog legs I'll probably eat it."

"Mrs. Jones, you've never eaten catfish?" Joe asked.

"I've never eaten a cat either," she smiled.

"You should try some catfish, it's delicious."

"You eat the catfish; I'll stick with a sirloin or a t-bone."

"Well, up ahead is Vickie's Country Kitchen. Linda, how does that sound?"

"It sounds fine—especially if they have a good clean restroom."

"Good afternoon," said the waitress, seeing Joe and his party sitting at a table. "May I get your drink orders?" Each of them told the waitress their preferences in something to drink.

When she returned with their drinks the waitress looked toward Little Joe. "That is a beautiful baby! Look at those gorgeous blue eyes! Mister, I see you've got brown eyes. Perhaps this little fellow got his blue eyes from his mother or the grandparents."

Joe hung his head downward for a few seconds. Linda and Grace were well aware of what he may be thinking. "Waitress, I believe everyone is ready to order," said Grace.

"What are you ordering, Joe?" He seemed to be puzzled about something. "Joe, I asked you what you were ordering."

"I'm sorry, Linda, I didn't hear you. Waitress, I'm having today's special." Linda realized that no matter how much Joe loved their baby he still had that big question on his mind, who is little Joe's father?"

It was two hours later when Joe's car pulled into the parking lot of the mountainous retreat.

Mr. Cyrus Owens was standing by the lake observing a family of mallard ducks as they paddled along. "Linda, look over by the lake, it's Mr. Cyrus Owens. Mrs. Jones, that's the man I was telling you about. He's one of the nicest individuals I've ever met."

"Does he work here?" Grace asked.

Joe winked at Linda, and then he said, "Yes, Mrs. Jones, he works here. Now, isn't it beautiful up here?"

"It certainly is!" Mr. Owens happened to turn around and saw Linda and Joe standing by their car. Joe wasted no time heading toward him.

"You're right on time, Joe!"

"Yes sir, I told you that we would be here." Joe shook his hands, and then he gave Mr. Cyrus a hug. "Walk with me to my car, Mr. Owens; I want you to see Linda and little Joe. Also, I brought a dear friend of mine."

At the car, Linda hugged Mr. Owens' neck. "Sir, this lady here is Grace Jones, she's my mother."

He removed his hat. "Mrs. Jones, it's a pleasure meeting you. Linda, you or Joe never mentioned in your letters how beautiful Mrs. Jones is."

Grace had a big smile on her face. "Thank you very much, Mr. Owens, I appreciate your compliment."

"Now, I want to see little Joe," said Cyrus. He saw the baby sitting in the car seat. "He's a beautiful baby boy. I know you two are very proud of him."

"I understand from my son-in-law that you work here," said Grace.

Mr. Owens feeling a little confused concerning the question, he looked toward Joe, and then he answered, "Yes, I work here a good deal of the time."

"Do the owners treat you nice?"

"Yes, Mrs. Jones, I should say they do. Joe, why don't you take everyone to your cabin so they can get settled in?"

"I'll do that. Mr. Owens would you do us the honor of having dinner with us this evening?"

"By all means, but provided you let it be my treat."

"That wouldn't be fair, Mr. Owens," Joe smiled.

"Why is that?"

"I asked first," he laughed.

"What time would you like to go to dinner?" Cyrus asked.

"We'll go at six o'clock this evening. We'll park in front of the office about that time, but soon as we get unpacked I'll be back to talk with you some more."

"I'm looking forward to that. Mrs. Jones, I do hope you have a pleasant stay here."

"Thank you, Mr. Owens, I appreciate that." Joe drove his car a couple hundred yards to their cabin.

"My goodness, what a beautiful cabin this is!" Grace said, excitedly. "On the other hand, it's not a cabin at all! This is a house! Linda, this place is bigger than my own home!"

"Wait until you see the bathrooms, Mother? There's five in this cabin."

"Why are there so many?"

"I don't know, but there are five bedrooms, also. Soon as we straighten up a little, we'll go outside and look at the Koi pond. Mother, what do you think about Mr. Owens?"

"What do you mean?"

"Well, do you think he's as nice as we said he was?"

"Yes, he seemed very nice. He's, also, a very handsome man."

"Did you notice that?"

"Well, I'm not blind. Where did Joe get off to?"

"He's at the cabin office talking to Mr. Owens."

"I wonder how long he's been working here."

"Well, at dinner tonight you can ask him. Would you believe there's fifteen cabins or more scattered throughout this general area."

"I guess different people own these cabins you're talking about."

"From what I hear the same organization owns all the cabins, the lake, and numerous houses around this part of the country. I think the same company owns businesses, and more properties in and around Mountain Bluff."

"If the companies own that much they certainly should pay Mr. Owens a decent salary."

"That's something else that you can remind him about during dinner this evening."

Joe and Mr. Owens were sitting under the shade of a mimosa tree. One of the attendants working in the rental office took two glasses and a pitcher of cold lemonade to them. "Mr. Owens, what do you think about Linda's mother?"

"She seems very nice. Joe, what did you and Linda tell her about me?"

"The honest truth, Mr. Owens, she thinks you're employed here at the rental office."

"That's very good. How old is Mrs. Jones?"

"She doesn't look it, but she's fifty-five years old."

"Mrs. Jones and I are about the same age. You say her husband has been dead for about a year now?"

"Yes, maybe a little longer."

"Mrs. Jones is a very shapely lady."

"You noticed that, too, Mr. Owens?"

"Believe it or not, I've still got outstanding vision. Joe, whatever you do—don't let her know that I'm worth millions of dollars."

"I promise, Mr. Owens. Well, I'll get back to the cabin so you can be ready for our dinner this evening."

Joe walked back toward his cabin. He saw Linda and Mrs. Jones looking out across the lake.

"Mrs. Jones, how do you like it here?"

"It's beautiful here, Joe. I'm so glad that you brought me with you. Linda, where is the baby?"

"He's asleep in the crib."

"I'll go watch little Joe. Linda, why don't you and Mrs. Jones walk over to the rental office and get us some soft drinks? There are several vending machines in that office."

"Mother, are you going to walk with me to the office?"

"Sure, I'll go with you."

Mr. Owens saw Linda and her mother walking toward the rental office. He hurried inside and told the two employees to go take a thirty minute break somewhere. Mr. Owens was standing behind the office counter when Linda and her mother came inside the rental office. "Mr. Owens, how do you like your job here?"

"I enjoy meeting people, Mrs. Jones."

"Linda told me that some large organization owns all this property around here. In fact, according to her, that same organization owns the lake, too."

"I believe your daughter is correct, Mrs. Jones."

Linda gathered up a half dozen soft drinks from the cooler. She laid seven dollars on the counter to pay for the drinks. "I'll pay for the drinks, Mrs. Wilson."

"Mr. Owens, Linda should pay for them. You shouldn't spend part of your salary to pay for other people's stuff."

"That's okay, Mrs. Jones, I certainly can pay for six drinks," he smiled. He handed Linda her money back.

Joe drove his car in front of the rental office at six o'clock that evening. Mr. Owens walked outside; he quickly noticed that there was no room in Joe's car for him to sit. "Joe, I'll follow you in my car. What restaurant are we going to?"

"If you don't mind I would like to eat at Daisy Mae's Country Kitchen. Is that okay with you?"

"That's a fantastic choice."

"Mrs. Jones, would you mind riding with Mr. Owens?" Joe asked. "I feel awkward having him ride there by himself."

"No, I don't mind. Will that be okay with you Mr. Owens?"

"It will be my pleasure." Mrs. Jones exited Joe's car and then got into the front seat of Mr. Owens car. "You've got a beautiful car, Mr. Owens."

"Thank you very much." They followed Joe's car out of the parking lot. "May I call you Grace?"

"Yes, that will be just fine."

"In that case, just call me Cyrus."

"Cyrus, Joe and Linda sure do like you a lot."

"I like them a lot, too."

"Have you ever been married?"

"Yes, I was married to a wonderful woman, but she died some years ago. It broke my heart when that happened."

"I'm surprised you haven't remarried."

"Grace, for a long time following my wife's death I wasn't interested in a relationship with a woman. Joe tells me that your husband passed away a little over a year ago. I know it must have been tough on you."

"Yes, it certainly was. He and I were very close. I've got two wonderful daughters, a grandchild and Joe, but my life is still filled with loneliness. Cyrus, do you know what I'm talking about?"

"Yes, Grace, I know exactly what you're talking about. Well, we're at Daisy Mae's Country Kitchen." He parked his car next to Joe's vehicle. "Grace, I enjoyed our little talk while driving here. Would you do me the honor of riding back with me?"

"Yes, Cyrus, I will do that."

He hurried around to the passenger side of his car, he opened Grace's door. "Thank you," she said.

"Mother, you're going to really love this place. Joe and I ate here when we were on our honeymoon."

"Linda, I see little Joe is wide awake," said Mr. Owens.

"He wants to see what's going on around here," she responded.

"Mrs. Jones, how did you like Mr. Owens car?" Joe asked.

"It's very nice. I could never afford a car like that. I'll bet Cyrus had to do a lot of saving before he bought that car." Shaking his head and smiling, Joe gave Mr. Owens a wink.

Chapter 26

Joe and his party had finished eating, but they were still sitting at their table. "Mrs. Jones, how did you enjoy your food?" Joe asked.

"It was simply delicious. I'm a very good cook, but I couldn't have done better than Daisy Mae's Country Kitchen. Cyrus, I bet you eat here quite often."

"I do, as a matter of fact. The food here is always delicious. I see little Joe has fallen asleep."

"Joe, I guess we're ready to go soon as you pay the bill," said Linda.

"I'll be more than happy to use my card, Joe."

"Thanks anyway, Mr. Owens, but this is our treat."

"Linda, I'm going to ride back to our cabin with Cyrus."

"That's fine, Mother. Mr. Cyrus, I'll bet my mother would like to see that big, beautiful house that you showed Joe and me on our first trip. Mother, he said it was owned by a very rich man. In fact, that same man owns the lake, at least fifteen cabins around the lake, and business properties in several states."

"I, definitely, would be afraid of him!"

"Why would you be afraid of someone like that, Mother?"

"I wouldn't even know how to talk around someone that rich. I would feel very uncomfortable around someone that had that much money."

"Why would you, Mrs. Jones?" Joe asked. "Just because someone is rich doesn't mean that they think they're better than you."

"I know that, but I've always lived by modest means. I'm afraid I might feel a little insecure around someone with that much money. Anyway, who is this rich man you've been talking about?"

"I believe his last name is Billingsley," said Joe. Linda nearly knocked over her glass of tea, trying to keep from laughing at what Joe said.

"Grace, it is a beautiful house, would you like to drive by it?"

"Yes, Cyrus, I would like to see this house."

"Joe, Linda, would you pardon us if we took off now to see the house?"

"That will be just fine, Mr. Owens. Linda and I are about to leave anyway."

Cyrus opened the passenger door so Grace could get inside the car. His mannerly ways had not gone unnoticed by Grace.

"That big house is not very far from where you all are staying," said Cyrus. "Grace, how do you like it here?"

"I like it a great deal. It's so beautiful here."

About ten minutes later, Cyrus stopped his car on the side

of the road. He pointed to a well-lighted, gigantic sized brick house, located at the end of a paved driveway. "Grace, how do you like that house?"

"It's beautiful, Cyrus. I've never even been in a house like that! The man that owns that house must be very, very rich! Have you ever been inside that house?"

"As a matter of fact, I have. As you walk into the foyer there's a very large chandelier hanging overhead. The brilliance and elegance of the lighted chandelier is simply amazing."

"I would hate to be that man's wife!"

"Why is that, Grace?"

"A house that big, how would I ever be able to keep it clean?"

"You wouldn't have to. A man that rich would be able to afford maids or a butler."

"Well then, married to a man like that wouldn't be so bad after all, but I would never marry someone just because they had a lot of money. Cyrus, have you ever dreamed of having a house like the one we're looking at?"

"Yes, Grace, I had that dream when I was a very young man."

"You don't need to be rich to find yourself a nice woman companion. You're a very handsome man. There are plenty of women that would like to be part of your life."

"Do you really think so?"

"I most certainly do! Maybe we should head back toward the cabin. Looking at this beautiful house is getting to be depressing."

"Why is that?"

"The house is very beautiful, but I couldn't even pay the utility bill on it."

Mr. Owens stopped his car in front of Joe's cabin. He got out, and then opened Grace's door.

"Cyrus, I really did enjoy myself this evening. I really appreciate you taking me by that rich man's house. Now I know why Joe and Linda like you so much."

"Thank you, Grace; I had a wonderful time as well. I have access to the company boat, how about all of us going for a ride on the lake tomorrow?"

"I'm a little afraid of the water. Is this a fairly good sized boat?"

"Goodness yes! This boat can carry fifteen people very comfortably."

"Cyrus, I would love to ride on the lake, but are you sure you can take off from work?"

"I believe it will be okay for me to do that. May I walk you to the door?"

"Thank you. That would be very nice." They stopped on the porch.

"Goodnight, Grace, I'll see you tomorrow."

Joe and Linda's eyes lit up when Grace walked inside the room. "What are you two looking at?"

"Mother, did you see that colossal sized house?"

"Yes, it was very, very beautiful! Cyrus said that rich man had servants working there. Guess what, he's taking us on the lake tomorrow. Apparently, his employer trusts him with their boat."

"Mrs. Jones, did you have a good time this evening?" Joe asked.

"No, I had a wonderful time! Cyrus is a charming man! I'm concerned about him though."

"Mother, why is that?"

"I hope we don't cause him to lose his job at the rental office." Joe looked at Linda and winked. "Mrs. Jones, I don't think Mr. Owens is going to lose his job. He's been with his outfit far too long for that to happen. I'm sure the company knows what a valuable man he is. Are you glad you came with us?"

"I certainly am! I won't get a wink of sleep tonight!"

"Why won't you be able to sleep tonight, Mother?"

"Too much excitement I guess."

"Mrs. Jones, I couldn't help but notice how Mr. Owens was looking at you during dinner. I'm not an expert on such matters, but I believe he likes you."

"You do! I mean—you do. What makes you think he likes me?"

"Well, for one thing you're a very attractive lady."

"Linda, did you hear what Joe said about me?"

"Yes, Mother, Joe has always said you were a gorgeous looking woman. Since the subject has come up, how do you like Mr. Owens?"

"I think he's very nice."

"You did use the term 'very'. Does that mean you like him?"

"Linda, I've known him for only one day, but yes—I like him. He's sweet, kind, mannerly, and he's good looking, so why wouldn't I like him?"

It was nine o'clock in the morning. Joe, Linda, Grace and Little Joe were at the boat dock. They were looking around for Mr. Owens, thinking that he would be there on a rather small boat.

"Hello there!" Mr. Owens called, standing on a 32-foot Tiara 3200 open boat.

"My goodness, Cyrus, are you telling me that we're going to ride on that beautiful ship?" Grace asked, excitedly.

"The answer is yes, but it's not a ship. It's just a boat. You nice people walk down the boardwalk to the boat and I'll help you onto the Lucky Lady." He assisted each one as they crossed from the boardwalk to the boat.

"My goodness, Mr. Owens, this is a gorgeous boat!" Joe said.

"Cyrus, are you sure you know how to drive this big thing?" Grace asked.

"Yes, I have a little bit of experience running this boat."

"Mr. Owens, where does that little stairway lead to?" Linda asked.

"Oh, that leads to a sitting area or sleeping area. This boat sleeps four very comfortably. Well, let's get underway. Joe, if you will undo the anchor rope we'll go for a scenic drive."

Mr. Owens turned on the powerful engine, and then placed it in gear. "Linda, you can take little Joe down below if you like. Grace, how do you like this toy?"

"It's a beautiful boat, Cyrus. I'm surprised that rich man will let you use it like this."

"I'll be honest with you, Grace, that old rich man is not all bad. He owns two more boats down at the beach much larger than this one. Would you like to sit in the seat next to me?"

"I will if I won't be in your way."

"Heavens no, you won't be in my way. Come on up. Joe, I brought fishing equipment and plenty of bait. I'll take you to where the big ones are."

"Mother, look over there!"

"I see them, dear! Aren't those deer beautiful? Cyrus, those four deer are standing in the edge of the water, but they're not afraid of us or this boat."

"That's because hunting is totally prohibited around here. Grace, look to your right about sixty yards."

"What in the world is that thing?"

"It's a river otter."

"Mr. Owens, if it's a river otter why is it in this lake?"

"Linda, that's a good question, but I'm afraid I don't have the answer. Grace, we're not going very fast, would you guide the boat for a minute?"

"Me! Guide the boat! What do I do?"

"Just hold your hand on the steering wheel like you would your automobile." She grabbed the steering wheel. He turned around toward Joe and Linda. "Joe, those two large coolers contain drinks and our food. The large red one has all kinds of prepared food for our lunch. The large blue one has a variety of drinks, orange juice and sweetened tea. Feel free to eat or drink whenever you all choose to." Mr. Owens turned back around. "Grace, how are you doing?"

"This is the most excitement I've ever had. When do you have to take this boat back to the dock?"

"There's no real hurry for me to take it back to the dock. Linda, how is little Joe doing?"

"He's doing just fine, Mr. Owens. Wow, a fish jumped clear out of the water! Joe, did you see that?"

"I sure did. I believe it was a large mouth bass. Mr. Owens, are there some big fish in this lake?"

"Yes, I've caught some fish out of here that topped thirteen pounds. A friend of mine caught a catfish out of this lake that weighed thirty four pounds."

"Cyrus, don't you think you should take the wheel?"

"Grace, you're doing just fine. By the way, I've noticed something about you."

"You have?"

"Yes. You have the prettiest smile that I've seen in years." Joe winked at Linda, and then he gave her thumbs up.

"Mr. Owens, how soon will we get to that fishing spot that you were talking about?"

"Joe, I'm glad that you mentioned that because we're there now." He cut the engine. "Grace, pull that blue lever down, please." She lowered it and the anchor dropped slowly until it was lying on the bottom of the lake.

"Cyrus, what did I just do by pushing that lever down?"

"You dropped the anchor."

"Goodness that was very easy. How do we get the anchor back up when we're ready?"

"Reverse action. Moving the lever in the opposite direction brings the anchor back up. Joe, there are several reels and rods in that compartment next to your right leg. Open it up and I'll help you get the ladies equipment ready to fish with. Grace, I'll rig your pole up first. Do you have a preference as to what kind of bait you would like to use? I have crickets, fishing worms, shrimp and cut bait."

"I'll use whatever you put on my hook."

"In that case, I'll put a fishing worm on your hook." He handed her a light weight fishing tackle. "All you have to do is let your weight touch bottom, and then wind your line in about a foot. This far out I seldom use a bobber. Linda, how are you doing?"

"I'm doing just fine, Mr. Owens. I've already had a bite, but I didn't hang the fish."

"Oh, my goodness," Grace remarked. "Cyrus, I've hung something big!"

"You're doing just fine. Hold your pole up a little. That's it! Uh-oh, he's taking your line out! I'll tighten your drag a little." He reached around her to get to the drag. Momentarily, Grace looked into his eyes. He stared back at her for a couple of seconds.

"Mother, your line is still going out!"

Cyrus tightened the drag on her reel a little. "Reel fast, Grace, he's headed back this way! That's it! That's it! Keep your pole up some! Joe, get the fish net. Your mother-in-law has hung into a whopper. Keep winding your line in. There he is! Goodness gracious, Grace you've got yourself a nine pound bass, maybe ten pounds." Using the net, Joe lifted the fish inside the boat. "Linda, I see you've got your camera around your neck. How about taking a picture of your mother's fish? I'll hold him up so he'll show up real good."

"Mother, stand beside Mr. Owens as he holds your fish up." She snapped several pictures of her mother and Mr. Owens standing together.

"Cyrus, will it be okay if we release the fish?"

"Of course it will, Grace I do that all the time."

"Linda, you and Joe keep fishing, I'm going to take Little Joe below. It looks like he's wide awake now."

"Mother, are you sure?"

"Yes, I want to see what it looks down there anyway."

"In that case, I'll escort you down there," said Mr. Owens. Grace took the baby down below. Mr. Owens followed her.

"How do you like it down here?"

"It's beautiful, Cyrus. I had no idea that a boat could look so attractive."

"Please excuse me for asking, but you have tears in your eyes. Why?"

"Cyrus, I'm not sure myself."

"Is it something that I said or did?"

"No, it's none of that. You're a wonderful man! Maybe you're too wonderful."

"Is that all bad?"

"It's not bad at all, but—."

"But, what, Grace?"

"I've only known you for two days, but it seems like it's been much longer than that. I'm sorry; I'm so confused I don't know what I'm saying." Tears slid down her face.

Mr. Owens moved next to her. "Grace, I wouldn't hurt your feelings for anything in the world." He placed his hand on hers. "It has only been two days, but already I like you a lot. You are the woman that was mentioned in my dream months ago."

"Cyrus, what woman in your dream are you talking about?"

"Linda wrote me a letter about a week after her father died telling me the sad news. The fact that she had lost her father really did upset me. If I had known about it sooner I would have attended the funeral. Anyway, I placed the letter inside the envelope and laid it on a small table near my bed. I guess it was about one o'clock in the morning when I had this dream. Well, it was more like a nightmare. All at once a glowing figure appeared before me. In my dream I tried to scream, but I couldn't. I tried to wake up, but I couldn't! It was then that a man's voice said that in the months to come I would meet a wonderful lady that would bring happiness back to my life. I wanted to ask the apparition how he knew, but I couldn't open my mouth. As if the apparition could read my mind, he answered, 'For only I know the purity of this woman, and what I say will come to pass.' By now, I was no longer afraid. I wanted to ask this figure how he knew it would come to pass, but I couldn't. Again the apparition said, 'There will be signs that will let you know. Two people you already love. Third person, you will love at first sight. The fourth one is the woman in your dream. You will love her—she will love you. Be good to her—for I will never come again.' I strained as hard as I could to ask him who he was, but my mouth wouldn't open. Right out of the clear blue he answered, 'She will know.' Grace, the apparition disappeared and I've never seen it again. Don't you see I love Joe, Linda, and little Joe? That's three; you have got to be the fourth one. Grace, do you know who it was that came to me in my dream?"

She nodded her head, indicating yes.

"Who was it, Grace?"

She squeezed against his hand. Tears slid down her face as she looked Cyrus in his eyes. "It was my husband."

"How is everything down there?" Joe asked loudly, from upper deck.

"Grace, is everything alright?"

"Yes, Cyrus, everything is just fine."

"Grace, are you the woman mentioned in my dream?"

"Yes, I believe I am."

"Joe, we're doing just fine down here!" Cyrus said. "You and Linda keep on fishing."

"Why are you so sad?"

"Grace, I'm happier than I've been in years."

"If that's so, why do you have tears in your eyes?"

"Because if that apparition was right I'm going to have myself a real family. I'm hoping I'll have myself a wife to go with that family." He rubbed the top of Grace's hand.

Chapter 27

It was their third day in the mountains. Linda was feeding little Joe near the breakfast table. Joe and grace were eating their breakfast. Joe's cell phone rang, it was Mrs. Delores Sweeney. Delores was the wife of Sergeant Horace Sweeney, Joe's military buddy that was shot and killed in Iraq. "Mr. Wilson, I called your house several times, but there was no answer. Fortunately, I had written down your cell phone number as well."

"That's perfectly okay, Mrs. Sweeney. How are Michael and Gail doing?"

"Mr. Wilson, they're doing just fine. I'm calling you for two reasons. First, I want to thank you for your generous check that you sent me a short time ago. However, I did get the money from Horace's insurance policy. As you recall it was a lot of money. I will be more than happy to return your money if you need it."

"No, Mrs. Sweeney, I want you to keep the money and

use it to educate your two children. I promised you and your children that I would always be around if you needed me. Horace and I were the best of friends. I hope that money will help you and your children to have a better life."

"I will never forget how good you have been to me and the children since Horace was killed. I really do appreciate it. Mr. Wilson, I'm getting married again, but I won't have to change my married name."

"Why is that, Mrs. Sweeney?"

"I'm marrying Horace's brother. His name is Alvin. Mr. Wilson, I want you and your wife to come to our wedding."

"When is the wedding?"

"It's in three months from now. You and Mrs. Wilson will come if I send you an invitation, won't you?"

"Yes, Mrs. Sweeney, she and I will come. Congratulations to you and Alvin!"

"Thank you, sir. Goodbye, Mr. Wilson."

"Did I understand that Mrs. Sweeney is getting married?"

"Yes, Linda, she's marrying Alvin Sweeney."

"She's marrying another Sweeney?"

"Yes, he's Horace's brother."

"Joe, I'll bet you gave Mrs. Sweeney your reward money," said Grace.

"Yes."

"Linda, you are one lucky woman."

"Why is that, Mother? Is it because my husband gives other women money?" She asked, laughing.

"No, you silly thing, you're lucky because you're married to a wonderful man. Joe, wouldn't you like to own a big boat like the one Mr. Owens borrowed yesterday?"

"It would be very nice if I had the money needed to run it. It would break my bank account to just fill it up with gas. Mrs. Jones, what are your plans for today?"

"Cyrus has asked me to go dining with him this evening."

"Mother, that sounds like a date!" Linda smiled.

"Do you think I should?"

"Are you asking my opinion?"

"Joe, does your wife have a hearing problem? Linda, I asked you if I should go with Cyrus to dinner."

"Yes, I think you should. Mr. Owens is a very nice gentleman. I don't see how you could even ask me that question. Mother, I believe he likes you a lot. The question is this, how do you like Mr. Owens?"

"I don't know how to answer that. On one hand it seems like I've known him for years, but then again, it's like I'm just getting to know him."

"Mrs. Jones, I believe you like Mr. Owens quite a bit."

"Why do you believe that, Joe?"

"Your eyes and expression is a dead giveaway. He's a wonderful man, Mrs. Jones. I hope you don't let him slip through your fingers. Men like Mr. Owens don't come along very often."

"Mother, Joe is right; you need a man back into your life."

"What would Doris think if I were to get involved with a man?"

"Mother, Doris wanted me to fix you up with Gary Humperdinck a month ago."

"Gary Humperdinck! Just wait until I get home! I wouldn't go three steps with that tobacco-chewing, bow-legged, snaggletooth nitwit! Just wait until I get home!"

"Mother! Mother, tone down a little! Doris didn't say that at all. I just made the whole thing up!" Linda and Joe were laughing like crazy.

"I'm beginning to get the picture now."

"How is that, Mother?"

"Now, I know why I was invited on this trip. You two wanted me to meet Cyrus, didn't you?"

"Mrs. Jones, I'll answer that," said Joe. "The plan truth is—yes, we wanted you to meet Mr. Owens, but only because we both love you. Mr. Owens is a wonderful man, and I truly believe that you and he have matching chemistry. He's a wonderful man that hasn't known a woman in years, but he sees something in you, Mrs. Jones. He sees the same thing that Linda and I see in you. You're a good, sweet, caring, God-fearing woman that loved your husband as much as any woman could have loved their man. Mrs. Jones, it's been over a year, you've got your husband's memory locked inside your heart, but it's time to move on. It's time that you filled that void in your life. Mr. Owens is exactly the man that could and would fill that void. Linda, why are you crying?"

"I'm crying because that was most beautiful thing I have ever heard. I wish Doris could have been listening."

"Mrs. Jones, are you mad with me for saying what I did?"

"No, Joe Wilson, I'm more proud of you now than ever before. Linda, will you help me figure out what I should wear this evening?"

"Mother, I would be happy to."

Linda and her mother were back in the kitchen a few minutes later. "Mrs. Jones, did you determine what you will wear this evening?"

"I did with your wife's help. I've got my clothes laid out on the bed."

"Joe, how come you've got your new pair of slacks and new shoes on this morning?" Linda asked.

"Mr. Owens wants me to ride with him this morning."

"Where are you going?"

"I have no idea, but he did say it was important that I go with him."

"I'll be surprised if Cyrus doesn't lose his job the way he takes off from work," said Grace.

"Mrs. Jones, maybe what he's doing this morning is job related."

"That could very well be."

"It's a beautiful morning; I think I'll walk over to the rental office. Linda, I should be back around noon or shortly thereafter. I'll bring some food when I return. How does some fried chicken, mashed potatoes, string beans and corn on the cob sound?"

"It sounds wonderful, but you left out one item."

"Which item?"

"I want sweetened tea from Daisy Mae's Country Kitchen. That is where you're going to get our food, isn't it?"

"That's right. Well, I'll see everyone after a while." Joe headed out the door. He stopped, momentarily, as he observed a flock of Canadian geese swimming about twenty yards offshore.

Overhead were two grey squirrels playing in the tree tops. The beauty of the landscape had captured his heart as he breathed in the clean morning air.

"Joe, I was just about ready to drive to your cabin."

"It's a beautiful morning; I decided to walk over here. I just saw about twenty Canadian geese out on the lake. That was a beautiful sight to me. I'll need for you to stop at Daisy Mae's Country Kitchen on the way back from our trip. I told Linda that I would bring food when we returned."

"That won't be a problem at all. Nelson, are all the cabins rented now?"

"Yes, they certainly are, Mr. Owens. Excuse my manners, Joe, this is Nelson Whittaker, he's the manager of my cabin rentals. He's been working with me for fifteen years or more. Where, is Clara Jones this morning?"

"She's not feeling well this morning. I told her that I would fill in for her today."

"I hope it's nothing serious."

"She told me it was a migraine headache."

"Joe, we need to leave now to get to my meeting."

Five miles down the road Mr. Owens turned toward Joe. "How is Grace this morning?"

"She's just fine. I believe she's looking forward to yours and her dinner date tonight."

"Splendid! I guess you must know by now that I'm quite fond of Linda's mother. I don't know how you and she have kept my secret for so long about me being rich and all. It's quite obvious that Grace doesn't know about it. I asked you and Linda not to tell her and you didn't. I really appreciate that. Now, I'm wondering what her reaction will be when she finds out the truth about me. At least I'll know she's not interested in me just because of my money."

"Mr. Owens, I don't know what her reaction will be, but I know she would never be interested in a man just because he had a lot of money. I believe she likes you a great deal already.

Her eyes seem to sparkle each time your name is mentioned. In fact, yours and her attraction to each other may be the fastest on record."

"Joe, we're going to Haleyville this morning. I have several businesses there and I'm going to chair a board meeting this morning. I have my reasons for wanting you to attend."

"How much farther is Haleyville?"

"It's about thirty miles from here. The meeting will only take about an hour."

Mr. Owens and Joe were in Haleyville about twenty-five minutes later. Mr. Owens parked his car in a private parking place that had his name on it. Joe couldn't help but notice that the building had Owens's Enterprises written on it in great big letters. They took the elevator to the fifth floor. Mr. Owens and Joe walked down the hallway to a conference room. Five men and three women stood up when they walked into the room. Mr. Owens sat at the end of the table. He motioned for Joe to sit down in a vacant seat next to him. Everyone else took their seats.

"Good morning, ladies and gentlemen. I appreciate your attendance today, especially since some of you had to drive several hours to get here. The very first thing I want to do is introduce my very good friend, Joe Wilson. He's married to a lovely lady and they have a beautiful baby boy. I mentioned his name at our last quarterly board meeting. Joe, please stand up. Now, one by one I want you to come shake hands with Joe because you're going to hear more and more about him as time goes by." Mr. Owens was the last one to shake Joe's hand. "Joe, I would like for you to go downstairs and see Mrs. Julia Lauren, she will be expecting you. I've arranged for you to visit three of our stores here in Haleyville while I conduct this board meeting."

As Joe got on the elevator to go downstairs he wondered what Mr. Owens meant about the board members going to hear more and more about him as time went by. He got off the elevator and walked down the hallway toward the front entrance of the building. Two women were sitting in an office area. A middle-aged woman stood up. "Mr. Wilson, my name is Julia Lauren, I've been expecting you."

"Judy, Mr. Wilson and I will be back after awhile. Mr. Owens wants him to see three of his stores here in Haleyville." They started walking toward the front door. "Mr. Wilson, where is your home?"

"I live in a town named Adamsville."

"What a coincidence. Mr. Owens owns a large department store there."

"I didn't know that! What is the name of the store?"

"Charlotte's Clothing Store. Do you know where it is?"

"Yes! I live within two miles of that gigantic store! In fact, I bought the pants and shoes that I have on from that store. Are you saying that Mr. Owens owns that big store?"

"Yes. The store was named for his wife, Charlotte. Mr. Wilson, not only does he own that store, he owns many stores. Some people think he's a millionaire, but he isn't. Your good friend couldn't be a millionaire."

"Why is that Mrs. Lauren?"

"It's quite simple, Mr. Owens is a billionaire! All three of his stores are in walking distance. We'll go to the nearest one first. It's a large drugstore. The name of it is True-Aide."

"Great day in the morning!"

"What's the matter, Mr. Wilson?"

"This drugstore is bigger than any one we've got in Adamsville. There must be over a million dollars of inventory in this store."

"Mr. Wilson, the inventory would be more than three million dollars in this store. Mr. Owens owns six drugstores named True-Aide. We better hurry along before Mr. Owens gets through with his board meeting. The next store we will stop at is his top of the line clothing store. The name of it is Gallagher's Clothing Store."

They walked two blocks and there was the store. "Mrs. Lauren, don't Mr. Owens own anything that's small?"

"I'm not sure about that since he owns properties in other states." They walked inside and were met by the store manager.

"Mrs. Lauren, this must be Mr. Joe Wilson."

"Indeed it is, Mr. Peterson. Do you have a package for Mr. Wilson?"

"Yes, but I had one of the employees take it to Mr. Owens car already." He extended his hand to Joe. "Sir, it's a real pleasure meeting you. Mr. Owens has said some very nice things about you and your wife, Linda."

"Thank you, I really do appreciate that."

"Mr. Owens helped me pick out two of our nicest suits for you. In fact, he picked out the shirts and ties himself. Mr. Wilson, you're very fortunate to have a friend like Mr. Owens."

"I couldn't agree more."

"Mr. Peterson, we'll have to move along before Mr. Owens gets through with his board meeting."

"I understand, Mrs. Lauren. Mr. Wilson, I'm looking forward to seeing you again."

"Thank you, sir." Mrs. Lauren and Joe hurried out of the busy store.

"Mr. Wilson, the next store is our newest one here in Haleyville."

"Where is it located?"

"It's around the next block." Joe was shocked when he saw the name on the store. In big, bold letters was 'WILSON'S SPORTING GOODS STORE.' Mr. Owens named this store in honor of you." Tears came into Joe's eyes. Mrs. Lauren handed him some tissue.

The large store was filled to capacity with all kinds of sporting equipment and accessories. Every known name brand of athletic shoes and socks were on display. "Mr. Rollins, guess who this gentleman is that's with me?"

"Mrs. Lauren, would I be very far wrong if I said his name was Mr. Joseph Edward Wilson?"

"You hit the nail right on the head."

"Mr. Wilson, my name is Tommy Rollins. I'm the manager here at Mr. Owens' newest store."

"It's a pleasure meeting you, Mr. Rollins. How many employees do you have in this store?"

"Including me, there are ten full time employees in this store."

"Mr. Wilson, I think we should head back to the corporate office before Mr. Owens gets through with his meeting."

"Mr. Rollins, it was a pleasure meeting you."

"Thank you, Mr. Wilson. I believe I'll be seeing you again." There again, Joe wondered what Mr. Rollins meant by his comment that he would be seeing him again.

Mr. Owens was getting off the elevator when Mrs. Lauren

and Joe entered the lobby of the corporate building. "Well, Joe, did you go into all three stores?"

"I sure did. One store had a very familiar name."

"I'll tell you about that name on the way home. Mrs. Lauren, did Joe's package get placed into my car?"

"Yes sir, it sure did."

"Joe, let's head toward home. Let's not forget to stop at Daisy Mae's Country Kitchen."

Chapter 28

Mr. Owens and Joe were four miles out of town and Joe hadn't said a word. "You seem troubled, Joe, what's the matter?"

"Mr. Owens, I'm simply overwhelmed about you being so rich. I knew you were probably a millionaire, but I was told that you were a billionaire. In comparison, that reduces me down from the size of a volley ball to a solitary peanut. "

"There's no reason you should feel that way, Joe. You already know that I don't flaunt my money around. Besides, you're a lot richer than you know about."

"I'm rich alright; I've got six thousand, three hundred and forty two dollars in my checking account."

"You should have a good deal more than that in your checking account now."

"Mister Owens, the truth is—I didn't keep a single penny of my reward money, I donated it."

"I'm quite aware of that, Joe. You signed the check and

mailed it to Mrs. Delores Sweeny. She's the wife of your military buddy. I, also, know that he was killed standing beside you. He asked you to tell his wife and children that he loved them. That's when you stood up behind that brick wall and started firing your weapon. You killed several of the enemy before you were shot yourself."

Joe's eyes bulged. "Mr. Owens how could you possibly know about those things you just told me? It's impossible! Unbelievable!"

"It's very easy for a man like me to find out things about a person. You're a good, kind-hearted man, and so is your wife. I even know about you finding Mr. Jim Turner's body in the river. Soon afterwards, Linda had a visit from Grace Turner, Jim's wife. The poor woman didn't know which way to turn until Linda gave her peace and comfort by accepting her as her friend. I still say you don't know how much money you have in your checking account."

"Mr. Owens, believe me I know right to the penny how much is in my checking account."

"Son, you really don't know because I have wired one million dollars into your checking account. Soon as you get home I advise you to put part of the money in your savings account and the rest in high interest bearing CD, s."

"Mr. Owens, as much as I appreciate it, why would you give me so much money?"

"I like you a lot, Joe. Charlotte and I didn't have any children. I've got everything in the world that any man could ever hope for, except for a family. In you, Linda, and little Joe I have found the family that I have always wanted. It is my sincere desire and fondest wish to ask Grace Jones to be my wife. I know I'll have to go through a reasonable wait period, but she is the one that I have chosen to be my mate."

"Joe, what are those tears for?"

"I'm happier than I have ever been, Mr. Owens! I never thought one second about asking you for any money. It never crossed my mind."

"I know that. That's one more reason that you'll go back to your cabin as a millionaire. Whatever you do, don't let Grace know about the money that I gave you. By the way, Joe, I'm opening up a new business in about a month. This one is a nice restaurant. Guess what the name of this business will be."

"I have no idea."

"The name of it will be, 'Little Joe's Family Style Restaurant'. Do you like the name?"

"I like it a lot, Mr. Owens! I like it more than I can ever explain!"

"Well, Joe, there's Daisy Mae's Country Kitchen up ahead."

Mr. Owens dropped Joe off in front of his cabin. As he stood there holding the food trays and a gallon of ice tea, Mr. Owens waved goodbye, and then he drove off.

"Joe, we had just about giving up the idea of having lunch today. It's one o'clock already. What took you so long?"

"Linda, I'm sorry it took so long."

"That's okay—now that I smell fried chicken in those trays. Mother, let's eat!"

"Where is little Joe?"

"Mother has been playing with him on her bed."

"Daddy, would you like to hold your jovial little son?"

"I certainly would." Grace handed the child to Joe.

"Mother, this chicken is delicious. I see Joe didn't forget to get my tea."

"That's because I'm very attentive to detail, isn't that right little Joe? Look at my baby's little smile, Mrs. Jones. Isn't he the cutest thing you've ever seen?"

"He most certainly is! Linda, I can't eat all this food."

"Mother, you don't have to eat all of it. Joe, where did Mr. Owens take you today?"

"We mostly rode around looking at the country side." He caught Mrs. Jones not looking, and then shook his head, indicating to Linda to not ask any more questions concerning his trip with Mr. Owens.

At 5:45 that evening Mrs. Jones was sitting on the couch. Joe and Linda were sitting across from her. "Mother, you seem to be nervous, why?"

"Well, it's been a lot of years since I've been on a date with a man, except for my husband."

"You'll be just fine, Mrs. Jones."

"Thanks, Joe, I need that reassurance."

"Mother, where did Mr. Owens say he was going to take you?"

"All I know is he said it would be a surprise."

It was exactly six o'clock that evening when Mr. Owens arrived at the cabin to take Grace Jones on a date. Joe answered the door, and he let Mr. Owens inside the cabin. "Grace, you look absolutely gorgeous in your pretty blue dress."

"Thank you, Cyrus, you look handsome yourself. I'm ready to go if you are."

"Mother, you and Mr. Owens have fun. I don't want you worrying about a single thing while you're gone."

"Thanks, Linda."

Joe and Linda watched from the doorway as Grace accompanied Mr. Owens to his car. Joe and Linda waved bye as they headed toward the main road.

"Cyrus, how are you feeling this evening?"

"I feel fine, but I am a little nervous."

"You have no reason to be nervous around me."

"I know that, Grace, but I want tonight to be very special for you and me."

"Have you decided yet where we're going this evening?"

"Yes, we're going to Tiffany's for dinner and dancing. After that I have a special place I want to take you."

Cyrus and Grace arrived at Tiffany's twenty minutes later. "Good Lord, Cyrus, are we at the right place? This restaurant looks far too expensive for ordinary people!"

"There's not one thing ordinary about you, Grace. I can afford to splurge once in a while, especially someone as good looking as you are. Let's go inside."

"Mr. Owens, lady, please follow the waitress to your table," said the hostess. "Grace was very impressed with the restaurant that Cyrus had taken her to. "Would you care to dance with me?"

"I would love to, Cyrus, but it's been quite a while since I last danced."

"You'll do just fine." He extended his hand to her. The four-piece band was playing an old waltz song. Cyrus and Grace started dancing. "Grace, you're a marvelous dancer."

"So are you."

They danced to two songs before sitting down to their table. "That was a lot of fun."

"Yes, it certainly was," Grace answered. "Cyrus, I'm confused about something."

"Why is that?"

"It's like I have known you for a long time, but I know I haven't."

"I know exactly how you feel."

"You do?"

"Yes, I feel exactly the same way about you."

"Sir, are you and your lady friend ready to order?" A waitress asked.

"Grace, have you decided what you're ordering?"

"I want the t-bone cooked medium well-done, a baked potato, and small salad with French dressing."

"Sir, what are you ordering?"

"I believe I'll have the very same thing that my lady friend is having."

"Very good, sir, I see each of you have tea already. May I show you our famous wine list?"

"Grace, would you care for a glass of dinner wine?"

"No thank you."

"We won't need the wine list," said Cyrus.

"Cyrus, you're looking at me with a little mischievous smile on your face."

"I was just thinking how lovely you look in that dress. You're the very first woman that I have been interested in since my wife died."

"Why am I so much different than those other women you had no interest in?"

"I still think it's got something to do with that dream I told you about. I was interested in you the very first minute I saw you. Grace, it's a lot more than just a passing interest in you. When I say I like you, I mean I really like you a lot."

"I like you too, Cyrus, but it's so soon since we've met."

"I've made up my mind, when we leave here I'm going to take you to a special place."

"What kind of place is it?" Before he could answer the waitress was there with their food.

"Grace, is your steak cooked the way you want it?"

"It's just fine."

For the next hour Cyrus and Grace ate, talked, danced and enjoyed each other's company.

"I really did enjoy my food," said Grace.

"I'm glad you did." The waitress returned with his credit card. Cyrus left a ten dollar tip on the table. "Now, we'll go to that special place I told you about."

"Cyrus, what is this special place that you're taking me to? We've been riding for about twenty minutes now."

"We're almost there. Grace, the rich man that owns that big house I showed you before is allowing us to go inside and look around. I want you to see the elegance and sheer beauty of that house."

"Are you sure it will be okay for us to go inside?"

"The owner is not there now, but he left the key underneath a flower pot on the porch."

"I've never been in a mansion before."

"The owner doesn't consider it to be a mansion. To him it's just his home."

"Cyrus, how long have you known this rich man?"

"I've known him for years and years. He's not an old stuff shirt like you may think he is?"

Cyrus parked his car in the driveway of the mansion sized house. "It was nice of him to leave the front yard well lighted," said Grace.

Just as Cyrus had told Grace, he lifted up a flower pot and picked up the house key. She was very apprehensive about going into someone else's house. Grace stood behind Cyrus as he unlocked the front door. He reached inside the foyer and turned the lights on. The room was breathtaking to Grace as she looked upwards at the large lighted chandelier. Never had she seen anything so beautiful as the multi-colored light reflected against the glass crystal. The foyer was a large room with expensive antiques and fine furniture. Cyrus observed Grace as the room décor seem to take her breath away. "Grace, how do you like this room?"

"It's breathtaking. I've never seen anything like this. How many rooms are in this house?"

"I'll have to do some counting. Let me see—I believe there are eight bedrooms, living room, dining room, office complex, den, weight room, sauna room, laundry room, sun room, kitchen and six bathrooms." Grace sat down on one of the leather couches. She seemed overwhelmed by what she had seen just in the foyer.

"Cyrus, why did you want to bring me in a place like this?"

"I thought you wanted to see what a rich person's house looked like."

"Tell me the honest truth, who actually owns this house?" Tears came into her eyes.

Cyrus sat down beside her, placing his hand against hers. "Grace, I'm—

"I feel like a fool! All this time I thought you were just a regular guy struggling to make a living."

"Grace, I am a regular guy! I'm sorry if I have been a little deceptive with you. I was afraid you might not be interested in me if you knew right away that I was rich. I'm in love with you!

I'm still the same man, rich or not! Grace, look at me, please!" She turned toward him. He pulled out a small box from his pocket, and handed it to her. Grace opened the tiny box to see an expensive, sparkling engagement ring inside. She had never seen a ring so beautiful. She slipped it on her finger, it was a perfect fit.

"Cyrus, why would you want to be engaged to a woman that never had more than a salaried person could afford?"

"It's very simple, Grace, I'm in love with you. I knew you were the woman for me when I first laid eyes on you. You're the woman from my dream. Grace, I love your daughter, Joe and little Joe as well as you. There are hundreds of individuals that would pretend they love me because of my money. Linda and Joe love me for who I am, not because I'm rich. Grace, I'm asking you to love me for whom I am, not for what I've got. Everything I've got I will share with you. You will never feel one second of inferiority to me because I had the money. We'll be on an even keel on everything." Cyrus pressed against her hand as tears slid down his face.

Grace could no longer control herself. She reached her arms around his neck; she kissed him passionately on his lips. Afterwards, they looked into each other's eyes for a few seconds, and then Cyrus leaned forward and kissed her on her lips. "Grace, you are going to be a very rich woman!"

"How rich are we talking about, Cyrus?"

"I hate to tell you this, but I'm not a millionaire."

"That doesn't matter to me because I still love you."

"The reason I'm not a millionaire is because I'm a billionaire."

"Does that mean I won't have to work night shift at a sewing factory?" She smiled.

"Grace, you will live like a queen for the rest of your life."

"There are two little problems," said Grace.

"What problems?"

"You haven't asked me to marry you."

Cyrus wasted no time placing his knees on the marble floor. "Grace, I'm asking—no doggone it, I'm begging you to be my wife, to love me, and to share equally everything I have or will ever have."

"Yes, Cyrus, I will marry you, love you, and be faithful to you as long as I live." Cyrus got up from the floor. Tears streamed down his face. "Why are you crying? I said I would marry you."

"I'm the happiest person in the whole world! Now, what was the second thing you were talking about?"

"Our courtship has been less than a week. What will people think?"

"Frankly, I don't give a crap what people may think! What about you?"

"Oh heck, I don't care either!"

"Grace, you set the wedding date."

"How about one month from today?"

"Fantastic! Grace, would you like to see the rest of your house now?"

"Yes, I can hardly wait. Cyrus, I'll need some help in this big house."

"You've already got help, my dear. Oscar and Nellie Johnson are man and wife, and they live in a suite here in the house. I let them off for tonight. Grace, you won't have to do a single thing if you don't want to. Now, let me show you your new home."

It was Eleven o'clock that evening when Grace opened the cabin door. Linda was holding the baby. "Mother, you've got a funny look on your face. What is that funny looking grin all about?"

Grace could no longer keep them in suspense, she held her hand outwards. Linda's eyes bulged when she saw the engagement ring glittering from the overhead light. "Linda, Cyrus asked me to marry him!" Grace was so excited that she could hardly control her emotions.

"Mother, that's wonderful!" She handed little Joe off to her husband. Tears came into Linda's eyes as she embraced her mother. "When is the wedding date?"

"One month from today. Linda, what will Doris say about me getting married so soon?"

"She will be very happy for you. I'm proud of you, Mother. You're marrying a very good man."

"By the way—you two had me going around like a pure idiot!"

"Why is that, Mrs. Jones?"

"Joe Wilson, you know darn well what I'm talking about! You and Linda let me go around worrying whether Cyrus would lose his job or not by spending time with us."

"Mrs. Jones, I've got just one question."

"What is it?"

"Are you happier now than when you first came here?"

"Yes, Joe, I really am. Thank you both for what you did for me."

"Mother, what are your plans?"

"We're going home day after tomorrow. Cyrus is going to show me some of his businesses tomorrow. He said that would take most of the day. He's going to show me the new location that will soon be opening. Joe, tell Linda what the name of that restaurant will be."

"It will be named, 'Little Joe's Family Restaurant.' He's naming it after our baby."

"Another place of his is named, 'Wilson's Sporting Goods.' Linda, I have a real big surprise for you."

"Mother, what is the big surprise?"

"Cyrus is going to give you a clothing store in your home town."

"He's going to do what?"

"Charlotte's Clothing Store in Adamsville, he's going to give you that big store and enough capital until you get on your feet."

"Why would he give me that store?"

"It's very simple, he loves you very much!"

"Joe, we're going to own that big store!" Linda was very, very excited. All at once she looked toward her mother. "Mother, I can't accept that store. It wouldn't be fair to Doris."

"Don't be too sure about that. Cyrus is going to buy Stapleton Furniture Company in Adamsville for her. Oh, my goodness, I'm so excited I don't know what to do! I'm coming back to the mountains in two weeks, along with all my clothes and stuff. I've got a wedding to attend."

"Mother, what about your house? What are you going to do with it?"

"It's going to be little Joe's house when he grows up. Until then, you and Doris can do whatever you want to with it. I'm going to bed now, but I won't sleep a wink all night long!"

Joe drove into his driveway two days later. His first stop had been to let Grace off at her house.

He got out of his car, and then he opened the passenger's car door. Linda unbuckled little Joe's car seat and removed him from the car. She got as far as the porch before she realized that Joe was at the mailbox. Linda unlocked her front door, and then she hurriedly placed a small blanket on the floor. She laid little Joe down gently, and then she hurried to her window, fearful that the DNA results were in the mailbox. Linda looked horrified when she saw Joe looking toward the house as he held a manila folder in his hand. She saw him shaking his head back and forth as he slowly tore into the folder. Tears were sliding down Linda's face. Her hands were trembling as he began reading the letter. All at once Joe dropped to his knees, still clutching the paper against his chest. Linda knew he was crying. Panic stricken, she ran out of the house. She could hear Joe crying out loud. Tears flowed down her face as she stood over him. "Joe! Joe, I'm sorry! I'm sorry!"

He stood up, wiped his eyes, and then handed the paper to Linda. She had so many tears in her eyes that she couldn't read what the letter said. "What does it say? Joe, tell me what the letter says?" Linda cried out.

"Linda, I'm little Joe's father! Did you hear what I said? I'm little Joe's father!" He grabbed Linda and twirled her around. "You don't have to cry ever again." He kissed his wife. "I love you, Linda! I love you with all my heart! Now, let's go inside the house. I want to hold my son!"

LaVergne, TN USA
19 October 2010
201312LV00003B/2/P